A ST...
LIK...

Paula Marshall

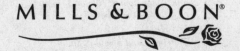

MILLS & BOON®

*First published in Great Britain 2000
Harlequin Mills & Boon Limited,
Eton House, 18-24 Paradise Road, Richmond, Surrey TW9 1SR*

© Paula Marshall 2000

ISBN 0 263 82318 0

*Set in Times Roman 10½ on 11½ pt.
04-0009-84038*

*Printed and bound in Spain
by Litografia Rosés S.A., Barcelona*

Prologue

Temple Hatton, near Brinkley, Yorkshire, 1839

'One of these days Eleanor Hatton, you will go too far,' sighed Mrs Laura Hatton to her daughter. She was trying to comb Eleanor's glossy black hair into some sort of order.

'Really, Mama, if you say that once again I shall have the vapours,' retorted Eleanor angrily, twisting in her chair.

'Do sit still, child. You look like an unbrushed pony. No one would think that you were nearly eighteen.'

'Well, I hate the idea of being eighteen. I'm sure that when I get there Grandfather will start making plans for my marriage to Stacy. He knows perfectly well that I don't want to marry him. I don't wish to marry anyone, ever.'

'I thought that you liked Stacy Trent,' sighed her vague, gentle mother, who found it difficult to understand her strong-minded daughter. However had she come to give birth to such a hoyden?

'Oh, I do, I do, as a friend—or as a brother—but not as a husband. Besides, I don't want a husband chosen for me by someone else. You chose to marry Father, I know.'

Her mother sighed again, and did not need to tell Eleanor that it was the worst mistake she had ever made, Eleanor's father having been an unfaithful, spendthrift rake of the first water.

'Really, Eleanor, I think that your grandfather did you no favour when he arranged that you should be educated with Stacy and Ned until they went to Oxford.'

Worse than that, not only did the three of them share a tutor, who had taught them Latin and Greek, but Sir Hartley, her grandfather, had insisted that they should be instructed in Natural Philosophy, or Science, as it was coming to be called, as well as in Mathematics.

Eleanor had been as quick and bright as Stacy, and far more so than her older brother, Ned who hated all forms of learning. She had a mind like a knife, said her grandfather proudly; he secretly wished that her brother, Ned, his heir, was more like her.

Her mother, though, deplored what education had done to Eleanor. It had made her, she frequently and despairingly said, a boy in girl's clothing, everything which was unfeminine. Besides, her wickedness was all the cleverer for her having been educated. It really served to show that girls should never be taught very much more than how to play the piano a little, paint a little, read a little and the proper way to conduct themselves in public—something which seemed beyond Eleanor.

Her frequent complaints to her father-in-law simply resulted in him saying gently, 'I have no wish for Stacy to marry a fool.'

Which was all very well, but neither should he wish Stacy to marry a freak. This thought was so painful that Mrs Hatton gave a little moan and dragged the comb through her daughter's hair more forcefully than she had intended. Eleanor twisted away from her again.

'Do sit still, child. You will never look like an illustration from *The Book of Beauty* at this rate.

Eleanor pulled a face. 'I shall never look like those simpering creatures if I live to be a hundred.'

'Well, you certainly won't look like a beauty if you do live to be a hundred! Concentrate on looking like a beauty at seventeen. There, that will have to do. And remember, you must be ready for tea. The Lorimers and some of their friends are coming.'

Eleanor ignored this, racing out of the room and up the stairs, two at a time, shouting as she went, 'I'll be back in an instant. Don't worry so, Mama.'

On reaching her bedroom, she hung out of the window, calling down to one of the stable boys working in the yard below: he was her frequent companion in naughtiness.

'Nat! Nat! Did you get it?'

'Yes, Miss Eleanor, you can see it later...'

'No, I want to see it *now*. Wait there. I'll be down presently.'

She shot down the stairs even faster than she had mounted them and ran through a side door into the yard, where she found Nat cuddling an animal which was squirming beneath his jacket.

Nat Swain was a stocky youth from a family which had worked for the Hattons for generations. Although he was three years older than Eleanor he was not much taller than she was, but he was broad and strong, the perfect shape for a stable lad. He, Ned, Stacy and Eleanor had birds-nested and played together as children, and until recently the four of them had been companions and apparent equals.

But then Ned and Stacy had left for Oxford and the wider world outside to which Nat had no access. Ned, nearly four years older than Eleanor, was now a young man about town, and Stacy, almost the same age, was growing up fast, too.

Eleanor, once the two boys had gone, had been forbidden the stables and Nat's companionship by both her grandfather, who was also her guardian, and her good-natured but ineffectual mother. She had responded by apparently agreeing with them—and then doing exactly as she pleased when no one was about. Sir Hart's warning that her friendship with Nat must be a thing of the past went unheeded.

Nat showed her his prize: a ferret. Eleanor exclaimed delightedly over it and was impatient to see it running free.

'No, Miss Eleanor, it's not safe; it moves so quick we might lose it.'

'Well, then, at least allow me to hold it.'

Nat looked doubtfully at her. He was well aware that Miss Eleanor was, as Ned, young for her age and that he was not. He had already pleasured one of the village girls out on the moors which surrounded the great house, and had pretended that it was Miss Eleanor in his arms, that grey eyes were really deep blue ones and russet hair was black.

He knew that to desire Miss Eleanor was crying for the moon, but there were times when his longing for her grew unbearable. He also knew that Sir Hart—as everyone called him—had forbidden them to associate with one another once Ned and Stacy had left, and that their recent return had not lifted his prohibition. If Miss Eleanor continued to ignore it, though, then so would he.

Unable to refuse her anything, he handed the wriggling creature over to her. Eleanor, ignoring her fine clothing and recent toilette, cuddled the feral thing, exclaiming over it until she almost drove Nat mad with desire for her, thus justifying all Sir Hart's prohibitions.

She petted and stroked the little creature, holding it up so that it hung slack from her hands, but her raptures were cut short when the impudent beast bit her finger. With a sharp cry she relaxed her grip. It leapt out of her arms and, before she and Nat could recapture it, the little animal scuttled away in the direction of the house.

Nat's desire for Eleanor was replaced by an even greater desire to catch the ferret before he could be in trouble for involving Eleanor in this escapade!

Alas, it was more nimble than they were. Scurrying and flowing along, it turned the corner of the house, found the tall glass doors opening on to the Elizabethan knot garden and ran through the drawing room, where Eleanor's mama was entertaining the Lorimers, the Harshaws and other gentry of the district to tea.

Feminine screams bore witness that the arrival of the ferret had devastated the party.

In the middle of the noise Eleanor's mama appeared at the doors to face her daughter and Nat, who were both transfixed by the enormity of a prank which had gone sadly wrong.

'Run, Nat, run,' Eleanor had said, once the outcry had begun. 'It was my fault, not yours.'

Too late! Even as he turned her mama said, in a voice severe for her, 'Miss Hatton, did you release that animal? Shame on you. Is that Nat Swain with you?'

'Yes, but it was my fault, Mama, not his. It was an accident. I did not mean to upset the tea party. I am sorry.'

'Sorry! Yes, you should be sorry, Miss Hatton. Swain, you had better come and rescue the tea party by taking the animal away. Sir Hartley must be informed of your misbehaviour once you have removed it. Having done so you will report immediately to him. And you, Miss Hatton, will go to your room at once. At once, I say.'

Her mother was rarely firm, but today she showed no signs of relenting.

Obedient for once, Eleanor, her head hanging, walked to the stairs, where she met Ned and Stacy attracted by the uproar.

'Well, you've really done it this time, little sister,' said Ned, grinning.

Stacy, just behind him, was more serious. 'Oh, Eleanor, you've got poor Nat into trouble again! You know what Sir Hart said last time.'

'Oh, Stacy, don't preach,' exclaimed Eleanor sharply. 'It wasn't deliberate. It was an accident.'

'Which will cost Nat a thrashing,' returned Stacy bluntly. 'It will cost you, as well. Sir Hart won't be best pleased. You're not fair to Nat, you know.'

He was not referring to the prank, but Eleanor was too immature to grasp his real meaning—that she was a temptation to him.

'Oh, Nat'll take it in his stride,' said Ned carelessly, nearly as blind as Eleanor. 'Best you go to your own room, Nell. Mama was really in a taking this time.'

It was nearly an hour before her mother's maid came knocking on her bedroom door to tell her that her grandfather wished to see her in his study. By then Eleanor had begun to regret her recent rash behaviour and the tears were not far away.

She made her way slowly downstairs, through the long picture gallery and past the giant Gainsborough portrait of Sir Hart's father, Sir Beauchamp. Sir Beauchamp always frightened Eleanor: he was so cold, so stern and so handsome. It was strange that Sir Hart resembled him so much in appearance but was so different in his kind goodness from his redoubtable and severe father.

Sir Hart's goodness was legendary; Sir Beauchamp's ruthless will was equally so. Even in the days when Sir Hart had been a member of Lord Liverpool's government his virtue had been a byword. It made it difficult to oppose him.

What was remarkable was that Sir Hart had always stuck to his principles first in his difficult youth, under Sir Beauchamp, and then with his equally difficult problems with his two worthless sons, one of whom had been Eleanor's father. Both of them had died young as a consequence of their dissolute lives.

It must be hard, thought Eleanor, to have had someone like Papa to contend with. And for the first time she felt guilt at her own thoughtless conduct. She wondered how Sir Beauchamp would have dealt with her.

Her great-aunt Almeria, Sir Beauchamp's only daughter, had said once to Eleanor's mama that he had never suffered nonsense from anyone. She had added that he'd had the coldest heart she had ever encountered. Eleanor thought that her great-aunt resembled Sir Beauchamp—but was a little kinder.

By the time she had reached Sir Hart's study door Eleanor was in a mood which was new to her. Seeing Sir Beauchamp as though for the first time had set her thinking of how unsatisfactory Ned was. With his easy charm and his heedlessness of the consequences of his rash actions, he was behaving exactly like their dead father.

Worse than that, she was suddenly unhappily aware that she was following the same path as Ned—and that would never do. The deeper implications of her friendship with Nat and her own thoughtless conduct were presenting themselves to her for the first time. Later she was to think that her life changed fundamentally on that afternoon—and all because Nat Swain had brought her a ferret!

She found Sir Hartley Hatton standing by the window looking out over the moors: his favourite position. He was in his late seventies but was still a handsome man, nearly as straight and tall as he had been in his prime.

'Pray sit down, Eleanor.'

She chose a high-backed chair opposite to his desk, clasped her hands loosely in her lap and hung her head. Sir Hart thought that she might be so subdued because for the first time she was questioning her own conduct, and was wondering, perhaps, why she had behaved so wildly. It was plain that she was feeling shame for more than the silly prank itself. It was a good sign.

He came straight to the point. 'I don't often give you an order, Eleanor, but I gave you one over young Swain. Why did you disobey me?'

His voice was so kind that the tears threatened to fall immediately.

'Oh, I don't know, Grandfather. I thought that it was unkind of you, when I was lonely once Ned and Stacy had gone, to deny me Nat as well.'

'Why do you think I gave it?'

Sir Hart's voice was still kind, but there was a hint of sternness in it.

Eleanor twisted her hands, and said painfully, 'I suppose it was so that I shouldn't play a silly prank, as I did with the ferret. It wasn't intended, though, Grandfather, and it wasn't Nat's fault. Please don't punish him for it.'

Her grandfather waved a dismissive hand. 'Oh, the business with the animal was stupid, and caused distress, but that was not the fault, only the symptom. Pray answer my question.'

Her eyes full of tears, Eleanor murmured, 'I suppose because I'm too old to play childish tricks and run wild...' She faltered to a stop.

'Indeed, but more than that you are being unfair to young Swain. He is not of your world, Eleanor. What was innocent and passed the time when you were children became less so as you grew older. It was positively wrong once Ned and Stacy had left and you were on your own.'

Sir Hart paused. It was plain to him that Eleanor did not know what a temptation she presented to the lad now that she was growing into a beautiful young woman. What she must also understand was that he could not agree to young Swain going unpunished.

'You must be aware that you have left me with no alternative but to instruct Hargreaves to give him a thrashing. He was expressly ordered not to associate with you once Ned and Stacy had grown up. He disobeyed me, so he must be punished as well as you. How shall I punish you, Granddaughter?'

'In my grandmother's day they did not hesitate to thrash naughty young ladies,' she said steadily, her face white.

'That is true, but it is not the fashion now, and I do not think that it is required. I believe that you understand that you have done wrong, and worse, I suspect, than you intended. No, what I have in mind for you is both more and less severe. I propose to send you to your great-aunt Almeria Stanton in London—without your mother. She cannot control you, I know, and that is bad for you, for you can control her. Almeria will teach you to be a young lady and prepare you for life. She is strict, but kind. You shall have your come-out, and she will make you ready to marry young Stacy—which is, as you know, my dearest wish.

'Stacy is both good and steady, which is what you need in a husband. You have a fine mind, Eleanor, but you have been misusing it. On the other hand, apart from this folly with young Swain, you do not lack application. I have no wish for you to go the way that Ned is going.'

Eleanor was now crying bitterly. 'Oh, no, Grandfather, I don't wish to live in London. I've always hated it there. Please let me stay here. I promise to be good in future.'

'No, Eleanor. You would have had to leave soon in any case, with or without your mother. You are merely going earlier than I intended. Your mother has been told and she does not like this, either, but she lost control of both you and Ned long ago, and we must all, I fear, pay for our failings as well as our sins.'

That was the end. There was no use in pleading—and

no dignity, either. Kind Sir Hart might be, but he was also
firm, and what he decreed was law.

'You may go, Granddaughter. Tomorrow you must prepare to leave.'

Eleanor rose and walked to the door, where she turned
and looked at him. Her face was white but the tears had
stopped falling.

'I will be good, I promise. I don't want to be a fine lady,
I despise them, but I will become one for your sake, Grandfather.'

'And for yours, too, Eleanor. For yours, too.'

Chapter One

London, 1841: Monde *and* demi-monde

Mr Alan Dilhorne, 'the person from Australia', as some butlers were later to call him, stood in the foyer of the Haymarket Theatre, London, on his second night in the capital.

Tired after the long journey from Sydney, he had gone straight to bed at Brown's Hotel when he had arrived there, but a day's sleep had restored him to full vigour and a desire to explore the land which had exiled his father. He looked eagerly about him at the fashionable crowd, many of whom stared at his clothing which, however suitable it had been in Sydney, branded him an outsider here.

Curious stares never troubled Alan. His confidence in himself, helped by his superb physique and his handsome face, was profound. It was backed by the advice offered him by his devious and exacting father.

'Work hard and play hard' was his maxim, which Alan had no difficulty in following. He had come to London to carry out a mission for his family which promised him a busy time in the old country. He was not going to allow that to prevent him from enjoying life to the full while he executed it.

He had walked through the *demi-monde* on his way to the theatre, and it was obviously much larger and livelier than its counterpart in Sydney.

A hand fell on his shoulder and spun him half around. A man of his own age, the late twenties, fashionably dressed, slightly drunk already, was laughing in his face.

'Ned! What the devil are you doing here so early, and in those dam'd awful clothes, too?'

'Yes,' chimed his companion. 'Not like you, Ned, not at all. Fancy dress, is it?'

'Ned?' said Alan slowly. 'I'm not Ned.'

The small group of young gentlemen before him looked suitably taken aback.

'Come on, Ned. Stop roasting us. What's the game to-night, eh?'

'Not roasting you,' said Alan firmly. 'I'm Alan Dilhorne, from Sydney, New South Wales. Don't know any Neds, I'm afraid.'

He had deepened his slight Australian accent and saw eyes widen.

'Good God, I do believe you're *not* Ned,' said his first accoster.

'Bigger in the shoulders,' offered one young fellow, who was already half supported by his friends. 'Strip better than Ned, for sure. Bit soft, Ned.' Other heads nodded at this, to Alan's amusement.

The first speaker put out a hand. 'Well, Not Ned, I'm Frank Gresham, and you're like enough to Ned to deceive anyone. I'd have taken you for him on a fine day with the hounds running.'

Alan liked the look of the handsome young man before him, whom he took to be younger than he was—in contrast to himself; he looked more mature than his years.

'I'd like to see Ned. Ned who?'

'Ned Hatton. Not here yet, obviously. Always late, Ned. Look here, Dilhorne, is it? Meet us in the foyer in the first interval and you shall see him. And if this play is as dam'd boring as I expect it will be, we'll make a night of it together.'

Most of them looked as though they had made more than a night of it already.

'You got that shocking bad hat and coat in Australia, I suppose?' said Gresham's half-drunk companion, introduced as Bob Manners. 'Better get Ned to introduce you to his tailor—won't want his face walking around in that!'

'Shame on you, Bob,' said Gresham genially. 'Fellow can't help where he comes from.'

He put his arm through Alan's—he had obviously been adopted as 'one of theirs' on the strength of his likeness to Ned—whoever he was. 'Buy you a drink before the play, Dilhorne—girls'll look better with a drop inside.'

Bells were already ringing to signal the start of the entertainment, but Gresham and his chums took no notice of them. The man at the bar knew him.

'Yes, m'lord, what is it tonight?'

So Frank, who had walked him over, was a lord and Ned, who had still not arrived, was his friend. The foyer emptied a little, but Alan's new friends continued to drink for some time before they decided that they were ready to see the play.

He made his way to his seat as quietly as he could, so as not to disturb the audience or the others in the box. Frank and his companions, who were a little way away from him, were not so considerate. They entered their box noisily and responded to the shushing of the audience by blowing kisses and, in Bob Manners' case, by dripping the contents of a bottle of champagne on to the heads of the people below.

Alan, looking eagerly around the garish auditorium, expected them to be thrown out, but the other people in his box, half- amused, half-annoyed, knew the revellers.

'It's Gresham's set again,' said one stout burgher wisely to his equally plump wife.

'Disgusting,' she returned. 'They should be thrown out, or not allowed in.'

'Manager can't throw Gresham out—too grand.'

The spectacle on the stage amused Alan, although it did not engage him. Half his mind was on his recent encounter, and when the curtain fell at the first interval he was down the stairs in a flash to see Ned, who wore his face.

Gresham's friends, who had quietened a little after their entrance, had further annoyed the audience by leaving noisily before the first act ended, and were already busy drinking when Alan arrived in the bar. He was loudly greeted, and he guessed, correctly, that his new acquaintances were bored and needed the diversion which he was providing.

Well, that did not trouble him—who knew how this odd adventure might end?

'It's "Not Ned", the Australian,' proclaimed Gresham. 'Here, Ned, here's your look-alike.' And he tapped on the shoulder the tall man standing beside him.

Ned Hatton turned to confront himself. And it was a dam'd disturbing experience, he reported afterwards. All he said at the time was, 'Jupiter! You've stolen my face.'

Alan was amused as well as startled by seeing his own face without benefit of his shaving mirror.

'As well say you've stolen mine.'

'Not quite your voice, though,' offered Manners. 'Nor your clothes. But, dammit, you're even the same height.'

'I'm Alan Dilhorne, from Sydney, New South Wales,' said Alan, putting out a large hand to Ned for it to be grasped by one very like his own. Yes, Manners had been right: Ned was softer.

Fascinated, Ned shook the offered hand. 'Well, Alan Dilhorne, what you most need is a good tailor.'

'And a good barber,' commented Gresham critically. 'Although nothing could improve the colour—as shocking as yours, Ned.'

General laughter followed this. Alan's amusement at their obsession with his clothes and appearance grew.

The bells rang for the start of the next act. None of his new friends took the slightest notice of them. Alan debated with himself. Should he go back, alone, to his box? Or stay with this chance-met pack of gentlemen and aristocrats whom in normal circumstances he would never have met at all?

Fascination at meeting his exact double kept him with them. *Almost* exact was more accurate, for Manners was right: Ned was certainly not in good shape, would not strip well, and was, in all respects, a softer, smoother version of himself.

'Well, my boys, let's be off,' said Gresham. 'A dam'd dull play, and a dam'd unaccommodating audience. Give it a miss, Dilhorne, and come with us. Let's find out if you can hold your drink better than Ned. Looking at you, I'd bet on it.' He clapped the protesting Ned on the shoulder. 'Come now, Ned, you know you've less head for it than Manners here, and that's saying something!'

He removed the stovepipe hat which Ned had just put on and tossed it into the street. 'Last one to leave pays for the rest. First one buys Dilhorne a drink.' And the whole company streamed convivially out of the theatre, bound for another night on the town.

A couple of hours later Alan found that he could hold his liquor better than any of them, including Ned, which was not surprising, because although he appeared to keep up with them he took care, by a number of stratagems taught him by his father, not to drink very much.

They had been in and out of several dives, had argued whether to go on to the Coal Hole or not, and at the last moment had become engaged in a general brawl with some sturdy bruisers guarding a gaming hell just off the Haymarket. Ned expressed a wish to go to Rosie's. Gresham argued that Rosie's was dull these days. Alan intervened to prevent another brawl, this time between the two factions into which the group had divided.

His suggestion that they should split up and meet again another night met with drunken agreement. He announced his own intention to stay with Ned.

'Mustn't lose my face,' he announced, and accordingly the larger group, under Gresham, reeled erratically down the road, to end up God knows where. Ned and another friend, whose name Alan never discovered because he never met him again, made for Rosie's, which had the further attraction for Ned of being near to where they were, thus doing away with the need for a lengthy walk or a cab.

Rosie's turned out to be a gaming hell-cum-brothel similar to many in Sydney, though larger and better appointed. Hells like Rosie's were sometimes known as silver hells, to distinguish them from the top-notch places to one of which Gresham had led the other party. Ned, though, liked the easier atmosphere of these minor dives rather than the ones which the great names of the social world patronised. Besides, they were rarely raided by the authorities.

The gaming half of Rosie's was a large room with card tables at one end and supper tables spread with food and drink at the other. The food was lavish, and included oysters, lobster patties and salmis of game and salmon. The drink was varied: port, sherries, light and heavy wines stood about in bottles and decanters.

Alan, who was hungry, sampled the food and found it

good. The drink he avoided, except for one glass of light wine which he disposed of into a potted palm, remembering his father, the Patriarch's, prudent advice.

Disliking bought sex—another consequence of his father's advice—he smilingly refused Ned's suggestion that he pick one of the girls and sample the goods upstairs.

'I'm tired,' he said. 'Much too tired for exhausting games in bed. I think that I'd prefer a quiet hand of cards—or even to watch other people play.'

'Suit yourself,' said Ned agreeably. He was always agreeable, Alan was to find, and this was a handicap as well as a virtue, since little moved him deeply.

'Play cards by all means,' Ned continued. 'Girls are better, though. I always score with the girls, much more rarely at cards. Don't wait for me, Dilhorne. I'll see you tomorrow afternoon at Stanton House.' He had earlier invited Alan to visit him at his great-aunt Almeria's, his base when he was in London.

He went upstairs on the arm of the Madame, a pretty girl in tow, leaving Alan with the other highly foxed member of the party slumped on a bench near the gaming tables. Alan made himself comfortable in a large armchair which gave him a good view of the room. Sitting there, half-asleep, he watched two well-dressed members of the *ton* enter. One of them flapped an idle hand at him, and murmured, 'Evening, Ned.'

Alan did not disabuse him. He could tell that they were both slightly tipsy, at the voluble stage, and when they seated themselves at a table near him the larger, noisier one began chaffing the other about a visitor he was expecting to arrive at his office on the following morning—'Or rather, this morning, to have it proper.' He had apparently reached the pedantic stage of drunkenness.

'From New South Wales, I understand, Johnstone.'

The other laughed humourlessly. 'Yes—if it isn't bad

enough that I have to earn a living at all, I'm expected to dance attendance on a pack of colonial savages who have set up in London and are sending one of their cubs to tell us our business. I understand that Father Bear went out there in chains. What a set!'

'And when do you expect Baby Bear?'

'Tomorrow, as I said. He sent me a note today, telling me that I am to have the honour of his presence at ten. The honour of his presence! And at ten! I don't recognise the time. Well, Baby Bear will have to wait. He proposed the time, not me. The honour of his presence, indeed!'

He choked with laughter again, spluttering through his drink, 'Young Master Alan Dilhorne must fancy himself.'

Alan had early begun to suspect exactly who Johnstone was speaking of, and this last sentence confirmed it. The true son of his devious father, he gave nothing away. Johnstone had risen, looked over at him and said, 'A game of cards, Ned?'

Alan nodded. At some point he would have to speak. He, and not his older twin, Thomas, had inherited their father's talent for mimicry. He tried out Ned's voice in his head. It was light and careless, higher than his own, a very English upper-class drawl. He thought that he could pull it off. Impersonating Ned would be harder than some of the tricks he had played at home—but it would give him a different form of amusement.

Meantime, he warned himself, he must watch his vowels—it wouldn't hurt to appear to be a little drunk. Johnstone and his pal called in another man so that they could sit down in pairs to play piquet. Johnstone against Alan, and his friend against the stranger. Alan prayed that Ned would not return; he had said that he would not, but one thing was very plain: he was not reliable and said whatever pleased him at the time.

It soon became equally plain that, for Johnstone, Ned

was a pigeon to be plucked. He assumed that Ned was both drunk and careless and his manner was lightly contemptuous. Well, he might be in for a surprise. Alan began by knocking over his glass of light wine and dropping his cards. He fell on to his hands and knees in order to pick them up, exclaiming, 'The devil's in them tonight.'

He heard Johnstone and his friends, Lloyd and Fraser, laugh while he continued to offer them the picture of incompetence which they both expected from flighty Ned Hatton. All three, indeed, obviously regarded Ned as little better than a fool. Lloyd even winked at Johnstone when Alan dropped his cards again.

By the end of a couple of hours, though, they were all frowning. Stupid Ned Hatton was having the devil's own luck, and was far in advance of the game, having consistently won despite muttering and moaning, losing his cards and once depositing all his gaming counters on the floor.

'Hands and knees business, again,' he announced cheerfully. 'Rising like Venus from the waves,' he drunkenly told them all, before he began winning again. In his last hand, before he broke Johnstone completely, he even Rubiconed him—a feat rarely performed.

'By God, Ned, you've got the cards tonight,' exclaimed Johnstone, unable to credit that it was skill and not luck which was defeating him.

'Fool's luck,' muttered Alan, picking up yet another of Johnstone's IOUs with shaking hands. His father's tuition and his own mathematical skills, honed by several years of running the money-lending side of his father's business, gave him a good edge over most card players—even those as skilful as Johnstone, who was obviously unused to losing.

Towards the end Alan began to suspect that Johnstone's friend was shrewd enough to guess that there was something odd about Ned Hatton that night, and when Lloyd's game came to an end, with him as winner, Alan announced that he was too tired to continue. Since Johnstone had also had enough, they finished playing in the early hours of the morning.

Stone-cold sober, as he had been all along, Alan was careful to stagger out of Rosie's some little distance behind Johnstone and his friends. The Haymarket was alive with light and noise—he was in the midst of the *demi-monde* about which his father had warned him. Chance and his strange resemblance to Ned Hatton had brought him here— and had also given him a strange opportunity.

He laughed to himself all the way to Brown's. Not only would he be better prepared to meet Johnstone in the morning, but he was relishing the prospect of watching the other man's reaction when someone with Ned Hatton's face walked into Dilhorne and Sons' London office.

And in the afternoon he was due to visit Stanton House off Piccadilly. It should be an interesting day.

Although perhaps not quite so surprising as the one just past!

'You're up early today,' Eleanor Hatton commented to a yawning Ned, who had come down for breakfast in the middle of the morning and not at its end.

He took a long look at her and said inconsequentially, 'I still can't get used to how much you've changed.'

Eleanor smiled somewhat ruefully. She was remember- ing the first occasion on which Ned had visited Stanton House after her great-aunt Almeria had taken her over. She had only been away from Yorkshire for three months—the longest three months of her life, she had thought at the time.

At first she had fought and argued in her determination not to be turned into a fine lady. She had hated London and longed for her carefree life in the country. Worst of all had been to be told to forget notions of educating herself beyond the mere demands of most fashionable women's lives.

Finally she had confronted her great-aunt with an ultimatum. 'If you will allow me to spend a few hours each week with Charles and his tutor, Mr Dudley, then I will agree to be groomed for the life of a fine young lady. Otherwise…' And she had shrugged.

Almeria Stanton, faced with a will as strong as her own, had capitulated.

'A bargain then,' her aunt had agreed, amused by Eleanor's strange mixture of learning, and athleticism, both qualities totally unsuitable for the lady of fashion which she was destined to be.

Charles was Lady Stanton's grandson, a lively twelve-year-old who had been left behind in England when his soldier father had been ordered to India. His tutor, an earnest young man, had been pleased to teach her once Eleanor had proved that her interest in learning was genuine. He had also, much against his will, fallen in love with the lively young woman who was so far beyond his reach.

Eleanor kept her promise. Ned, meeting her again after nearly two years, had barely recognised her. She had entered the room where he'd been reading the *Morning Post*, stripped off her gloves, pulled off her poke-bonnet to reveal her fashionably dressed hair, and smiled at him in the cool, impersonal way she had learned from her great-aunt.

'Oh, Ned, how nice to see you,' she'd murmured, graciously offering him two fingers and her cheek.

Ned had been lost between admiration and horror. Where had tomboy Nell gone to?

'Good God, sister, what have they done to you?'

'I'm a lady now, Ned. I've had my come-out and two proposals of marriage. Both unsuitable, I hasten to add. I've also got a marquess dangling after me. Not that I care about *him*; he's as old as the hills.'

Almeria had surveyed her transformed charge approvingly. 'Well done, my dear—although we could have done without the bit about the Marquess.'

'Well done?' Ned had exclaimed scornfully. 'What do you think that Stacy will have to say about this?' He had flipped his hand derisively in his sister's direction. 'I thought that you, at least, were a girl of sense. Never thought that propriety would overtake you, Nell.'

'Eleanor,' she'd said automatically, colouring faintly and moving away from him. 'Nell's days are over. Sir Hart was right. My behaviour was not proper. In any case, I have to leave now. I need to change for Lady Lyttelton's soirée.'

'Oh, you'll come about, I'm sure,' Ned had said uneasily, but she hadn't. Some of their old rapport had returned, but the Nell who had romped with Ned, Nat and Stacy had gone for ever.

Now, sitting opposite to her, months later, drinking coffee and nursing a thick head after the previous evening's debauchery, he asked, somewhat blearily, 'Going to be in this afternoon, Eleanor?'

She looked up from her plate. 'I shall be with Charles and his tutor until four-thirty, and then I'm free. Why?'

'I've invited an Australian friend I made last night to meet me here around half past four. I promised to take him to Cremorne Gardens this evening. Thought that you might like to meet him before we go.'

He did not say so, but Ned was hoping to play a jolly jape—his words—on his sister when Alan arrived. It was all that she deserved for turning herself into such a fashionable prig.

'An Australian?' said Almeria Stanton doubtfully. 'Is he a gentleman, Ned?'

'As much as I am,' returned Ned ambiguously. 'Which isn't saying much, I know. But I think that you'll like the look of him.'

He laughed to himself when he said this, and watched Nell rise gracefully from the table. She and Great-Aunt Almeria were about to spend the morning shopping in Bond Street, an occupation which the Nell who had once been Ned's boon companion would have rejected completely.

Never mind that, though. Ned nearly choked over his coffee when he thought of the shock she would get when she met Alan Dilhorne. He wondered idly what his new friend might be doing on this bright and shining early summer morning.

Alan was enjoying himself by combining business with pleasure. He rose early, ate a large breakfast and arrived at Dilhorne and Sons' London office promptly at ten. They were situated in one of the rabbit warren of streets in the City, at the far end of a filthy alley. This appeared to signify nothing, since several of the dingy offices sported brass plates bearing the names of businesses equally if not more famous than Dilhorne's.

He still wore his disgraceful clothes, and the clerk in the outer office gave him a look which could only be called insolent.

'Yes?' he drawled, not even putting down his quill pen. His contemptuous look dismissed this poorly dressed anonymous young man.

'I have an appointment with Mr George Johnstone at ten of the clock,' Alan announced without preamble.

'Doubt it.' The clerk's drawl was more insolent than ever. 'He never gets in before ten thirty, mostly not until eleven.'

'Indeed.'

Alan looked around the untidy, disordered room, and listened to the staff chattering together instead of working. He noted the clerk's languid manner and the idle way in which he entered figures into a dog-eared ledger. He reminded himself that his father, always known to his family as the Patriarch, had sent him to England with instructions to find out what was going wrong with the London end of the business.

He wondered grimly what the Patriarch would do in this situation. Something devious, probably, like not announcing who he was in order to discover exactly how inefficient the business had become. Yes, that was it. They could hang themselves, so to speak, in front of him. Yes, deviousness was the order of the day.

'I'll wait,' he offered, a trifle timidly.

'I shouldn't,' said the clerk, grinning at Alan's deplorable trousers. 'He won't see you without an appointment—and I've no note of one here.'

Alan forbore to say that, judging by the mismanagement he could see in the office and its slovenly appearance, the clerk's list might be neither accurate nor reliable.

Time crawled by. When the clock struck eleven the clerk looked at Alan and said, 'Still with us, then?'

'Nothing better to do.' Alan was all shy, juvenile charm, which the clerk treated as shy, juvenile charm should be treated by a man of the world: with contempt.

'Pity.' The clerk's sympathy was non-existent.

Everyone stopped work at eleven-thirty. One of the junior clerks was sent out for porter. Alan looked around, identified where the privy might be, used it, and came back again to take up his post before the clerk's desk.

'Thought you'd gone,' tittered one of the younger men, currying favour with the older ones, waving his pot of porter at him.

No one offered Alan porter. He resisted the urge to give the jeering young man a good kick and sat back in his uncomfortable chair.

It was twelve-fifteen by the clock when George Johnstone entered, blear-eyed and yawning. The clerk waved a careless hand at Alan. 'Young gentleman to see you, Mr Johnstone.'

Johnstone looked at Alan in some surprise.

'Good God, Ned, what are you doing here? Still wearing those dreadful clothes, I see. Lost all the Hatton money?'

'I came to see how hard you businessmen work.'

Alan's imitation of Ned's speech was perfect enough to deceive Johnstone.

'Come into my office, then. Thought that I'd have a visitor waiting to see me. Some colonial savage—but he's obviously given me a miss. Or he's late. You can entertain me until he arrives.'

Alan followed him into his office. It was little cleaner or tidier than the one which the clerks occupied.

'Have a drink,' offered Johnstone, going immediately to a tantalus on a battered sideboard. 'Must get ready for Baby Bear.'

'Not in the morning,' said Alan, still using Ned's voice.

'T'isn't morning,' said Johnstone, sitting down and swallowing his brandy in one gulp. 'By God, that's better. Hair of the dog. But have it your way, Ned.'

'I fully intend to,' returned Alan, in his own voice this time. He rose abruptly: now to do the Patriarch on him. He leaned forward, seized Johnstone by the shoulders and hauled him to his feet with a jerk. He let go of the astonished man and stood back.

'Stand up when you speak to me, you idle devil!'

His cold ferocity, so unlike Ned Hatton's easy charm, was frightening in itself. Coming from someone with Ned's face it was also overpoweringly disconcerting.

'You aren't Ned!' squeaked Johnstone, beginning to sit down again.

'How perceptive of you. No, I'm not. And stand up when Baby Bear speaks to you.'

'Oh, by God, you weren't Ned Hatton last night, were you?'

'No, I wasn't Ned Hatton last night, either. I am your employer, Tom Dilhorne's son Alan, come over without his chains to find out what has gone wrong with the London end of the business. I only needed to look at you to find out. Would you care to explain how a worthless fine gentleman like yourself came to be in charge here?'

'But why do you look exactly like Ned Hatton? Are you his cousin?'

Alan surveyed Johnstone wearily. 'No, I'm not his cousin. It's just a strange likeness, that's all. Pure chance. And I'm not a pigeon for the plucking like poor Ned, either—which you found out last night.'

'Doosed bad form that, pretending to be Ned Hatton.'

'You called me Ned first. You were so dam'd eager to fleece him that you couldn't look at him properly. You haven't answered my question.'

'What question?'

Alan sighed. 'How you came to be in charge here? Good God man, where's your memory?'

'I was Jack Montagu's friend. He knew I needed to find work so he made me the manager here when he married his heiress.'

'I suppose you think that you've been working. Good God, man, you don't know the meaning of the word, but you will by the time that I've finished with you.

'I want to inspect all your books and papers. I want to interview every clerk in your employment, see all contracts, bills of sale, be given a full account of all transactions, wages, rents, and what you're paying for this hole—it had better be cheap. In short, I want a full account of the whole business, and I want everything ready for inspection by ten of the clock tomorrow. Not ten-thirty, mind, but ten. You take me, I'm sure.'

This last sentence was delivered in a savage imitation of Johnstone's own gentlemanly drawl.

Johnstone blenched. 'I can't, Dilhorne, you're mad.'

'Sir, to you,' said Alan, in the Patriarch's hardest voice. 'You can and you will, or it will be the worse for you.'

'Good God, sir, it will take all night.'

'Then take all night. You and the rest of the idlers in the other room have wasted enough of the firm's time and money. Now you can make some of it up.'

Johnstone sank back into his chair, his face grey.

'I didn't give you leave to sit, you idle devil. You'll remain standing until I leave.'

Mutinously Johnstone rose, silently consigning all sandy-haired young Australians to the deepest pit of Hell.

'Now mind me,' said Alan pleasantly. 'You'll jump when I say jump, and you'll say please nicely when I ask you to if you don't want instant dismissal. And if you think that Baby Bear plays a rough hand I can't recommend you to meet Father Bear. He'd not only eat your porridge, he'd eat you, too.'

He strolled into the outer office, leaving behind him a stunned and shaken man. The clerk, quite unaware of what had taken place in Johnstone's room, gave him yet another insolent grin, and said, 'Got your interview, did you? Not long, was it?'

'Yes,' said Alan sweetly. He looked judiciously at the clerk, registered his leer, leaned forward, picked up his ink-well and slowly poured its contents over the page of ill-written figures which the clerk had been carelessly copying from various invoices, receipts and notes of hand.

'What do you think you're doing?' yelped the clerk. 'That's my morning's work ruined.'

'Well, you ruined my morning's work,' said Alan reasonably, head on one side, surveying the havoc he had wrought. 'You can do it again, legibly this time.'

He turned and shouted at the door behind him, 'John-stone! Come here at once!'

To the clerk's astonishment the door opened and a respectful Johnstone appeared.

'Sir?' he said to Alan, and the office fell silent at the sound.

'What is this man's name?' asked Alan.

He still had the inkwell in his hand and he leisurely began to pour the remains of the ink on to the clerk's head. The clerk let out another strangled yelp and looked reproachfully through the black rain, first at Alan and then at the subservient Johnstone.

'Phipps,' Johnstone said. 'Nathaniel Phipps.'

'Phipps,' said Alan thoughtfully. 'Dirty, isn't he?' He critically surveyed the ruined ledger and the ink dripping down Phipps's face.

'Yes, sir,' agreed Johnstone nervously.

'You did it,' squealed Phipps at Alan. 'He did it, Mr Johnstone. Not I.'

'"You did it, *sir*," is the correct usage,' said Alan, putting down the empty inkwell. 'Say it after me, please.'

'Mr Johnstone, sir,' roared Phipps desperately. 'Please stop this madman.'

'Madman? Tut-tut,' said Alan. 'And if I *am* mad you've driven me into that condition, what with making me wait over two hours in a dam'd uncomfortable chair and enduring your insolence while I did so. I've a short fuse, which anyone who works for me soon finds out.'

This was a lie, but Phipps was too agitated to care.

'Works for you! I don't work for you! I work for Mr Johnstone.'

'And he works for me,' said Alan gently. He picked up the clerk's quill pen, and with the whole office and Johnstone watching him silently, breath drawn in, he rolled it in the ink and negligently wrote his initials on Phipps's forehead.

'Yes, he works for me, and so do you now. You're mine, Phipps. Alan Dilhorne's property so long as you're in this room. Unless, of course, you care to resign.'

The silence in the room grew more deathly, broken only by the clerk's whimpering while he scrubbed at his face with his handkerchief. 'This can't be true, Mr Johnstone.'

'Oh, but it is,' said Alan. 'Now clean up your disgusting person and your disgraceful work and do it again: properly this time.'

'It's not fair,' said Phipps tearfully. 'You should have told me who you were.'

Alan's face was suddenly like stone. 'Ah, but you see, I needed to know how you would treat someone whom you didn't know was your employer's son, and I found out, didn't I. Didn't I, Phipps? And if you can't see what was wrong with what you've just said, then we shall never get Dilhorne and Sons' London branch straight again, shall we?'

He swung round and addressed his staring staff. 'The rest of you can get down to it immediately, and do an honest day's work for once. You're none of you fit to work in my Sydney office. Mr Johnstone will tell you what I expect of you by tomorrow, and God help you all if it's not ready by ten.'

He walked to the door before turning and delivering his parting shot.

'Oh, and by the by, mid-morning porter is out, from to-day!'

Chapter Two

That afternoon Eleanor left the schoolroom, where she had been working with Charles and young Mr Dudley, and decided that, four-thirty being almost upon her, she would not trouble to change her clothes in order to meet Ned's Australian friend. She was still wearing her deep blue walking dress and that would have to do.

She had reached the last step of the graceful staircase which spiralled to the top of the house when she met Staines, the butler. He bowed and said 'Mr Ned is in the drawing room, Miss Eleanor, awaiting his friend, and asks you to join him there.'

Somehow Eleanor gained the impression that he was enjoying a small private joke. She immediately dismissed this notion as fanciful and walked across the stone-flagged hall to the drawing room door.

She should have trusted to her instincts. Ned had spent the afternoon avoiding her. He had also given orders to Staines for Mr Alan Dilhorne to be taken straight to the small drawing room with the message that Mr Ned Hatton would shortly join him there.

He had taken care to tell Staines of the likeness and to

warn him not to inform anyone else of it before Alan arrived.

'For,' he had said ingenuously, 'I wish to tease the family a little and you must not spoil the fun.'

Staines had agreed to be discreet. All the servants liked Ned: he was so easy, jolly and kind, although some worried what would happen to the Hatton fortune when Sir Hart had gone to his last rest.

Eleanor said over her shoulder to Staines, in a sudden access of her old impetuous spirit, 'Australian, is he? D'you think he'll be wearing his chains?'

Staines, bowing his head again, opened the double doors for her, and she entered the drawing room to find not the Australian guest but Ned, standing in front of the fireplace studying Lawrence's portrait of Great-Aunt Almeria in her youth, which hung above it.

Eleanor resembled her father's aunt a little, but Almeria Stanton was sterner-looking, and even her airy draperies and the posy of flowers which she was holding did not soften her austere expression. Ned had his sandy head tipped back, the better to inspect it, which struck Eleanor as amusing—as did the outlandish clothes he was wearing.

She gaily continued teasing him when he turned towards her, his back to the light so that his features were a little obscured. 'Wearing fancy dress so as not to discommode your new friend, are you, Ned? Why didn't you put chains on, too? Then he would have felt really at home.'

Ned looked at her. His eyes seemed bluer than ever, and they roved over her in a manner which, had he not been Ned, would have made her blush.

Alan found her enchanting. She did not resemble Ned in the least, either in manner or appearance. She was a tall girl, beautifully proportioned, elegantly dressed, from the crown of her glossy head to the toes of her well-shod feet. Ned had spoken of a sister and this must be her. Her colouring was deeper and richer than Ned's and her hair was a raven-black in colour.

It was very plain that naughty Ned had told her of a visitor from Australia but had not seen fit to mention the likeness. His mouth twitched in involuntary amusement, but before he could identify himself Eleanor spoke again.

'I understand that you're taking him to Cremorne Gardens. Tell me, don't you think that your colonial friend will be overset by such worldly sophistication?'

Before she could commit herself further, and add to her ultimate embarrassment, Alan spoke at once, privately deciding to reproach Ned for putting his pretty sister in such a false position. He had already learned enough about him to know that what had been done was deliberate.

'You mistake, Miss Hatton,' he told her, 'I am not Ned.' And he deepened the accent which he had not known he possessed until he reached England.

Eleanor's hand flew to her mouth in an embarrassed reversion to childhood.

'Not Ned? Then you must be the Australian visitor of whom he spoke. Oh, dear, I have been so mannerless, so *gauche*. How can I apologise? On the other hand you are so like Ned I can be forgiven for being tactless. Only your voice is different, and, yes, I do believe that you are even bigger than he is.'

Alan decided not to favour her with his wickedly accurate imitation of Ned's light drawl.

'Yes,' he said, smiling. 'It's too deep. The voice, I mean. It's the chains. They weigh it down, you know. They took them off…'

He paused tantalisingly, still smiling. He had two sisters whom he liked to tease gently, and he wanted to see how this poised and pretty girl would react to similar treatment.

Eleanor took the bait.

'The chains? Took them off?'

'Yes, when we boarded the ship for England. They said that if we wore them during the journey they'd slow us down too much. The weight again.'

'They did?' said Eleanor, fascinated by this young man who looked so like Ned but who was yet utterly unlike him when he teased her. On closer inspection he looked very much more severe than Ned, but there was a gentleness in his manner to her which her wild brother had never possessed.

'Yes. Sorry to disappoint you by not having 'em on.'

'I'm not disappointed,' said Eleanor truthfully.

'I can see that. The Patriarch says—'

'The Patriarch?' Eleanor was fascinated all over again.

'M'father. We call him the Patriarch occasionally—he does come on rather patriarchal at times. He also says that they slow you down when you're working. So they took them off him soon after he arrived in New South Wales. More trouble than they were worth, he said.'

'Do stop,' said Eleanor faintly, trying not to laugh. Great-Aunt Almeria insisted that young ladies never laughed. Lord Chesterfield wouldn't have liked it, she said. 'You're not a bit like Ned now that I've got to know you.'

'No, I'm not,' agreed Alan cheerfully.

'But you do look very like him.'

'Yes—but it was a naughty trick to play on you—and so I shall tell Ned.'

'Well, I wouldn't have said all that to you about chains if I hadn't thought you *were* Ned.'

He agreed with her, head on one side judiciously, adding, 'Not to my face, perhaps, but afterwards.'

'Yes, no. Oh, dear.' She laughed out loud this time, but was saved further embarrassment by the arrival of a grinning Ned.

'I see you've found one another,' he offered carelessly.

'Too bad of you, Ned,' Eleanor began.

'Miss Hatton found me,' said Alan. 'I didn't do any finding. Our resemblance confused her somewhat.'

Ned's grin was wider than ever. 'Thought it might. Bit of a shock was it, Nell?'

'My name is Eleanor,' she said repressively. 'You are quite disgraceful, Ned. I behaved very badly as a consequence of your silly trick and Mr—?' She looked at Alan.

'Dilhorne, Alan Dilhorne,' he told her. 'But then I behaved badly, too. I was a dreadful tease, I fear.'

'Indeed you were,' she agreed, captivated by his charm. No, he was not really very like Ned, despite the resemblance.

'So, we are quits,' he said to Eleanor, ignoring the grinning Ned, who was beginning to annoy him.

'Quits,' she agreed, and put out her hand to take his and shake it, which pleased Alan mightily.

There was no false affectation about her, despite her overwhelming air of fashion and consequence. He looked at Ned and said, only half-jokingly, 'Beg both our pardons, Ned, and introduce me properly to your sister, there's a good fellow.'

The note of command in his voice was such that Ned had begun to obey him when the doors opened again, and Almeria Stanton entered. Her eyebrows rose alarmingly when she saw Ned and Alan standing side by side, their two faces and figures so alike. Yet she thought that there was no doubt which was Ned. The face on the right possessed a power and a strength missing in her great-nephew's.

Almeria sighed. Inconvenient likeness were the bane of the aristocracy's life, but if this were the Australian visitor of whom Ned had spoken then the likeness had to be put down to chance.

But she would still like to know more of the origins of Ned's new friend...

'I understand that you are taking Mr Dilhorne to Cremorne Gardens tonight, Ned. I must remind you that you were out late this morning. I'm not sure that your grandfather would approve of your way of life.'

'I'm well of age,' said Ned sulkily.

Watching him, Alan thought that Ned Hatton was strangely juvenile, for all that he had reached his mid-twenties.

So, apparently, did his formidable great-aunt.

'You must remember, Ned, that you are dependent upon Sir Hartley for your income—and that you do little in return for it. You make no attempt to begin to learn the management of the estate which you will one day inherit. Besides, if you are living in my home you must respect my wishes. No, I propose that you ask Mr Dilhorne to dine with us instead. Should you like that, Mr Dilhorne?'

Alan looked from Ned's scarlet and embarrassed face to Almeria Stanton, so serene and sure of herself.

'If Ned does not mind forgoing our entertainment this evening—and I'm sure that Cremorne Gardens will be there for another time—I should be honoured to dine with you. Although, as you see, I am not properly dressed for it.'

'No matter. I will ring for Staines and tell him to see that another place is laid at table.'

Having done so, she sat down and began to draw out this young man who so improbably possessed her nephew's face.

'Since Ned has been as mannerless as usual and has failed to introduce us, I must introduce myself. I am Almeria, Lady Stanton, Ned and Eleanor's great-aunt, and you, I believe, are Mr Alan Dilhorne. I seem to remember, from my childhood in Yorkshire, that it is a surname commonly found there, but I have not come across it in the south.'

'It is not common where I come from, either,' Alan told

her. 'I have no knowledge of any relatives of that name in England.'

'I presume that you are in England on pleasure, then?'

'Not at all,' said Alan. He was beginning to admire this forthright old lady. He thought that Eleanor Hatton might grow to be like her in time. 'I am here on two pieces of business. My first relates to the London branch of the family firm.'

Ned was struck by this. 'Of course, Dilhorne and Sons! What a forgetful ass I am. My friend, George Johnstone, is manager there.'

'Yes,' said Alan with a small smile. 'I know.' He thought that the friendship revealed a great deal about Johnstone.

Almeria Stanton knew that one should not ask someone from New South Wales about his family's origins, but she cared little for society's rules and regulations. Besides, the resemblance was beginning to make her feel uncomfortable, and the more she could discover about this self-controlled young man—so unlike Ned in that—the better.

'You must be a member of the Dilhorne family which, I understand from my brother-in-law, who is at the Board of Trade, runs something of an empire in Sydney and district. Pray where did your father originate from, Mr Dilhorne?'

Alan was amused, although he could see that Miss Eleanor was shocked by her great-aunt's bluntness. The people whom he had met so far had danced around the tricky subject of his origins. He decided to give the straightforward old woman a straightforward answer, however much it might shock her or his hearers.

After all, the Patriarch had never repudiated his origins, nor sought to hide the fact that he *had* arrived in chains. He was always frank about his past, being neither proud nor ashamed of it.

'I believe my father lived in London before he was transported to New South Wales.'

It was as much of the truth as he was prepared to give. Later, he was to be grateful for this early reticence.

Eleanor's face was shocked when her unfortunate gaffe about chains came back to haunt her. Ned would have guffawed had Alan made his answer in male company, but being in his great-aunt's presence always made his behaviour a trifle more reticent than was habitual with him.

For her part, Almeria Stanton was cool. 'I collect that he was the architect of your family's fortunes, Mr Dilhorne. I find that most praiseworthy, given his unfortunate start in life. But you spoke of two reasons for your visit?'

Alan was pleased to hear her ask this question. Now for the second and somewhat different bombshell.

'My second reason is perhaps why I am here at all. I have come to clear up the business of my mother's inheritance.'

He paused, watching for—and finding—the twitch of surprise on their faces.

Eleanor, throwing on one side all good manners which prescribed that you did not bombard new acquaintances with personal questions, but fascinated by Ned's new friend who looked so like him but was really not like him at all, took up the inquisition.

'Your mother's inheritance? May we know of it, Mr Dilhorne? It must be substantial to bring you all the way from the Southern hemisphere.'

'Indeed. My mother happens to be one of the Warings of Essendene Place in Surrey. By chance she has fallen heiress to the entire estate since Sir John Waring, who never married, left it to her. She is the daughter of Sir John's younger brother, my grandfather, Frederick Waring, who died in Sydney before I was born. I understand that there are some distant cousins of mine in the female line who were unaware of my mother's existence until her name appeared in Sir John's will and who had consequently hoped to inherit Essendene. They are rightly demanding proof of her existence and I have come to furnish it.

'I also understand that Sir John had only lately decided to leave everything to my mother, and that this, too, is causing friction. My mother hopes that if her claim is substantiated I can bring about a reconciliation of sorts, once I have settled the legal situation to the satisfaction of us all.'

Ned was looking fuddled at the end of this precise and exact recital. The two women thought all over again how little the two men really resembled one another.

Almeria's expression was one of astonishment for another reason. 'You are saying that your mother is one of the Warings of Essendene? I had understood that it was the Lorings who stood to inherit—through their grandmother.'

'You mean my friend, Victor Loring?' Ned offered. 'I had heard that he'd had a great disappointment recently over a will. They're as poor as church mice.'

He looked respectfully at Alan, who, despite his apparently dubious origins, had turned out to be related to one of the oldest families in England.

Alan was amused to notice by their changed expressions that his worthless grandfather, Fred, a remittance man who had died of drink, having gambled away what little he had left, leaving Alan's mother penniless, had given him an introduction into high society which his own father's sterling qualities could not have achieved for him.

'Fancy that. Related to Caroline and Victor Loring,' laughed Ned. 'You have a whole pack of relatives over here whom you do not know. And plenty more cousins to discover, I'll be bound. The Warings married into all the best families.'

Unspoken was the question, How did your mama come

to marry an ex-felon? Politeness rendered them all silent, but left them bursting with curiosity.

Alan decided to be downright. 'They can scarcely be expected to wish to know an Australian cousin who has come to dispossess them—for that is how they will see it.'

'Nonsense,' said Almeria sharply. 'If your mother's claim is a true one, then the laws of succession must hold.'

'With respect, Lady Stanton, my father would not agree with you. The women in our family have been given the same rights as men. They, and my elder twin brother, Thomas and myself, all have the same legal standing. He does not hold with primogeniture or the subjection of women.'

'Your twin,' said Eleanor, sparkling at him. 'Is he Ned's double, too?'

'Fortunately not. Begging your pardon, Ned. He is very much like my mother—and her long dead brother Rowland, she says. Except that Thomas is tall and dark while she is little and dark. Had he gone to the theatre no one would have taken him for Ned.'

Eleanor pursued a point. 'You said that your sisters were equal in law with you and your brothers. Can that really be true? We women have so many constraints and Mr Dudley, Charles's tutor, tells me that we have no legal existence at all.'

'My father had contracts and settlements drawn up for them. One of his sayings is, "In matters of judgement sooner a clever woman than a dull man."'

'Is this commonplace in the colony, Mr Dilhorne?'

'By no means, Lady Stanton. I fear that our women are under even more constraints than they are in England, and are even less regarded. The Patriarch—I mean my father— is, however, very much his own man.'

'Well, he would be my man,' said Eleanor decidedly, 'if he treats women so well.'

'Eleanor, you forget yourself,' said Almeria, ever ready to rebuke her great-niece when she showed her old outlaw spirit.

Alan regarded Ned's radiant sister with approval. There was obviously much more to her than there was to her charmingly lightweight brother.

'With respect, Lady Stanton, I think that the Patriarch would admire Miss Hatton greatly.'

The look Eleanor gave him was glowing. His smile made her tingle all over in the oddest manner. No man had ever affected her in such a strange way before.

Throughout the dinner which followed, where Alan knew how to use all the right knives and forks—doubtless his mother's influence being Almeria's inward comment—the good impression which he had made on the two women grew with each passing moment.

By unspoken agreement Alan was quizzed no further until, sitting over their port, the women having retired into the little drawing room, Ned remarked, a trifle roughly for him, 'Do you always make such a good impression on the ladies, Dilhorne?'

Alan's answer was an oblique question. 'Lady Stanton and Miss Hatton approved of me, then?'

'You know dam'd well they did.'

'Excellent. It's nice to know.'

The contrast between the two men could not have been more marked. Ned drank heavily of the port, Alan drank little, and by the time they rejoined Almeria and Eleanor in the drawing room Ned's drawl was already blurred. He was not entirely sure that he liked his women approving so much of his new friend—it took a little of his pleasure in him away.

Alan, meantime, contented himself with admiring both Miss Hatton and her great-aunt, for entirely different reasons!

* * *

Eleanor Hatton had to admit that she was fascinated by Ned's new friend. It was not the likeness which intrigued her, but the differences between them. Not only was Alan so much cleverer than Ned, but she also liked Alan's easy athletic carriage, which was such a strong contrast to Ned's slouch.

For the first time in her short life she found sleep slow in coming. She relived her first meeting with Alan: something which she had never done before. Her great-aunt had said to her after he had left, 'Mr Dilhorne seems to be a worthy young man, my dear, despite his doubtful origins. We must not condemn a man because of his father's mistakes.'

'The Essendene connection must count for something, too,' Eleanor had said, trying not to sound too eager.

'If it's proved,' Almeria had replied dryly—although she had no real doubts. 'It's hard on the Lorings, though.'

Eleanor agreed. Caroline Loring, a shy, pretty girl, was one of her London friends—although she had told Eleanor nothing about the problem of the Essendene inheritance. Consequently, the next afternoon Eleanor took the Stantons' carriage and was driven to Russell Square, where the Lorings, Alan's cousins, lived.

They were all at home: tea was just being served. Victor, who had been about to go out, put down his gloves, hat and cane when she was announced, and returned to the drawing room.

'I've decided to stay for tea after all,' he said.

He was already half in love with Eleanor, and the fact that she was Sir Hartley Hatton's granddaughter, and would have a good dowry when she married and stood to inherit even more when the old man died, was an attraction to a man whose family was perennially short of money.

Eleanor was not sure how much she liked Victor. At first she had been drawn to him, because he was not only tall and dark, but handsome as well. Unfortunately he did not improve on further acquaintance, and if she was not sure whether or not she wished to marry Stacy she had no doubt that Victor would not do as a husband. His manner to his mother and his sister was frequently unpleasant and dismissive.

That his manner to Eleanor was always charming and courteous somehow made matters worse, not better. Only pity for Caroline kept her friendly with the Lorings at all. Victor, armoured in conceit, was quite unaware of her aversion to him.

Today the conversation turned immediately to the question of Hester Dilhorne's claim to the Waring fortune and estates. It was like a sore tooth to Victor, and to a lesser extent to his mother and sister. Their father had already succumbed—at a relatively early age—to his dissolute life. He had been a boon companion of Ned Hatton's father and uncle.

Before Eleanor had time to tell them that she had met Hester Dilhorne's son, Victor exclaimed viciously, in the middle of a long tirade, 'How do we know that the dam'd woman, her felon husband, and the whole Dilhorne family aren't gross impostors anyway?'

'Oh, Victor, we've been over all this before,' said his mother wearily. 'You know that the lawyers have affidavits from Sir Patrick Ramsay and Colonel Frank Wright testifying that they knew your great-uncle Fred, and Hester. Colonel Wright was even a guest at her wedding to Tom Dilhorne. There's no real cause for doubt, I'm sorry to say.'

'Then why did your cousin Hester forget herself and marry a dam'd ex-felon is what I want to know?' said Victor ferociously, forgetting his manners and his speech before ladies. 'And why did Sir John lose his mind and settle everything on her?'

'I expect that there were few others she could marry,' said Caroline quietly.

'Well, she should have had nothing to do with the brute, remained a spinster and not done us out of what we had come to expect.'

Eleanor decided that this was one of the days when she disliked Victor. She was remembering the pride and affection with which Alan Dilhorne had spoken of his father, the man Victor was calling a brute.

'I met Hester Dilhorne's son last night,' she said at last, when Victor had run down.

Victor was incredulous. 'Met him? Here? In London?'

'Well, I could hardly have met him in Sydney, Australia, could I?' asked Eleanor reasonably, unable to resist teasing Victor a little, even at this serious juncture. 'Ned met him by accident at the theatre the other evening and brought him home to dinner last night. Only fancy. He is Ned's double, but bigger, I think. His name is Alan Dilhorne.'

'Looks like Ned, only bigger, named Dilhorne, and here in England. The whole thing grows more unlikely every minute—which I have already told you, Mama.'

Really, thought Eleanor, Victor can be very wearisome at times.

'He can scarcely be a gentleman if he comes from Botany Bay and is an ex-felon's son,' ranted Victor. 'How in the world did Lady Stanton allow such a creature to sit down to dinner with her at all?'

'His manners are perfectly good, although I admit that his clothes are odd,' said Eleanor, suddenly indignant on Alan's behalf. 'He struck me as remarkably clever, although Ned laughed when I said so. "No one with his face could be clever," he said. Great-Aunt agreed with me, not him.'

She did not add that her great-aunt had said that the young man was inconveniently clever, and was apparently not aware of it. Almeria had noticed, even on this short acquaintance, that young Dilhorne appeared to be able to control Ned, a feat which no one else had ever performed.

He had reconciled Ned to his loss of the Cremorne expedition, and had quietly checked him at dinner when Ned had begun to speak of unsuitable topics before Eleanor. Later, when Charles had come down into the drawing room after dinner, he had entranced him by telling him of his intention to inspect railway lines and engines while he was in England, Charles being of a mechanical bent.

His charm was enormous, and it had certainly impressed Eleanor and Almeria, as well as Ned and Charles. Eleanor found herself spiritedly defending him.

After Victor had indulged in some further rant, for his anger at being dispossessed had been fuelled by the arrival in England of one of his dispossessors, Eleanor said quietly, 'You know, Cousin Clara—' she was distantly related to Victor's mother '—I think that Victor wrongs him. Mr Dilhorne said that his mother was all for a reconciliation with you, and with his other relatives in England whom she does not know, and that he hopes to achieve one before he leaves.'

'A likely tale,' sneered Victor, 'and easy for him to say when he has taken all.'

Eleanor decided all over again that this was one of the days when she definitely disliked Victor. 'Seeing that he is the younger twin, and that his father apparently does not believe in primogeniture, he will only take his share. Furthermore, since the lawyers took some time to trace his mama, she could scarcely have connived at influencing Sir John.'

Clara Loring took a hand when Victor, red in the face, began to answer Eleanor.

'You have to admit that it is quite beyond us to affect matters now, Victor,' she said wearily. 'The young man must have brought proof of Cousin Hester's existence and her marriage, so we must reconcile ourselves to accepting that Sir John's will must stand. It is both unmannerly and fruitless to continue to rail at fate. It is certainly not poor Eleanor's fault that Ned has become acquainted with him. If it proves that the lawyers are satisfied by the young man's evidence, it will be our duty to receive him, once at least, for my cousin Hester's sake. Let that be all for now.'

'But, Mama,' began Victor.

'No, that is quite enough. There are other topics to occupy us. Eleanor will think us all savages to go on so. Tell me, my dear, when do you hope to return to Yorkshire? I know how much you miss the country.'

'I don't know exactly when I shall go home,' murmured Eleanor, relieved that the question of the Waring inheritance had been dropped. 'I suppose when Great-Aunt thinks that I am sufficiently polished.'

'You look remarkably well polished to me,' said Victor, who was suddenly worried that his recent churlishness might have put Eleanor off him. He was not wrong. Eleanor did not like this new face which Victor had shown her, so different from that of his usually easy self. His anger over the whole business seemed excessive.

Victor could have told her that it was not. The Lorings had been financially desperate even before his own folly had made matters worse. The prospect of inheriting Essendene, and his possible marriage to Eleanor, were the only things which had kept them going.

They had borrowed heavily on their expectations.

Their creditors would allow them no more rope once Hester Dilhorne's claim had been proved. What would happen to them after that Victor dared not imagine. Only a rich marriage could save them, otherwise they were ruined.

He devoted his efforts to trying to charm Eleanor again, but she left earlier than she had intended. Her manner to him was as pleasant as usual, but he was unhappily aware that that meant nothing: Almeria Stanton had turned her into the very model of a complete young lady of fashion, who never gave any of her true feelings away.

By the way that Eleanor had carried on about that colonial swine, Dilhorne, he had obviously made it his business to win her over—which was another nail in the coffin of Victor's hopes.

Chapter Three

Eleanor was delighted to discover that her great-aunt was also impressed by Alan Dilhorne.

'If Ned is determined to be his friend, then I must launch him into good society,' Almeria said decidedly to her niece. 'He cannot be left to wander about the *demi-monde*, which is all that Ned can introduce him to. He deserves better than that. Ned must also introduce him to a decent tailor, since he plainly does not lack money. I shall speak to Lady Liston about him. She is the hostess of the biggest reception of the season next week, and for him to be received at Liston House will give him all the social cachet he needs.'

The shrewd old woman was not thinking solely of assisting Alan. It was plain to her that he was a steadying influence on Ned, and for that reason alone the friendship ought to be encouraged.

Ned did more than introduce Alan to his tailor. A fortnight after meeting Alan he asked him to Stanton House, took him to his rooms, called for his valet, Forshaw, and said in a manner which brooked no opposition, 'Come on, Dilhorne, if you're going to visit the best houses, and given that it will be some days before the tailors have your new

clothes ready, you might as well be outfitted in my spares.
I've enough to fit you up twice over, haven't I, Forshaw?'

'Certainly, Mr Ned, and no problem about the size, either.'

Alan began to demur, but the prospect of wearing clothes
which would not raise eyebrows was too much for him.
Ned and Forshaw danced around, sorting out shirts, jackets,
trousers, socks, shoes and assorted underwear as assidu-
ously as a pair of drapers in one of the new shops which
were beginning to arrive in Oxford and Bond Street.

Forshaw also trimmed what he privately called young
Dilhorne's 'errant hair', and when he was togged out to
their mutual satisfaction a trunk was filled with more of
Ned's 'spares' and the two of them set off to see the town.

They met Almeria and Eleanor in the hall. They had just
come back from a similar expedition—ordering two more
evening dresses for Eleanor to dazzle the *ton* in.

They both stared at the handsome pair. Almeria said
faintly, 'Properly dressed, Mr Dilhorne, it is quite impossible to tell which of you is which.'

Eleanor, on the other hand, had no such difficulty. She
exclaimed, 'Oh, no, Mr Dilhorne is the one on the left. I
can't understand, begging your pardon, Great-Aunt, how
anyone could mix them up!'

'Alan, please, Miss Hatton. We have gone beyond Mr
Dilhorne, I think,' Alan said quickly, before naughty Ned
could begin to tease his sister by falsely claiming that, not
at all, *he* was the man on the left. He was delighted, and a
little surprised that Eleanor could immediately, and correctly, identify him. A girl of common sense as well as
spirit, he decided.

Eleanor blushed charmingly, 'Then if you are to be Alan,
I must be Eleanor.'

'And all the more so,' he returned gallantly, 'as a reward
for your good sense in distinguishing me from Ned.'

'Dam'd odd that,' Ned told Alan, when they had made their adieux to the two women and set off together for an evening on the town. Later they were going on to a reception at the Ailesburys', to which they had both been invited and where they would later rejoin Lady Stanton and Eleanor. 'No one else can tell us apart, even when we're wearing quite different clothes. Wonder how she does it?'

Alan could offer no convincing explanation, and nor could Eleanor, when Almeria Stanton quizzed her later.

'Oh, it's simply a feeling I have when I look at them,' she offered hesitantly. 'I can't explain it. It's something which goes beyond reason, I think.'

Her tough old great-aunt thought that there might be a very down-to-earth explanation which the innocent Eleanor was not yet mature enough to understand. She had already noticed that her charge sparkled whenever Mr Alan Dilhorne walked over the horizon, and that her eyes followed him around the room.

Whether his apparent attraction for her niece was a good thing or a bad thing she was not yet in a position to say. Though his influence on Ned was so beneficial that she decided to give him *carte blanche* to visit Stanton House whenever he pleased.

Others at the function were obviously ready to accept him in society: he was rapidly surrounded by a group of fascinated members of the *ton*, most of them women.

'He's already got La Bencolin after him,' grumbled Ned to Frank Gresham, having met with a polite refusal himself from the lady who was the merry widow of Lord Bencolin, who had left her his not inconsiderable fortune.

'Oh, Marguerite's always after the latest sensation,' drawled Frank, who had once scored with the lady himself, 'and Dilhorne's certainly that.' He admired Ned's look-alike: talking to him was always refreshing. One never knew what he was going to say next.

Frank had found Alan a body-servant, Gurney, who had been a professional boxer, with whom he sparred in a gymnasium off the Strand—much to Frank's amused admiration.

'How the devil did a great bruiser like you, Dilhorne, acquire such a head for figures? You certainly don't resemble Ned: he possesses neither talent,' Frank had said after watching Alan work out one afternoon. 'Ned tells me you spend the morning grinding away in the City. He says that the rumour is that your father's rich enough for you never to work again.'

Alan, towelling himself off, had stared at young Gresham, armoured in idleness like all the young men whom he had met through Ned.

'Now where would be the fun in that? Look at the trouble that fellows like you and Ned have in filling your days. Some useful occupation would certainly do *him* a world of good.'

'Ned? Useful occupation!' Frank had snorted. 'You're light in the attic. He hasn't the brains of a flea, poor fellow.'

'Now, how do you know that?' Alan had queried. 'I doubt whether anyone ever troubled to find out.'

'Well, he made a dam'd poor fist of it at Oxford, I can tell you, and I was there with him.'

Alan raised his eyebrows. 'Now, what do you think that proves? That he can't construe, or write Latin verses. What in God's name has that got to do with anything?'

'Better than nothing,' Frank drawled. 'Though I confess that my ability to recite pages of Livy isn't exactly helpful—though it'll be pretty impressive when I do choose to sit in the Lords, even though half my audience won't know what on earth I'm spouting about. Be off with you, then. If you aren't going to be a bruiser you can concentrate on making yourself even richer than you are. Better than being like Victor Loring, perpetually strapped.'

Alan asked, apparently idly, 'The Lorings? Poor, are they?'

'Church mice,' agreed Frank cheerfully. 'And there's you, you devious devil, filthy with it, doing them out of that, too. Life isn't fair, else I shouldn't be ready to take my seat in the Lords and live on milk and honey.'

Alan thought that Frank was a little devious himself. He might be living a rackety life around town, but he possessed a good brain beneath his idly cheerful façade. He suspected that it would not be long before his wild life palled, and Frank, Lord Gresham, would place his obligations and duties first, and not second.

Meantime he was a jolly companion, and it was he who had introduced Alan to La Bencolin at the Ailesburys': a kindness which Alan had already begun to appreciate before Eleanor and her great-aunt arrived.

'So that's Ned's discovery and his improbable look-alike,' said George Johnstone's older brother, Sir Richard, who was a great friend of Lady Stanton's. He was amusedly watching Alan charm the ladies before taking La Bencolin off to supper. She was hanging on to his arm as though she never meant to let go of it.

'You know that my brother George is working in the City, Father having left him nothing. He's been entertaining us all with the goings-on at Dilhorne's ever since young Master Alan arrived there one fine morning.

'He entered the office like a whirlwind and frightened everyone to death. Told 'em they were all slackers,' Sir Richard continued cheerfully, 'which wasn't surprising considering George's attitude to life. He got the job by accident, and being George, didn't even try to do it properly. Young Dilhorne made 'em work all night, not once, but twice—took off his coat and worked with 'em in his shirtsleeves. He made George do the same—now, that I would like to have seen. Then he sent them all home, and worked most of the next day himself—God knows when he slept, because he was on the town with Ned Hatton the same night!

'When he'd got everything straight again, after making them work like coolies for the rest of the week, they arrived one day to find that at lunchtime he'd arranged a dam'd fine meal for them all, with enough drink to stun several horses, never mind some half-starved City clerks.

'He told them afterwards he'd put their pay up if they carried on as devotedly as they had been doing. George thinks he's God, and has begun to work for his money. What's more, some whippersnapper of a clerk he'd assaulted on the first day got up and made a drunken speech on Mr Alan, thanking heaven for the day he'd arrived— seems he'd grasped that young Master D had saved the London branch from bankruptcy, and all their jobs into the bargain.

'I want to meet this paragon, Almeria, and soon. Anyone who is the spit image of Ned Hatton and can make George work must be worth seeing. Tonight he's walked off with La Bencolin after five minutes' conversation with her! What will he get up to next?'

'He can tame Ned, too,' Almeria said quietly. 'The only question is, how soon will it be before he leaves Ned behind, or Ned begins to resent him?'

She said nothing of her suspicions that Eleanor had fallen in love—and at first sight, too—with Sir Richard's paragon. It was perhaps fortunate that Eleanor had missed his encounter with La Bencolin, nor did she see him leave with her later, having been cornered by Victor and Caroline Loring.

Sooner or later the gossip would reach her. Later would be better, when the first gloss of Mr Alan Dilhorne's arrival had worn off—or so Almeria hoped.

* * *

The gloss was not wearing off for Alan. His days were full and he had begun to discover that there were opportunities in London which did not exist in Sydney. And they were not all to do with getting into bed with one of society's most famous beauties.

His brother, Thomas, had commented shortly before he had left home that a buccaneer like Alan would be able to pillage the pillagers, and he was rapidly beginning to see ways of accomplishing this!

One duty, rather than pleasure, saw him making his way to the Waring family lawyers, who had their offices in Lincoln's Inns Fields. He dressed with some care, not in Ned's presents, but in the new suit which his tailor had made for him. Gurney had even tamed his unruly sandy hair, so like his father's. Thus respectable, he was ushered into the rooms of Hallowes, Bunthorne and Thring.

There were three people waiting for him, and two of them were obviously lawyers. One was sitting at a large desk, the other, holding a pile of papers, was perched on a high stool next to an over-full bookcase, and was obviously the junior of the pair.

The third man was tall and silver-haired. He was in his late fifties or early sixties and the expression on his handsome face could best be described as sardonic when he saw Alan come through the door.

All present rose to their feet.

'Mr Alan Dilhorne, I believe?' the senior lawyer said. Alan nodded agreement. He continued, 'May I present myself? I am Mr John Bunthorne, at your service, and this is Lewis Thring, my junior partner.'

Alan bowed and acknowledged them both.

Bunthorne turned and identified the third man in the room. 'May I have the honour of presenting you to Sir Patrick Ramsey, KB, once of the 73rd Foot, the Royal

Highlanders, stationed in Sydney when Lachlan Macquarie was Governor there. He has come to help us in our duties.'

Sir Patrick bowed gracefully to Alan. Alan responded; the lawyer waved him to a chair before his desk.

'Being a businessman yourself, Mr Dilhorne, you will, of course, understand that we have a duty to protect the Waring estate from possible impostors.'

He paused, and Alan said, 'Of course,' and tried not to look at Sir Patrick who appeared vaguely amused by the whole business.

'Since we discovered your mother's existence—Sir John having left her everything without ascertaining whether she was alive or dead—we have taken a number of affidavits from persons resident in Sydney at the time of her marriage but who have now returned to England. These appear to be satisfactory on the face of it.

'I am sure, though, that you will understand that it seemed wise to ask Sir Patrick Ramsey to meet you as further confirmation, since Colonel Wright left for service in India some six months ago. That is correct, is it not, Sir Patrick?'

Sir Patrick flapped a hand in agreement.

'Now, as I understand it, Mr Dilhorne, you are here on behalf of your father, Thomas Dilhorne Esquire.'

'No,' said Alan, throwing both lawyers into a temporary fluster. 'My father is Tom, not Thomas, and I am not here on his behalf. It is my mother who inherits the estate, and I represent her.'

Sir Patrick gave a short laugh on hearing this.

Bunthorne favoured Alan with a patronising smile.

'Not so, Mr Dilhorne. But your mistake is quite understandable, since you may be unaware that under English law your mother's rights are subsumed under your father's.'

'It is you who mistake,' said Alan gently. 'At home my mother's possessions have been contractually reverted back to her. She is a free agent, and, as such, is as full a partner in my father's firm as myself or my brother Tom.'

Sir Patrick's laugh was not stifled this time. Memory moved in him when he surveyed Tom Dilhorne's son.

The lawyer was only temporarily embarrassed. He began again.

'Your mother's inheritance. So be it. And you are her representative. Very good.'

He gave a half-bow in Sir Patrick's direction. 'Now, Sir Patrick, you see Mr Alan Dilhorne before you. Have you any comments to make or questions to ask?'

Sir Patrick rose negligently. Alan saw that he had been an athlete in his youth and was still supple for his age. He walked to Alan and put out his hand. Alan took it. They shook hands gravely.

'Only,' said Sir Patrick, 'that Mr Alan Dilhorne is the image of the Tom Dilhorne I once knew—only larger. I suppose that, like me, he is feeling his years.'

The lawyer smiled. 'That merely proves Mr Alan here to be his father's son, and not necessarily Miss Hester Waring's.'

Alan looked at Sir Patrick, who said, 'I remember Miss Waring's wedding, and also the birth of twins to her. This is the younger twin, I am sure.'

Alan thrust his hand into the pocket of his beautiful coat and took out a locket, which he handed to Sir Patrick. Sir Patrick opened it to find there Tom and Hester, painted as they had been nearly thirty years ago when he had known them.

'Sarah Kerr's work, I take it,' he said examining the portraits carefully. 'A beautiful woman, your mother,' he added, handing the locket to the lawyers for them to inspect it. 'I was right about your resemblance to your father. Is your older brother like him, too?'

'No. He is like my mother's brother, who was killed in

the Peninsular War before I was born. He is very like my father in character, though.'

'Both are truly your father's sons, then,' said Sir Patrick. 'When I heard George Johnstone speaking of you in admiration, although God knows why after the way in which you treated him, I was back in Sydney nearly thirty years ago. Tell me, are you as dangerous as he was?'

'No,' said Alan. 'I haven't had his provocations. My life has been easier.'

The three men were struck by him: by his maturity compared with that of most of the young men in their twenties whom they knew.

The lawyer handed the locket back. Alan passed to him the notarised copies of the documents relating to his parents' marriage, his mother's birth certificate, and the records of his own and his siblings' births. He also passed to the lawyer the power of attorney signed by his mother, setting him out as her agent to act for her in any problems concerning the Waring estate, and a similar document from his father relating to his power over the Dilhorne branch in London.

All the time he felt Sir Patrick's humorous eye on him.

'Done, then?' said Sir Patrick at the end, pulling out his watch. 'Luncheon calls.'

'Indeed,' agreed Bunthorne. 'A piece of advice for Mr Alan here, which it would not go amiss for you to hear, Sir Patrick. The Loring connection are resentful that the estate on which they counted passes to your mother. It would be wise to be wary, Mr Alan.'

'So noted,' returned Alan coolly. 'Do I take it that you are satisfied with my credentials?'

'After meeting your good self and hearing what Sir Patrick has had to say, and having seen these documents, there can be no doubts in the matter. There remain only the final legal moves—including the granting of probate—which will place the estate in your mother's hands. The title, of course, died with Sir John.'

'Of course,' said Alan gravely, and Sir Patrick cocked a sardonic eye at him.

'You will be staying some little time in England, Mr Dilhorne?' pursued the lawyer.

'Until this and other matters are settled,' said Alan cheerfully.

'We shall, then, remain in touch. I gather that your firm employs its own solicitors in London? Pray keep our office informed of your own address, and your movements, if you would be so good.'

Alan assented to this, and they all bowed at one another.

Sir Patrick took Alan's arm. 'I insist that we dine at my club, Master Alan. You can tell me the latest news from Sydney. Particularly anything about your redoubtable father and your beautiful mother.'

'Certainly, Sir Patrick. I believe that you left Sydney shortly after my birth,' he said, adding slyly, 'You do not object to eating with the felon's son, I take it?'

Sir Patrick dropped Alan's arm and turned to face him. 'I grew to admire your father before I left. Although I'm bound to say that he frightened me, too. In an odd way, that is.'

Alan laughed. 'He frightens us all. But the Patriarch is a great man.'

Sir Patrick stopped short and began to laugh. 'The Patriarch, is it?' he choked. 'Let me tell you later of one of my favourite memories of your father. He was pretending to be dead drunk when lying under the gaming table in Madame Phoebe's brothel. The Patriarch! Well! Well! And do you play, Master Alan? Are you a fly-boy, too?'

'A little,' replied Alan modestly. 'Only a little.'

So it came to pass that he dined with a laird of thirty thousand acres in Scotland, twenty thousand in England, who owned two castles, three country houses, four follies, who had a clever and beautiful wife, and whose happiest memories were of his days as a penniless officer in a frontier town in the Pacific when all the world seemed young and merry.

Alan liked visiting Stanton House. Its interior was beautiful after a fashion quite different from his home in Sydney, which was furnished in the Eastern style. Instead it contained all that was best in European taste, from the paintings on the walls to the *objets d'art* which stood everywhere, and the furniture on the elegantly carpeted parquet. Best of all he liked its owner, Almeria, and her charge, Eleanor Hatton.

Shortly after Almeria had launched him on London society she invited him to dinner to introduce him not only to Sir Richard Johnstone, but also to his Loring cousins.

'It will be a splendid opportunity for you to make your peace with them,' she had said.

He arrived promptly, wearing his new evening clothes. Eleanor, greeting him, thought that, while in one sense it was necessary for him to conform to the society in which he was now mixing, they diminished him in another. He looked more like the smooth young men she knew, and less like the strange, exciting man she had first met.

'Ah, Mr Dilhorne, you are as prompt as I expected you to be,' Almeria told him. Privately she contrasted him with careless Ned and other members of the Hatton family, who had been asked to be sure to arrive in the drawing room in time to meet Alan and her other visitors but who had not yet come down.

Alan, indeed, soon became aware that beneath her usual calm manner she was vexed about something. Finally, in a lull in the conversation, she rang the bell for Staines and asked him to enquire of Mrs Henrietta Hatton whether she had forgotten that she had promised to come down early for dinner in order to meet Mr Dilhorne before Sir Richard and the Lorings arrived.

He bowed deferentially. 'I believe, m'lady, that they are on their way downstairs. I gather that there was a slight misunderstanding involving Master Beverley when they first set out, but that has now been overcome.'

Young Charles Stanton, who was being allowed down to dinner that evening, gave a slight guffaw. His grandmother said, 'Thank you, Staines,' before looking over at him and remarking glacially, 'You wished to say something, Master Stanton?'

'N…n…not at all, grandmother,' he stuttered. He was so unlike his usual well-behaved and quiet self that Alan wondered what was wrong with him. Eleanor, as well as Charles and Almeria, was also on edge. Her welcome to him had seemed somewhat distracted—which was most unlike her. He was soon to find out why the atmosphere in the pretty room was so tense.

Mrs Henrietta Hatton burst into the room all aflutter, immediately behind her unruly son whom she was unsuccessfully pursuing. She was, Alan later learned, Eleanor's aunt by marriage, having been the wife of her father's younger brother John, who had died in a drunken prank involving a curricle, two ladies of easy virtue and half a dozen equally overset friends. As if this was not bad enough he had done so on the day his wife was giving birth to their only child, known to all and sundry as Beastly Beverley.

He had been taken up dead after trying to manoeuvre through the gateway of Hatton House, off Piccadilly, when he could barely stand, never mind drive.

Henrietta had mourned her faithless husband as though he had been the most sober and loving of men. She had transferred her unthinking love to their son, with the result that the child, naturally headstrong, was rapidly transformed into something of a monster.

Although only eleven years old, he was already obese through self-indulgence, and had been informed by Almeria Stanton that he would not be allowed to sit down to dinner as he could not be trusted to behave himself. She had given way, regretfully, to his fond mother's insistence that he might be allowed in the drawing room before it was served, so that he could meet the guests.

Beastly Beverley, living up to his name, walked up to Alan and thrust his scarlet face at him. Before he could speak Alan forestalled him by putting out his hand, taking Beverley's flaccid one, and saying gravely as he shook it, 'Hello, old chap. I'm Alan Dilhorne. Pray who are you?'

Beverley wrenched his hand away. 'So *you're* Ned's convict look-alike. Where are your funny clothes? Ned said that you had funny clothes.'

He began to laugh loudly, pointing at Ned and choking out, 'Got it wrong again, Ned, didn't you? No funny clothes.'

Charles, sitting quiet and obedient by Mr Dudley, plainly did not know whether to laugh or to cry at this exhibition. Almeria Stanton shuddered. His mother said weakly, 'Oh, Beverley, do try to be more polite.'

Beverley, who made a point of never listening to a word his mother said, opened his mouth to speak again, but before he could do so Alan said gravely, 'Ned kindly introduced me to his tailor. Sorry to disappoint you.'

For once his already famous charm did not work. Beverley gave a shriek of laughter in order to demonstrate that nothing would be allowed to put him down.

'Oh, I'm not disappointed. I never expect anything from convicts.'

At this Almeria Stanton said in her most severe voice, 'Behave yourself, Master Beverley Hatton.'

Beverley's response was to put his tongue out at her and shout, 'Shan't,' before retreating behind his mother.

She said nervously, 'Beverley always behaves well—unless, of course, someone provokes him.'

Presumably I provoked him when I came in fashionable clothing, thought Alan wryly.

Rational conversation proved impossible in Beverley's presence, until Almeria said to Mrs Hatton in her coolest voice, 'I think that, after all, it would be best, Henrietta dear, if you took Beverley to his room before our other guests arrive.'

This was only accomplished after a great deal of screaming and crying, and some reproaches from Mrs Hatton to her aunt concerning her disregard for poor Beverley's feelings.

The sense of relief at his departure was immense. The only sad thing was that in response to Hetta Hatton's demands for fairness, Charles and his tutor were asked to leave also. This was particularly hard on poor Mr Dudley, who had been looking forward to a good dinner and would now be reduced to dining on schoolroom fare again.

Sanity ruled at last. The Loring party and Sir Richard and his wife arrived to find a composed family ready to introduce them to the young Australian who was the subject of society's latest gossip.

'Yes,' Sir Richard said, shaking Alan's hand, 'you *are* like Ned—but there is an odd difference between you. I hear from my brother George that you have been enjoying yourself in the City.'

'Work to be done there,' agreed Alan. 'I like a challenge.'

'Apparently. I wish more of our young men did. We grow soft.'

'An old head on young shoulders,' Sir Richard told his wife later.

Introduced to his Loring relatives *en masse*, as it were, Alan told them collectively, 'It's a pleasure to meet my English cousins whom I did not know that I possessed.'

Victor frowned. Caroline, wearing a pink gauze frock which did her no favours, smiled admiringly at him.

Clara Loring said gently, 'We never knew your mama. She left England with her father after Fred's bankruptcy. I hardly knew him, either. I believe that he quarrelled with his family before he lost everything.'

Well, they certainly quarrelled with him *after* he was ruined, thought Alan, but being a polite young man he bowed and smiled at her. Both Loring women appeared to be faded and cowed, and the reason was obvious: the dominant and personable Victor, who stood over them full of himself. He was a bullying Beastly Beverley grown up.

'Must say that your arrival, as well as the news of Cousin Hester's family, was a great shock to us all,' was his grudging contribution to the conversation.

Alan nodded. 'Must have been,' he agreed: a statement which was laconic and cryptic enough to have pleased his father. 'My mother left England when she was so young that she scarcely knew what family she had. It was a great shock to her, too.'

This was something of a gloss on the truth, but it seemed the thing to say. Nothing ever shocked his strong-minded little mother—'surprised' would have been a better word.

Victor made a great effort to be civil to the sandy-haired barbarian who had diddled him out of a fortune. Yes, the wretch had Ned Hatton's face, but there the resemblance ended. It was as plain to him as it was to everyone else that he shared no other attribute with Ned. Side by side they were of a height, and a similar shape, but examined closely Alan's athleticism and his hard determination shone out of him.

A friend had told Victor earlier that day, 'Shouldn't be

surprised if that new cousin of yours was having it off with Marguerite Bencolin. I should be wary of him if I were you, old boy. Anyone who can have La Bencolin under him not long after meeting her bears watching.'

'Stuff,' Victor had said rudely. 'I can't see his attraction myself. Fools say anything about a new face.'

'He hasn't got a new face,' his friend had guffawed. 'Only Ned Hatton's old one.'

Now, meeting him at last, Victor thought glumly that it was bad enough to have an unknown cousin disinherit him, but even worse to discover him to be so formidable despite his lack of years. Victor, at over thirty, felt himself to be juvenile beside him. Were all Australians so indecently mature? On the other hand, perhaps Caroline could be persuaded to charm the swine and get the money back that way. Now, there was a thought worth having!

As the evening wore on, however, it became apparent to Victor that, La Bencolin or no La Bencolin, Alan's attention was fixed on Eleanor, and that Eleanor sparkled when he spoke to her. This added to the dislike he already felt for his supplanter.

He also feared that Eleanor was not so attracted to himself as she had once been.

He was not wrong. Eleanor was beginning to feel an even stronger disgust for Victor's unkind remarks. Alan was shrewd, but he tempered his knowledge of the world with a half self-deprecating, half-teasing humour.

Drinking their port after dinner, the gentlemen indulged in male gossip.

'Hear you spar a little,' said Victor, who was indulging himself with the Stantons' good port.

'A little,' said Alan.

'More than a little,' drawled Ned, determined to keep up with Victor. 'Shouldn't fancy going a round with him myself.'

Victor refrained from making the cutting remark about Ned's condition which trembled on his lips. Disappointment had made his speech reckless lately. If he wanted to retain some favour with Eleanor, however, then Ned had to be placated. He decided to turn on Alan.

'Hear you are a little *épris* with La Bencolin.'

'La Bencolin?' said Alan blandly. 'Now, which was she? The blonde at Lady Ailesbury's, or the brunette at Lady Palmerston's? I don't remember a Miss Bencolin.'

Both Sir Richard and Ned gazed sharply at him, but his manner was as easy and cool as he could make it. Alan had no intention of allowing two strenuous afternoons with Lady Bencolin to queer his pitch with Eleanor, to whom he was becoming increasingly attracted.

La Bencolin was all very well, but her practised charms were boring, and Alan was beginning to recognise that he was one of those men who needed more than an easily available body to attract him—and then to rouse him. He also needed some genuine rapport. So far he had only come across it once, and, sadly, that had been with someone who was married and wished to remain chaste.

His imperturbability annoyed Victor. 'You know perfectly well who I mean,' he said savagely. 'Marguerite, Lady Bencolin, or are you so involved with the ladies that you can't tell one from another?'

'Steady on, Victor,' said Ned indignantly. 'Alan here's such a busy man, what with sparring with Gurney, ruining his eyesight in the City and dancing about with your lawyers, that he's hardly had time to get into bed with anyone, let alone such an exhausting piece as La Bencolin is said to be. He don't look dead wore out, do he?'

Both Sir Richard and Victor, despite themselves, gave Alan a good hard look. No, he didn't took 'dead wore out'. But that proves nothing, thought Sir Richard cynically. He wouldn't, not he. It was quite plain that Victor was making such a dead set at young Dilhorne because it was beginning to look as though the Hatton girl was slipping out of his hand.

He promptly turned the conversation to other matters, and fortunately a sudden access of good manners prevented Victor from turning it back. In revenge he took Ned off to Rosie's as soon as he could decently prise him away from the aftermath of the dinner party. Once there he cheated Ned, now more than half-drunk, out of more money, playing piquet, than Ned could ever repay.

If playing clean wasn't going to win him Eleanor, playing dirty might!

Chapter Four

'Ned, a word with you,' said Almeria Stanton when he crawled downstairs well into the next afternoon after his misspent night.

'Yes, Great-Aunt,' croaked Ned, 'but make it short, please. I've a monstrous bad head on me.'

'So you should have,' she told him severely. 'Arriving home at five in the morning and disturbing the sleep of the whole house with your drunken nonsense. If you can't behave any better than that, I shall have to ask you to find rooms elsewhere. Apart from anything else, it's a bad example for poor Charles.'

'Good God!' Ned exclaimed, in a voice so loud and shocked that it set his poorly head thundering as though the Lifeguards were riding over it. 'You can't do that to me, Great-Aunt. I can't afford to stay in London on what Sir Hart allows me if you don't give me a home. You know very well that he saw fit to cut my allowance by over half after last year's season—which, considering I am his heir, I consider dam'd bad form.'

'He only did so because in your drunken folly you ran up debts playing cards which you could not afford to pay—as well as following a life nearly as dissipated as your late wastrel father's was. I tell you plainly that hard living is beginning to leave its mark on your face. Why don't you take a leaf out of young Dilhorne's book and try to be a little more responsible? He even manages to earn his own living while enjoying himself.'

Now, this was tactless, which Almeria realised the moment she had finished speaking. Ned coloured up to his hairline and said indignantly, 'He isn't such a paragon as all that. God knows what he gets up to in the City, if half I hear is true. What's more, he's Marguerite Bencolin's latest conquest—if it isn't the other way round, that is! You could really complain if I was dancing around with her!'

He realised as soon as he had come out with this that he should not have spoken so frankly before Beastly Beverley, who immediately began guffawing, Charles, who stared at him, eyes wide, and poor Eleanor, who suddenly turned quite pale. His great-aunt looked at him, acute distaste written on her face, but before she could begin to reproach him he added sulkily, 'Of course, that's only the gossip Victor Loring is putting about. There's probably nothing in it.'

He was too late. Almeria said with cold disapproval, 'I am only sorry, Ned, that you are too old to be sent to your room. Such conversation is quite improper when indulged in before Beverley, Charles and your sister. Besides, if it is only idle gossip you are repeating, it is quite disgraceful.'

At this Beverley roared, 'Why?' at the top of his voice, and struck at Charles, who tried to silence him out of respect for his new friend Alan, who was always kind to him. He was not quite sure what cousin Ned was talking about, only that it was unpleasant.

Ned's unpleasantness was like the black dog of legend riding on his shoulders. He felt so ill, and his memories of what he had got up to the previous night were so distasteful, that later that day, in an effort to clear his head, he made his way to Hyde Park where he immediately came across Victor Loring.

Since it was to Victor that he had gamed away what was left of his allowance, and a small fortune in IOUs on top of that, Ned dreaded speaking to him. Victor greeted him so cheerfully that Ned thought he must be mistaken about his gambling debts—perhaps they were simply part of a nightmare which had afflicted him after he had fallen into a drunken sleep.

This delusion was rapidly dispelled when Victor said, 'You won't forget to pay me as soon as you can, will you, Ned? I'm a little strapped for cash these days, what with the Waring inheritance going wrong.'

'The money,' said Ned dismally. 'Oh, yes. Cards last night. How much was it? I don't remember.'

'Made a note on your cuff, didn't you, old fellow?' said Victor cheerfully.

He knew that Ned had already run through his allowance, and that Sir Hart had said that he would not bail him out again, for Ned had obligingly told him so.

Victor did not want Ned's money. He wanted something else. And in his present state he knew that Ned would agree to anything rather than lose his inheritance from Sir Hart. Light in the attic, Ned—which created great opportunities for cleverer men, of whom Victor counted himself one.

He immediately told Ned how he could extricate himself from his present difficulties, before riding home, congratulating himself on his ingenuity in extricating himself from his own.

Eleanor, who had been looking forward to seeing Alan at the Leominsters' dance that night—for he was the pet of the moment—suddenly felt that she did not want to meet him at all if he were involved with someone of Lady Bencolin's known reputation.

Jealousy, she found, was a most unpleasant emotion.

Her first impulse when she saw him coming towards her at Leominster House was to turn and run—like the Nell Hatton she'd used to be. Common sense told her to speak to him graciously and coolly, as though her acquaintance with him was only slight.

Alan was sensitive enough to detect the reservation in her manner to him, and to wonder what had caused it. He found out soon enough, for after he had left her with one dance booked, where he had hoped for two, Ned came up to him, looking shame-faced.

'Sorry, old fellow,' he muttered. 'I did rather a rotten thing this afternoon. Great-Aunt provoked me and I had no more sense than to rant in front of Eleanor about you being involved with La Bencolin. I did say later that it was probably only Victor Loring's gossip—but you know what women are...'

Yes, Alan knew what women were, and he knew what Ned Hatton was, too, and was not surprised that he had blabbed about La Bencolin—which was probably what Victor had hoped for. Well, it was too bad, but there was no use in crying over spilt milk. Patience was everything in this life, and if fences had to be mended with Eleanor, then so be it.

It was perhaps unfortunate for Marguerite Bencolin that she approached him a few minutes after he had learned of Ned's indiscretion. She had seen him with that fresh young beauty, Eleanor Hatton, and was a little worried because the two pleasurable afternoons which she had spent with him had not been followed up.

On his second visit to her he had pleaded the need to work at Dilhorne's while it was being reorganised, and had promised to visit her later. Later, however, had never come.

She turned her fine eyes on him. 'You are neglectful, Mr

Dilhorne. When may I have the pleasure of entertaining you again at Connaught Street?'

Alan bowed over her hand. 'It will not be soon, I fear. My affairs are involved at present, and my afternoons are consequently busy—for the moment duty must come before my pleasure.'

His smile was gallant and his lips had lingered on her palm, but he saw that his answer displeased her. Had she known him better she would not have replied to him as she did.

'Why, I do believe that it is nursery matters which engage you, my dear.' She looked meaningfully across at Eleanor, who was talking to Victor Loring. 'I had supposed that you were attracted to more adult games!'

He looked her full in the face and she saw at once that she had lost him. His bright blue eyes were as hard as stone.

'As to that, Lady Bencolin, I have fond memories of childhood. Milk pudding is sometimes more of a treat than spicier foods. The stomach can so easily be overset.'

She was not used to being refused, and she had entertained hopes of a permanent liaison.

'You surprise me, sir,' she bit back at him. 'Are all colonials so naïve?'

'This colonial is but a simple fellow, I fear.'

Now that is a lie if ever I heard one, she thought bitterly. It is plain that he intends to cut line. I must not be importunate, nor let him see that I feel humiliated because he prefers the pretty debutante to me.

She bowed coldly to him and began to move away.

Alan was suddenly sorry for her, and for the first time regretted having started an affair so lightly. He had been told that she took her pleasures where she found them and was never serious in pursuing them. It was, however, obvious that what had passed between them had come to mean more to her than it had ever done to him.

There was a lesson to be learned here: not to be tempted too easily. For he had not meant to hurt her, merely amuse himself a little and please her whilst he was doing it. But the damage had been done, and he would remember to be more careful in future.

Marguerite Bencolin's brief moment with Alan was noticed by many, as was his apparent dismissal by her and his ready acceptance of it.

'Another piece of nonsense,' said Frank Gresham to a friend. 'Nothing in it after all.' It was one such comment among many, but unfortunately none of them reached Eleanor's ears.

She was charming but cool to Alan when he came over to her shortly before their dance to sit beside her. Her worries now were not over him, but over Ned, who had been approached by Victor shortly after they had arrived.

He had announced that 'This is a dashed dull do,' and had persuaded Ned to leave with him to visit other delights of a more racy kind. He had carefully waited until Almeria Stanton—and Alan—were otherwise engaged before he tempted his victim away.

That Eleanor was distressed about something, despite her bright chatter about nothing was plain to Alan. He feared that it might be his association with La Bencolin which disturbed her, and he decided to risk all by saying gently, 'You are troubled tonight, Eleanor. Is there anything I can do?'

It was not the first time that Eleanor had thought he was a mind-reader. Yes, she was troubled, but how could he tell?

'Yes, I am a little distressed.' She looked hard at him. 'Perhaps you might be able to help me. It's Ned. I don't know why, but he's beginning to worry me. He's gone off with Victor again, and every time he does that he's like a bear with a sore head the next day. I have a dreadful feeling that he's losing money—and heavily.'

I shouldn't be telling Alan this, she thought feverishly, especially after learning about La Bencolin, but somehow he radiates a kind of strength which is pleasant to lean on. Besides, who else can I confide in? I fear that Great-Aunt Almeria will cut Ned off for ever if what I believe about him and Victor proves to be true.

Alan said gravely, 'I can't reassure you. It would be insulting your intelligence for me to pretend that all is well. You are not Ned's keeper, though. He is of age, and is older than you are.'

'I know that it's stupid for me to worry about him,' she said miserably. 'What troubles me most is that I'm sure Sir Hart won't bail him out again, as he did last year. I never realised before what irresponsibility meant. Oh, dear, I must stop. We're not supposed to talk about such things at balls.'

Touched by her concern for her flighty brother, Alan decided to try to comfort her.

'Indeed, no. We are meant to chatter sweet nothings until dawn comes to relieve us. As, for instance, allow me to praise your turn-out this evening, Miss Hatton. Only elegant and beautiful young girls like yourself may dare to appear in pure white with few trimmings. All is of the most charming.'

He then offered her a simper of the kind with which more than one man had favoured her that night. On him, with his size and strength, it looked incredibly foolish, and Eleanor could not repress an unladylike laugh.

'There, that's better,' he said, leaning towards her, giving her a genuine smile this time, causing her to forget her jealousy of La Bencolin and to feel—oh, to feel she knew not what. A kind of paralysis of will, something which she had never experienced before: sweet, but dangerous.

Bother La Bencolin, she thought. If she is what he wants,

it's too bad, but I do so like talking to him, and being near him, for he never patronises me, and I might lose all that by giving way to silly folly. After all, he has never tried to court me!

She smiled back at him and stood up, giving him her hand, for her dance with him was about to begin. He bent his head towards her and said in his most sober voice, 'I'll try to keep Ned away from Victor, but you must know that he will resent me if I make what I am doing too obvious, and rightly, too. I cannot be his bear leader.'

Despite his reservations, this limited reassurance served to improve Eleanor's evening. The discovery that Alan, like many big men, was an excellent dancer, light on his feet, with a feeling for the music, also pleased her, and she readily granted him the second dance for which he asked, and went home, happier than she had felt since Ned's indiscretion in the hall.

She left behind her a man who was beginning to discover that his chance meeting with his double was giving him obligations as well as pleasures. The memory of her anxious face stayed with him, causing him to ask how and why it was that Eleanor Hatton and her worries about her wastrel brother should concern him so greatly.

He could find no easy answer. Eleanor did not rouse in him the immediate lust which he had felt for Marguerite Bencolin; rather he was finding in himself a quite different desire: a desire to protect her.

Yes, that was all it was. Ned's face must lie between them, he thought, preventing anything stronger. A bar which prevented her from seeing him as other than a new and more responsible brother. On the other hand she was the only person whom he had met who could easily and instantly distinguish between them—which told him what?

Certainly it was Eleanor, and to a lesser extent her great-aunt, rather than Ned, who had drawn him to Stanton House after his first days in London. He could only hope that her fears about Ned were ill-founded.

That they were not, Eleanor discovered the very next morning. Ned came down early for breakfast for once, looking ill, his hands trembling. Almeria had already retired to her room to prepare for a morning visit to an old friend. She had arranged for Eleanor to accompany her.

Ned caught at her hand when she rose to leave.

'Don't go, Nell. I need to speak to you. It's urgent.'

'Very well, but don't be too long. I am due to go out with Great-Aunt shortly.'

She sat down. Ned caught at her hand again, saying breathlessly, 'Good God, not here, where we may be interrupted.' He looked around with a haunted expression. 'In the study, perhaps.'

'Very well, if you must.'

When they reached the study, however, Ned hardly knew how to begin. He looked everywhere but at her. Finally, and unexpectedly, he came out with, 'You like Victor, don't you, Nell?'

Her answer dismayed him. 'A little, but not nearly as much as I did.'

'Oh, come on, Nell,' he ground out. 'You know you do.'

Eleanor's expression was a pained one. 'Do come to the point, Ned.' She was worried that she might be late, and she knew that her great-aunt deplored unpunctuality: 'the beginning of sin', she had once called it.

'Well, I'm horribly in debt to all sorts of tradesmen, and on top of that I've lost an awful lot of tin to Victor. There's no way I can repay any of it. Victor says he'll cancel all my debts if…if I…'

He stopped, his head hanging.

'Oh, Ned, if what?' she asked him, exasperated. 'If you can't come to the point I shall have to leave you.'

'If I persuade you… If you'll marry him. Oh, Nell, do say that you will—you know you like him. All my troubles will be over.'

Shocked, Eleanor sank into the nearest chair.

'No, Ned, no. You don't know what you're asking of me.'

He fell on his knees before her, clutching at her hands.

'Oh, Nell, do but consider. I shall be ruined if you won't accept him. I beg you, do but consider…'

She wrenched her hands from his and shook her head, unable to speak.

He was desperate.

'Say you'll consider, please, Nell, please… Sir Hart… I shall be ruined. It's little enough to ask of you…'

Somehow she managed to answer him. 'No, Ned, no. It's vile of him to suggest such a thing! How can I want to marry a man who would buy me after this fashion?'

His answer was to burst into tears, wailing at her through them. 'Please, Nell, please, for my sake, for Ned's sake, for all we mean to one another.'

'I will consider, but I can hold out no hope that I shall change my mind. I will give you my answer in two days' time, and you must accept it, whatever it is. Now I must leave you.'

Ned had to be content with that. Glum and ashamed, trapped in his own self-indulgence, he watched her leave the study. As for Eleanor, she was in a frenzy of anger and revulsion.

So the old alliance between Ned and Nell had come to this sorry end. Ned was prepared to sell her to Victor, for whom he knew that she did not care, to pay his gaming debts. Worse than that, she was sure that once they were written off Ned would start gambling again, by virtue of having once—no, twice—being saved from his folly.

Everything that Sir Hart had said to her nearly two years

ago, before he had sent her to London, came back to her in a new light. How would *she* have ended up if she had given way to every desire, every light and foolish impulse, as Ned was doing, which she *had* begun to do before Almeria had taken her in hand?

To what would she finally have stooped when matters turned sour—as they surely would have done? Would she have turned into her aunt Emily, always known as The Bolter, who had abandoned not one husband, but two, and who now lived in permanent exile and semi-poverty in a tiny German duchy?

She sent word to her great-aunt that she was taken ill and begged to be let off the morning's excursion. She was shivering so violently that the maid put a warming pan into her bed before she crept into it. All that she had recently learned about herself and Ned—knowledge recently gained—told her why Nat had been forbidden to her, and what Sir Hart had really been speaking of when he had reproached her.

Her answer to Ned must be no, whatever the cost to him. She could neither give way to him nor be his keeper, as Alan had said, but surely there must be some way out. She wrote a short note to the Lorings, regretting that she could not visit them that afternoon as she had promised, but she did not suggest an alternative date. After this morning's work she felt that she never wanted to see any of them again.

Briefly, she wondered what Alan's advice to her would be if he knew of this latest development.

Alan had an ability which had served him well in the past and would do so in the future. Worried though he might be about Ned and Eleanor, once away from them he filed them away in the back of his mind and concentrated on trying to put Dilhorne's on an even keel again: helping the Hattons was something he would think about later.

Dilhorne's London branch had been on the verge of bankruptcy when he had arrived in England, and although he had staved off immediate ruin he needed to exercise all his powers to restore them to a satisfactory state. Their rivals had found them an easy mark to exploit, and it would take time and trouble to teach them that those happy days had gone.

The day on which Eleanor was due to tell Ned of her decision over Victor saw him dealing with a firm of shippers who had come to regard Dilhorne's with contempt since George Johnstone had become its manager.

They allowed this contempt to show when Alan, a very young man in their eyes, arrived with George to negotiate a new contract with them. He allowed George to do the talking while he sprawled at ease, his eyes half closed, looking bored, and occasionally yawning openly.

Well, it was obvious to him that they thought that they had George sewn up—as they had in the past. They looked pious when they told him regretfully that their rates for carriage in the Far Eastern trade must rise yet again.

In the middle of their self-serving explanation he interrupted them—they knew who he was for George had introduced him to them when they had arrived—and remarked in a passable imitation of Ned Hatton at his silliest, 'Pray, Mr. Simpson, would you say all that again? Didn't quite get it.'

Simpson stared at him offensively, and repeated his outrageous offer.

Alan yawned. 'You've lost me, old man. Could you take me through it again—more slowly this time.'

George would have laughed at Simpson's expression if Alan had not warned him beforehand of what he proposed

to do. Simpson repeated what he had said as though Alan
were ten years old, and backward at that.

Alan picked up a piece of paper and began to write on
it, slowly, his tongue protruding between his lips as though
he were having acute difficulty in forming the words and
figures on paper. Simpson and his aides watched him, fascinated. They had heard that he was shrewd: they saw nothing shrewd here. Alan continued to struggle with the figures
before him, breathing heavily. He then gazed earnestly at
them, his face contorted.

'Profitable contract for you, would you say?' he managed
at last.

Simpson was careless. 'Profitable for both of us, Mr Dilhorne.'

Alan addressed his paper once again.

The mute hostility and impatience radiating from Simpson and his cohorts could almost be felt. Nothing daunted,
he struggled on, swore gently when his pencil point broke,
looked up and managed to avoid George's eye. George,
indeed, was purple in the face from suppressed laughter.

'I am a busy man,' announced Simpson repressively,
when Alan began working on his figures again from the
beginning, his face screwed up in almost palpable concentration on the task before him.

'I have already spent the best part of the morning on
this. I believe that Mr Johnstone understands the terms I
am offering, and why I have offered them. He knows the
market and the current rates. Pray save us all our time by
consulting with him and closing with us.'

Alan ignored him. Suddenly shouting a triumphant 'Yes'
he finished adding up a line of figures. He walked to the
window, holding the paper up to the light the better to
examine it.

'You are sure your figures are correct, Mr Simpson?' he
asked dubiously. 'I would not like to get my sums wrong.

Bad example for George here to discover that a member of the firm is not up to it and all that. Pray repeat them for me.'

He sounded more like fatuous Ned Hatton than ever.

George gave a curious muffled groan when Simpson, plainly nearing breaking point, repeated his figures for the fourth time.

'We have dealt with Dilhorne's for some years now, young sir. No one has ever expressed any reservations about our prices before.'

'I know,' said Alan, waving his paper about in a vague, happy manner. 'Begging George's pardon, and yours, too, I am sure, what puzzles me is not you, sir—I quite see your corner in this—but why Dilhorne's should ever have agreed to such prices in the first place.

'Now, this piece of paper would seem to show me that you have made something like five hundred per cent profit out of us in the last three years. A pretty little swindle, wouldn't you say? Taking advantage of poor George, here. Not really trained in all this, was he? He don't mind me saying that, I'm sure, he's learning fast is George.

'Why, just yesterday George helped me to negotiate a possible deal with your rival Jenkinson down the road, at half your price. You see, in the past George took your word of honour—a big mistake that—he knows better now, don't you, George?'

George, his face red with the effort of trying not to laugh at the expression on Simpson's face, nodded, and muttered, 'Yes, Mr Dilhorne, sir, I've learned a lot since you arrived in London.'

'Thank you, George.' Alan smiled. 'Now, let me explain to Mr Simpson that if he wants our business he'd better dip under what Jenkinson has to offer, and after that we'll see what Jenkinson has to say in the way of fresh terms. I'm sure, Mr Simpson, sir, that you will understand why I needed to know *your* exact terms. I thought at first that they were a hum, you see.'

His smile when he said this was so engaging that it nearly undid George.

It was Simpson who was purple now. 'No one from Dilhorne's has ever complained before. Not Mr Johnstone, here, nor his predecessor, Mr Montagu.'

'Well, Montagu wouldn't, would he?' said Alan agreeably. 'Seeing that you were giving him a cut of your profits to get him to sign preposterous agreements like the one you just offered me. Not preposterous for you, I do acknowledge. But you soon saw that George here was green—begging your pardon, George—and you offered *him* nothing. Another big mistake. Greedy, weren't you? Think how poor George felt when he learned what you'd been giving Montagu. I had to up his stipend to console him.'

He got up, tossing the paper on to the table before them and saying negligently, 'Think it over. You'll find my offer is at the bottom. I expect to hear from you, one way or the other, tomorrow.'

George bursting behind him, he swept out. It was not the first time, nor the last, that he was to leave a room in an uproar. The recriminations at Simpson were severe.

'Now how the devil did he find out that Montagu was on the take?' moaned one.

'Went through all the books like a hawk when he first got here,' said another. 'I always thought that we should have listened to the talk about him—and his father.'

'But who would have thought it?' wailed Simpson miserably. 'Perfect picture of a ninny when he came in, and then there was all that wretched business with the paper. He looked like Johnstone's worst.'

'Not giving Johnstone a cut was a big mistake,' said the first speaker, wise after the event. 'Bound to help that bastard of a boy crucify us when he found out.'

'Laughing their heads off at us this minute, no doubt,' said Simpson miserably. It was the truest statement he had made all morning.

'Never had such fun in all my life,' gasped George when Alan treated him to a drink in the City Road. 'You should have seen his face when you started writing on that piece of paper as though you didn't know what writing was, after you'd made him repeat his awful terms three times running. Once to me, and twice to you. You even got him choking out a fourth. You should be on the stage, Dilhorne. You looked like the village idiot at play. Where did you learn such tricks? God, you're a fly-boy. No one's safe around you.'

This was a sentiment echoed by an embittered Simpson at the end of the uproar.

Alan looked modest. 'I may be fly, but I never cheat— until I'm cheated, that is. Anything goes then—no ceiling to it. Mind that, George. Honesty first, last and always, if you can. It pays better in the long run—but take the dishonest for every penny. I'm sorry I had to cut you up a bit, but it was all in a good cause. Not your fault that you were brought up to live a soft life, not a hard one. At least you're learning fast.'

Unlike Ned Hatton, was Alan's private judgement.

George nodded, then exploded over his claret. 'Worried about getting your sums right, were you? That was the richest bit of all! I've never met anyone faster with figures than you.'

Alan nodded, amused by the pleasure of his recent recruit to hard work and common sense. When George asked him if he thought that Simpson would agree to the terms he had offered, he answered him plainly.

'Bound to, aren't they? They need our business. They won't want to lose it—particularly since somehow the truth about today will get out. Biter bit, and all that.

'Close with us and they get something. Lose us to Jenkinson and Queer Street might beckon. Question really is,
do we want them? Think it over, George, and let me know
in the morning. Home now. Dilhorne's is on the up and up
at last and we've earned the right to play a little.'

Eleanor had spent two sleepless nights worrying about
Ned and his monstrous offer. She acknowledged that when
she had first met Victor she might have agreed to marry
him, but the more she knew of him, the less she liked him.
He was rude and unkind to everyone, family, servants and
even his horses. How, then, once he was married, would
he treat his wife?

She could not help comparing him with Alan Dilhorne.
She was well aware from the gossip which ran round society that he was a hard man in the City, but he treated
everyone he met, including scapegrace Ned, with unfailing
civility. Almeria's head groom had commented in her hearing on his considerate treatment of the horse which Ned
had lent him until he had acquired one of his own.

To refuse Ned's wishes meant condemning him to social
ruin and a debtor's prison, since, for the life of her, she
could think of no way of saving him. She thought of asking
Alan for help, but this was family trouble—and how could
she reveal to him that Ned was, in effect, trying to sell her?

The other question was, how would Sir Hart take this
latest piece of folly? He had already let Ned off so many
times. He seemed doomed to die disappointed in all his
descendants, and, looking at the trail of ruin which had
begun with his faithless wife—of whom her great-aunt
never spoke—and which had been continued by her father,
her uncle and Emily the Bolter, to say nothing of Beastly
Beverley, who looked set to follow the same dreadful path
as the rest, she could not repress a shudder.

Was all that was left to her to try to live a good life

herself, so that Sir Hart might have something to hold on to? Yes, she must disappoint Ned, and so she told him when he dragged her into the study again.

'No, you can't do this to me, Nell. He's ready to offer for you tonight and he's promised to tear up all my IOUs when you accept him,' shouted Ned angrily in the middle of their first real quarrel. 'You know that you like him— or you will when you marry him.'

'I can't like, or want to marry, a man who would stoop to blackmailing my brother to compel me to marry him. You should have thought of what you were doing before you wagered so much.'

'Dammit, Nell, I only did so because I lost so much to him that I believed that my luck must change and I could win it all back—only it didn't. I was hoping to clear all my other debts, too.'

'How do you propose to pay these other debts, Ned? Marrying me to Victor will only settle his.'

'Oh, good God, Nell, don't be such a flat. You know perfectly well that Sir Hart will settle a fortune on you when you make a good match. Victor comes from a good family, even if he is poor. You can help to bail me out when you're married.'

Worse and worse! Eleanor felt that she could sink through the floor at this revelation of how far Ned had sunk into moral idiocy.

'No, Ned. You must take this as final. If you and Victor have concocted this scheme between you then you are both even viler than I thought. That is my last word.'

Ned suddenly fell on his knees before her and, taking her hands in his, began to beseech her desperately.

'Oh, God, Nell, for old times' sake, do what I ask. You know that marriage is a lottery. As well marry Victor as another—and I shall be saved…'

As cold as ice, shivering between disillusion and shock,

Nell gazed down at him while he shrieked almost frantically at her to save him from the ruin which was about to destroy him.

Alan, his business with Simpson safely concluded, drove home to his rooms in the Albany to ready himself to visit the Hattons. At the Leominsters' ball he and Ned had agreed to pay their delayed visit to Cremorne Gardens that evening.

He arrived at Stanton House to be let in by Staines, who did not announce him—he was now one of the privileged few who came and went as the family did.

'Mr Ned and Miss Eleanor are in the study. I believe that you know the way, sir.'

Alan was later to wonder whether Staines knew something, and had steered him deliberately towards the confrontation between brother and sister. The noise of their quarrel came through the door carelessly left open by Ned in his excitement. He hovered for a moment, wondering whether he ought to leave and wait elsewhere, until the sense of what he was hearing had him standing silent and shocked.

So Ned Hatton was asking his sister to save him by selling herself to that swine, Loring, and was bullying her brutally in order to persuade her! To go, or to stay? The quarrel had reached the point where Ned fell on his knees and was wailing desperately at poor Eleanor.

Alan's disgust was extreme. He knew that Ned Hatton was weak—but this was beyond anything!

He pushed the door open and strode into the study to find a white-faced and shaking Eleanor standing over Ned, who had no more sense than to rise to his feet and say with his usual facile charm, 'Oh, you come *àpropos*, Alan. We were having a tedious argument. Eleanor, as usual, is being unreasonable.'

At this bare-faced piece of dishonesty Alan found himself gripped by something he had felt only once or twice before. He had told Pat Ramsey—incorrectly, although he did not know it—that he was not as ruthless as his father, that his response to life was easy and relaxed.

But the cold rage which flooded through him in response to Ned's careless words was frightening. It was as though he saw the whole world with dreadful clarity, with movement in it slowed down and himself the pivot of it. At the same time he felt a killing anger: a truly berserker rage.

He reached out and took Ned by his cravat with both hands, half lifting him off his feet. Behind Ned he saw Eleanor, her eyes wide and frightened. His face, although he did not know it, was almost unrecognisable: it was a cold mask of anger.

'What was that you said, Ned? Explain yourself. What was your argument with Eleanor really about?'

Ned was paralysed with fright. The transformation of easy, charming Alan into a cold and cruel stranger was the worse for it being his own face which looked at him. He put his hand up to try to relax Alan's grip on his throat. By now Alan's expression was such that any resemblance between the two men had disappeared completely.

'No, Alan,' cried Eleanor, 'let him go, please.'

He did not hear her. His whole attention was focused on Ned's face. The pivot of the universe was transferred from himself to that.

'I said, explain yourself, Ned.'

'Then let me go,' croaked Ned, 'and I will.'

'Not until you have explained yourself. What was that about Victor Loring?'

'I owe him,' mumbled Ned.

'Louder. You owe him what?'

'Thousands. He has my IOUs for thousands.'

'He has demanded that you sell Eleanor to him as the price for destroying them, is that it?'

'Oh, God, Alan, you put things so crudely.'

'Is there a way of putting it elegantly, then?'

Ned's eyes dropped.

'You've no need to pay him anything. You know that. Gambling debts don't exist in law.'

'They do in honour,' Ned moaned.

Alan's laugh was humourless. 'Honour? Are you all run mad in England? What honour is there in selling your sister to a vile bully to rid yourself of your gambling debts?' He shook Ned as though he were a rag doll. 'By God, I've a mind to thrash you before her.'

'No, Alan.' Eleanor's hand was on his arm. 'Please, Alan. Let him go. He's…'

'Weak,' said Alan, and shook his head. He still held Ned by the throat.

He turned to Eleanor and said, 'Tell me that you really wish to marry Victor Loring without Ned's pressure and his blackmail and I'll leave at once. Neither of you will see me again.'

Two pairs of eyes looked mutely at him. Both dropped before his own steady gaze. Eleanor sank into a chair and began to cry, speaking in a muffled voice through her sobs.

The whole sad story slowly emerged: she could not bear the notion of marrying Victor, he was repulsive to her, but what would become of Ned if she refused? It was all too much—particularly since Sir Hart would almost certainly disinherit Ned if he should ever find out the truth.

'Indeed!' said Alan grimly. 'Quite understandable if he did. Is this the whole truth, Ned?'

Ned lowered his head, mutely agreeing. Alan's rage drained out of him and he flung Ned away so that he ended up against the wall.

'Victor Loring! You were proposing to sacrifice your sister to that gentlemanly piece of filth who can't so much as treat a horse decently! He has your IOUs?'

Ned fingered his damaged throat and nodded a yes.

'Will you leave him to me?' The rage reared again inside Alan. It demanded satisfaction, was cold, not hot—which made it the more terrifying.

'What will you do?' quavered Ned.

'I don't know yet. Something.'

'Oh, God, Alan, if you could save me I'd be so grateful.'

That you would sell Eleanor to me instead, thought Alan disgustedly, but he did not say so aloud, wondering what all this had done to his growing rapport with her.

She stood up, drying her tears. 'Oh, Alan, please be careful. There is something else you ought to know. However tempted I might have been, I would never have obliged Ned in such a way—not even to save him.'

'But he asked you. I have no doubt, too, that Loring suggested the whole rotten scheme to him. No, you need not answer me, Eleanor, I know the truth now, about you and Ned both, and further talk will only cause you pain.'

You're the only man in the family, he thought, barring the unknown Sir Hartley Hatton, that is. He could not help comparing her favourably with feckless Ned. Likeable and charming he might be on the surface, but there was nothing to him, and by all accounts his grandfather, the poor devil, had no one who might be the family's saviour, given that Beastly Beverley was the next heir!

Below-stairs the duty footman from the entrance hall dashed into the kitchen where the staff, Staines included, were drinking tea.

'It's all gone quiet in the study,' he reported excitedly. 'I thought that young Dilhorne was going to murder Master Ned, that I did. One good thing—poor Miss Eleanor won't be marrying Victor Loring after all.'

'Listened at the door did you?' said Alan's servant Gurney, putting down his teacup. He did not expect an answer. 'Put things right, has he?'

'What I want to know,' said Staines magisterially, 'is how he does it? Young Dilhorne, I mean.' He looked expectantly at Gurney.

Gurney shrugged his shoulders. 'I dunno. I only know that he puts things right, does Golden Boy. Put things right for me, didn't he? When Lord Gresham couldn't. Put them right at Dilhorne's—and more beside.'

Golden Boy was his nickname for Alan, one which his hearers delightedly seized on.

'One thing,' said Gurney, hopefully holding out his cup to Cook for more tea, 'I wouldn't advise anyone to cross him, or get on the wrong side of him.'

'Handsome, though, isn't he? And he always speaks polite to me, too,' said one of the parlour maids dreamily.

'Polite to everyone,' said Gurney, 'except those he don't like, of course.'

'He didn't like Master Ned much this afternoon,' sniggered the footman. 'Good idea of yours, Mr Staines, to steer him into the study.'

Staines put a finger by his nose, and murmured, 'A good servant looks after the best interests of his masters.'

'Aye, aye,' said Gurney, and drank his tea down before conversation moved on to other upstairs gossip.

He wondered privately how Golden Boy was going to trick his way out of this mess and put things right for flighty Ned Hatton.

Chapter Five

Pushing Ned Hatton further and further into debt had seemed a good idea to Victor Loring. After that, piling pressure on him to persuade Eleanor to accept him had seemed an even better one. It appeared, however, that his plan was not working as well as he had hoped.

Eleanor was now avoiding the Lorings. She was not at home when they called, although an unhappy Caroline had discovered that she had been at home to others on the days when she had been refused. She had also ceased to visit them. She had deliberately avoided the whole family when they had seen her in Hyde Park and, all in all, it seemed that stupid Ned Hatton was living up to his name. He couldn't even persuade his sister to save him.

So Ned would have to be pushed even harder. He could threaten to write to Sir Hart, demanding that he pay Ned's debts of honour, or he could run him even deeper into the mire by persuading him to gamble at Rosie's yet again, with the bait that this time luck would be with him and he could recoup some of what he had lost.

The trouble was that Ned, strapped for cash, was now dodging him as well.

Alan was doing some planning of his own. Several options were open to him. He could pay Ned's debts himself, but that would merely serve to destroy Ned even further, by making him think that all his scrapes could be easily solved by the actions of others, not his own.

On the other hand he had promised to extricate Ned from this pit of his own making, but how? And by what means? And when—and if—he had done that, he might then try to steer Ned on to the straight and narrow path of virtue, by threats as well as bribes.

One ploy he could use was his strange resemblance to Ned, but Victor might be on the look-out for that, so it could be dangerous. On the other hand Alan knew that he was a better mimic than he had already revealed. It was not only voices which he could master, but body movements, too, and he was prepared to take the risk if Ned was. Ned, though, would always be the weak link. He would have to trust him to play his part correctly, and pray that his trust would not be misplaced.

His plan of action decided, Alan outlined it to Ned, and with all the foolish optimism which made him such a bad gambler Ned was mad to adopt it immediately, without even examining it for possible weak links.

Alan told him severely, 'Think it over. It might go wrong. You might end up in even greater debt to Victor, if, as I believe, he is rigging the cards.'

'Never,' said Ned with the sublime innocence of a pigeon ready for yet another plucking, 'not Victor. He wouldn't cheat, he's a gentleman.'

'Oh, yes,' said Alan sardonically. 'That makes him pure in heart, I suppose. Do you think that a man who would blackmail another man's sister into marrying him wouldn't stoop to cheat at cards?'

Alan was sure that Victor was a cheat. The Patriarch had spent many happy hours warning his sons of what card-sharps might get up to. He had shown them all the tricks of the professional gambler's trade, including rigging and marking the cards, false shuffles, false cuts, sleight of hand, how to cheat at Find the Lady as well as the cogging and switching of dice.

'I am telling you this,' he had said sternly, 'not so that you shall do it yourself, but so that others can't do it to you. Watch for the warning signs, and the moment that you see them make an excuse to leave the game at once.'

Alan had watched Victor at play, and had seen all the signs for which his father had told him to look.

It was Eleanor who almost prevented him from carrying out his daring plan of rescue for Ned. He had been working in the City and arrived at Stanton House in the late afternoon to find Ned was visiting Hyde Park but that Eleanor was in.

She had spent her day with Charles in the schoolroom and then in thinking about herself, Ned and the Hattons generally. She was compelled to acknowledge that her affections, even though she had known him for such a short time, were fixed on Alan.

Something in his manner, the affectionate way in which he teased her, as though he was the ideal brother whom she now knew that she had never had, encouraged her to think that he might have something of a *tendre* for her. The trouble was that she had seen little of him recently because he was so occupied by his responsibilities to Dilhorne's, and now by this wretched business of Ned's. But she was sensible enough to admit that the world was not only made for love and pleasure, however much the novels which she read might suggest.

She sighed. She also had to admit that men had the whole world to rove in. Alan, yes, and even Ned, had occupations and business to fill their days as well as a range of other interests. She, on the other hand, had had to fight in order to spend a few serious hours a week with Charles's tutor instead of spending her life talking about balls and bonnets, giggling over young men and engaging in the vapid world of making a good marriage where she would most likely be neglected in favour of horse and hound.

It might have been better for her to have been born a boy—until she thought that she could have turned out like Ned and, much though she loved her brother, that thought filled her with horror.

She was seated, trying to read, when Alan arrived. She put her book down and said in her pleasant and straightforward manner, which contrasted so strongly with that of most of the other women whom he had met in London, 'You always come at the right moment, Alan. Ned is still out, which is fortunate since I wish to speak to you privately—whatever the conventions dictate.'

The stigmata of tiredness were on her face, but somehow Eleanor seemed more beautiful in her worry than other women in their vapid serenity.

'Firstly,' she continued, 'I will ring for tea, so as to make things a little more proper. I know that men and women should never talk seriously to one another. Tea will confer frivolity.'

Alan laughed at that. 'Dinner, I suppose, being a stage further on, allows us to rise to higher things.'

'Quite so. Slightly weightier matters may be discussed. Tea is for bonnets and balls,' she finished, echoing her own thoughts of a moment ago.

'I must remember that,' he told her. 'What is this serious matter you wish to raise with me?'

Eleanor put her finger to her lips: Staines and the parlour maid were arriving with the tea-board. She was not surprised that Alan's answer had been a straightforward one. Most men would have responded by murmuring, Do not worry your little head about such serious matters, my dear. Leave that to us.

The servants gone, she began to pour the tea, saying, 'I am troubled that you might put yourself at some risk by attempting to help Ned. Whilst I want to save him from Sir Hart's anger, I do not wish it to be done at your expense. Pray do not think me forward in raising this matter with you—and alone. After all, Ned involved me, and then we both involved you—to my regret.'

Alan put his cup and saucer carefully down. He had not yet learned the art of talking whilst trying to balance tea, bread and butter and cake.

'I'm flattered that you should care enough to wish that I may not find myself at a loss. But I owe Ned a great deal, you know, and I would like to do him a good turn.'

'You owe Ned?' Eleanor was surprised.

'Yes. Oh, I suppose it happened through the chance re-semblance, and Frank Gresham mistaking me for Ned, but after that Ned chose to introduce me to his world, where I met his family and friends—and you. My life in England has been made pleasant and easier by his kindness.'

'That may be so, but still—' She looked at him, her eyes troubled.

His answer was swift and considered. 'I'm sorry to appear to rebuff you when you have done me the honour of considering possible consequences for me so carefully. Of course, you are right to be worried. I have warned Ned that matters might go awry. But...'

It was his turn to pause.

Eleanor finished the sentence for him. 'But Ned is fool-ishly optimistic, as usual. Tell me, Alan, why is it that although you are little older than Ned, Frank and the rest, you seem to be so much more worldly-wise and...harder? Forgive me for calling you that, but no other word will suit.'

This amused Alan, as well as revealing to him that
Eleanor was showing a shrewdness foreign to Ned. They
might be brother and sister but they could scarcely be more
different in character. He decided to tell her the unaccept-
able truth. She seemed to be able to take it.

'It is because none of you have genuine occupations or
responsibilities. You are all idlers for whom other people
do the real work. I was not brought up as a rich man's son,
Eleanor. When I was sixteen years old I was made to work
at Campbell's Wharf as a common labourer, lifting freight.
After that I did a stint in the brickfields my father owned
before I was promoted to hauling goods between Sydney
and Paramatta for him.

'At night I was made to study, not only Latin and Greek,
but book-keeping and mathematics. When I had mastered
them I became a junior clerk in my father's counting house,
no favours granted. My brother Thomas followed a similar
path. I was resentful of such drudgery, but he was not.
Thomas was always steady and serious whilst I was wild.

'I spent one summer as a deck-hand on the Macao run
and back, and saw the world with nothing in my pocket
but a deck-hand's pay. It makes a man see true to do that.
There were times I hated the Patriarch, when he allowed
his workmen to bait me on the wharf as though I were any
chance-hired boy—and for other humiliations, too. What
was I a rich man's son for if I were to suffer as though I
were not?

'But now? Now I cannot properly describe my gratitude
for what he made me do—and I know that I had it easy
compared with his life at my age. So, when I look at Ned
and the rest...'

He fell silent, but he did not need to finish.

'I see,' said Eleanor quietly. 'Yes, that explains a great
deal.'

That Alan had been wild surprised her, he seemed so

steady—until she thought of the way in which he had dominated Ned. Her understanding of his difference from all the young men she knew was heightened by what he had told her. It would have done Ned good to live like that, she thought, but the impossibility of it almost made her smile.

She said no more. Alan's plan to deal with Victor would go ahead.

Alan, drinking his tea and admiring her calm self-control, thought of all that he had not told her of that bygone summer on the sea. Of the hard work and the comradeship, the fun and the fighting and drinking in the ports they had visited. He remembered the rich man's widow in Macao who had taken the eager boy he had been into her bed.

He thought, too, of how he had argued and fought with the Patriarch to avoid going, before he gave in and finally consented. On his return, bronzed and muscular, a man among men, he had said simply to him, 'Thank you, Father,' because in some ways it had been the finest experience he had ever had, despite the hazing and the backbreaking work.

Dealing with Ned and Victor was child's play after what the Patriarch had put him through!

The plot against Victor Loring depended for its success on two things—making a successful switch between himself and Ned at some point in the evening, without Victor detecting it, and Alan's own ability to defeat a man who was cheating without being caught himself. One advantage was that if Victor thought that he was playing stupid Ned Hatton he would be careless.

Victor, determined to turn the screw on Ned, was delighted to find him willing to be friendly again. He was not to know that Ned was following Alan's instructions. So friendly was he that Victor found it easy to persuade him to indulge in yet another night's play at Rosie's, where he would consign Ned to a ruin so dire that even Eleanor's resolve might be broken.

'Time for you to try to get your revenge,' he said generously. 'Piquet shall be our game, and to give you a chance to recoup, let the winner take all.'

He was a little surprised that Ned agreed to these terms immediately—he must be even more desperate than Victor had thought he was.

He arrived at Stanton House to collect Ned, to find that that colonial savage Dilhorne was there: he had no wish to have him watching over Ned like a bear leader with his charge. He was only too relieved to learn that Dilhorne was going on to the Palmerstons' reception that night—every dam'd fool in London seemed to have nothing better to do than make a pet of him.

Eleanor was there, too, and greeted him so pleasantly that Victor's hopes rose again. She was not accompanying Alan to the reception—she said that she had a migraine coming and consequently Almeria would cancel also. Almeria was not in the plot, but had taken Eleanor's explanation at face value. Ned having cried off as well, Alan would have to go on his own.

Ned rapidly consented to visit a dive near the Haymarket before they went on to Rosie's, where they both drank heavily. At least Ned drank heavily, on Alan's instructions, and Victor was more careful. Rosie's was crowded when they finally reached it.

Several of the *habitués* shrugged knowingly when they saw Victor steering his unsteady pigeon towards the table of drinks whilst loudly promising the half-cut Ned a good game. The light in Rosie's was not good, a fact that had influenced Alan in his plan to change places with Ned before he began to play with Victor.

'Must go outside,' said Ned shortly afterwards, 'can't play you in this state.'

He stumbled into the smelly yard at the back, where a privy stood. Alan, having earlier shown his face at the reception, had already arrived there after scaling a low wall. He was waiting for Ned to appear.

Fortunately the night was fine, and they changed places as quickly as they could in the shadow between the wall and the privy. Ned was wearing a ruby stick-pin, distinctive rings, and a gold hunter given to him by Sir Hart. He pulled them all off and handed them over to Alan, whose clothing was identical to his own.

They had originally intended to change coats, but Alan's more massive shoulders had prevented that. Fortunately Ned's rings fitted Alan, just. Alan found that the seal ring with the Hatton eagle on it was the most difficult to force on to his finger, but he finally managed to make it fit.

Impatient Ned swore a little at the delay, but Alan was coolness itself. He hoisted Ned over the wall after he had promised to go home immediately by way of various back streets: it would not do for him to be seen.

Alan took a deep breath and made his faltering way back to the smoke-filled room.

'Thought you'd got lost,' drawled Victor.

'Dam'd buttons,' swore Alan, his mumble strangled. 'Ready to play old man. Want my revenge.'

They sat at one of the small tables and the game began, after Alan had fetched himself a glass of brandy. He tossed it down in one gulp—and, being stone-cold sober, he filled another and took it to the table—his breath was now as rank as Ned's had been.

He had been correct to believe that contempt for Ned would make Victor careless, for he switched the pack of cards provided by the house quite clumsily, and substituted his own marked one. His subsequent cheating was more skilful, but not skilful enough to deceive a man taught by a master. He was also under the disadvantage of playing against someone whom he thought was drunk but was sober.

Alan began by allowing Victor to win—a ploy designed to convince him that he was again about to take Ned Hatton for all that the fool decided to wager. He knew that to a certain extent gambling was as much a test of stamina as anything else. He had instructed Ned to drink heavily for he needed an excuse not to drink himself.

'Shan't last the night out if I take any more,' he claimed in a drunken mumble. 'Don't want to be incapable.'

The luck suddenly, and surprisingly, turned. From winning easily Victor found himself losing, just as easily. Ned's luck, indeed, was amazing. This was not surprising, for Alan, a far better player than Victor, was using the marked pack to his own advantage, as well as employing a few tricks of his own. A small crowd gathered round at the sight of Victor being taken by poor Ned Hatton for once. The pile of Ned's IOUs passed back to Alan, for this had been agreed beforehand, and then, in a desperate bid to carry on the game, Victor began signing his own, and these, too, swelled the pile in front of the supposed Ned.

Victor suddenly swore at the crowd pressing around them; their nearness was destroying his chance to cheat.

'Damn you all. A fellow can't play with you breathing down his neck. Get back, can't you?'

One of the club's minders, there to keep order, immediately pushed the crowd away, greatly to Alan's relief, for he thought that the game was reaching a climax, and he did not want curious eyes to see and hear exactly what was going on.

After one heavy loss, while Victor was desperately signing yet another IOU, he looked up unexpectedly to see Alan's hard, cold stare, so unlike Ned's, on him. In his turn he stared at the man opposite to him.

Understanding flooded in. He might have started the evening with the true Ned Hatton, but he had not finished it with him. Fortunately for Alan rage filled Victor to the degree that he could barely speak.

He put out his hand and caught Alan, who was gathering up the cards, by the wrist. Alan had known the moment that he had seen Victor's face change that, tired by the long night, he had dropped his guard and given himself away.

'You cheat,' whispered Victor, choked with a consuming anger. 'It's Dilhorne I've been playing, not Ned Hatton, who agreed to play against me. You changed over. I swear that it was Ned who came here with me. How…? Oh, the privy, of course. Just wait until I tell the room of this! No decent house in London will ever receive you—or Ned— again.'

Alan was ready for him.

'By all means tell them,' he whispered back. 'If you do I'll show them the marked cards, and the ones you're carrying in your sleeve. I'm a cheat, beating and cheating a cheat, I agree. Choose, Loring, choose! Expose us both, or leave us quits, neither of us to become outcasts—for who would receive you, either?'

Victor sat there in agony. Part of him wanted to jump up and expose the barbarian before him. The other part told him that he could not afford to do so.

'Cut your losses,' said Alan, picking up Victor's IOUs. 'End the game. Neither of us wishes to be socially ruined— I will survive it, but you can't.'

'You leave me no choice,' muttered Victor, aware that curiosity at this abrupt end to the game was drawing the spectators near to them again, now that they had stopped.

'Done,' said Alan. He picked up the cards and pitched them into the fire. Quite suddenly, and to Victor's astonishment, he turned into careless Ned Hatton again. He rose to his feet and shouted '*Io triomphe*—I win,' in exactly Ned's voice, and called for a taper and a bowl.

Winking at the shaken Victor, he picked up the two piles of IOUs, the one of Ned's, which he had won back, and the other of Victor's, recklessly given, and placed them in the copper bowl provided. Then, with a characteristic flourish, so that the whole room cheered, and agreed that mad Ned Hatton had never been madder, he picked up the taper, put it into one of the candles which lit the room—and set fire to both piles before handing the bowl and the ashes to the astonished Victor.

'Quits,' he proclaimed—and his imitation of Ned was perfect. 'I'll not play against you, Victor, ever again. The slate is clean between us, and will remain so. Now, who's for a drink on the winner?'

Delirious with laughter, he staggered across to the table laden with food and drink, the sound of the company's cheers following him.

Chapter Six

The gossip ran round London. The tale of how Ned Hatton had turned the tables on Victor Loring was too good not to pass on. If there were some, like Frank Gresham, who wondered which Ned Hatton had played Victor, the knowledge that he had seen Alan Dilhorne several times that night at the Palmerstons' reception—for Alan had returned to it shortly after midnight—made a switch seem unlikely.

Victor, of course, kept mum. Alan had not only saved his reputation, but had burned the IOUs which he might have retained—and then ruined him by demanding that they be repaid.

The big problem, as both Alan and Eleanor agreed, was trying to keep Ned mum! He was quite capable of blurting out the whole story after he had been drinking, however many times he assured Alan that he never would.

'Ned says that you burned Victor's debts,' Eleanor said to Alan when she met him again, several days later, 'but I'm worried about the Lorings. None of them have been seen in the Park since Victor lost to you. Do you think that he was going to pay his creditors with Ned's IOUs if I refused to marry him?'

'You mustn't feel guilty about that,' Alan told her earnestly. 'Ned was asking an impossible sacrifice of you.'

'Still…' said Eleanor sadly. 'It's Mrs Loring and Caroline who worry me. They are his victims, are they not?'

And Victor is mine, thought Alan, a trifle sadly. Aloud, he said, 'All things considered, it is kind of you to worry about them. I would like to help them but I fear that after that night they may not want to know me.'

'Life is hard, isn't it?' she said earnestly. 'And I used to think that it was simple and easy. You are teaching me otherwise. Not deliberately, of course. You see, when we spoke of saving Ned I didn't foresee that doing so would hurt Victor's mother and Caroline as well.'

After that they spoke of other, lighter things, but Alan remembered this conversation the next morning in his office at Dilhorne's when Phipps informed him that there was a young lady asking to see him.

What young lady could that possibly be? 'Did she give her name?' he asked.

'She wouldn't, Mr Alan. Just said that it was urgent, that she needed help.'

'Show her in, anyway.'

It was Caroline Loring, her face pale and her eyes red with weeping. Alan rose and showed her to the only comfortable chair in the room.

'How may I help you, cousin Caroline?'

'I have not come for myself but for Victor. The only person I could think of who might help us is you.'

Alan grimaced, remembering that in effect he had ruined Victor not once, but twice.

'I would scarcely imagine that Victor would accept help from me.'

'He would not welcome it from anyone—but we, the three of us, desperately need it. And you are our cousin, Alan, even if we did not really befriend you.'

'Tell me what is wrong, Caroline, and I will see whether I may be able to assist you. I suppose that Victor is in Queer Street financially?'

'Oh, Alan,' half-sobbed Caroline, 'it is much worse than you think. Victor is not only broken, he is ruined. We are all ruined. You see, he'd always expected to inherit Essendene. Sir John told him that he would. So he lived high and played deep—and lost. When he asked Sir John to bail him out, Sir John refused. He then went to the money-lenders and borrowed on his expectations—and when he couldn't pay the interest on his debts they wrote to Sir John.

'Sir John was furious. So furious he cut Victor and all of us out of his will. He had told him he would, but Victor hadn't believed him.'

She began to sob in earnest.

'And then Sir John left everything to your mama. Victor owes so much, and so do Mama and I. We have no resources at all other than a small annuity left to us after our father died. He was a younger son, too. We thought that the Essendene estates would save us.

'After you and he played at...at...Rosie's—' when Alan gave a start of surprise she said sorrowfully, 'Oh, yes, everyone knows; it's a great joke. Ned talked—did you think that he wouldn't? Victor came home and said that he would break the will. It wasn't right. Sir John was out of his head when he made it. He sent for the lawyers. He wouldn't go to their offices, he made Mr Bunthorne come to us.

'Mr Bunthorne told us that Sir John had written two letters as well as the will. One for him and one for Victor, if he tried to challenge it. He gave Victor his letter. It said that Victor wasn't fit to inherit, that the Warings had done Sir John's brother, Fred, a great wrong, and that as he had grown older he had remembered Fred. He remembered carrying him about as a little one at Essendene. He had learned that Fred died miserably, in great poverty, in Sydney, and had left cousin Hester destitute. It was restitution, he wrote. If cousin Hester was alive she was to have everything, and if not it should all go to charity.

'After the lawyers had left Victor was beside himself. Mama and I could not quieten him. He threatened to commit suicide. He said that the money-lenders had him by the throat and if he could not pay by next quarter-day they would send him to the Marshalsea Prison for debt. If they did we were all ruined, for he would never get out of the Marshalsea once he was in it.

'He has locked himself into his room and he has been drinking heavily. He will not answer and Mama is half-mad. I am afraid for her, too.'

She stopped. Alan looked at her, at her gentle, pretty face, now ruined by grief. When he had destroyed Victor in Rosie's, half in fun, he had not realised that it might come to this. Caroline was right. He was their cousin, and that must mean something.

'Don't cry,' he said gently. 'I will try to do what I can for you. After all, I pushed him to his final ruin. I will call on you tonight, but don't tell him so.'

'I couldn't, if I wanted to. He will no longer speak to us.'

'Don't cry, I beg of you. Phipps shall call you a cab, if you have not one waiting. You must go home and tell my cousin Clara that I shall do what I can.'

Alan was not hopeful, despite what he had said to Caroline, that he could do much to rescue Victor, but he left work early in order to reach Russell Square as soon as possible. His cousin Clara flew at him when he entered her drawing room.

'Oh, cousin Alan, Caroline should not have come to see

you, but I am so glad that she did. He is still refusing to answer us. I am afraid for him.'

Alan was not. In his experience, men like Victor threatened much, but did little. He was still bullying his mother and his sister and trying to avoid the unpleasant facts of his idle and useless life.

'Where is he?'

'Upstairs. I will take you there, but I am sure that he will not speak to you.'

'Leave that to me, cousin. Please lead me to him.'

Victor's room was off the main first floor landing. Both women, faces pale, eyes red, at the end of their endurance, would have stayed with Alan, but he did not want their loving, fearful presence to inhibit him in what he might say or do.

'Best you both retire, and wait for me in the drawing room.'

After they had gone he knocked on the door. He heard movement, but no answer. He knocked again, saying, 'Cousin Victor, it is I, Alan Dilhorne. I wish to speak to you.'

There was silence, and then a choked voice replied, 'Damn you, Alan Dilhorne, go away. I have no wish to see you again.'

Alan beat a tattoo on the door. 'And damn you, too, cousin Victor, but I intend to see you, and if you do not open this door at once I shall have it broken down. You know me well enough by now to know that any threat which I make I will execute. Do you want another scandal?'

There was a short silence and then the door opened. A haggard-looking Victor beckoned him into a disordered room, stinking of tobacco, alcohol and unwashed man. A pistol lay on a side table.

'What do you want of me now, Dilhorne? You've ruined me, isn't that enough?'

'You ruined yourself,' retorted Alan. 'I've come to stop you from ruining your mother and your sister, too. You've bullied them into a stupor, but, God forgive them, they love you and want you saved.'

'Saved!' The word was almost an obscenity. 'By you? I'd rather be ruined.'

Alan strode over and seized Victor by the collar. It appeared, he thought, to be his favourite occupation when dealing with gentlemanly fools in England.

'You're half-drunk, Victor, or I'd teach you manners. It's your mother and your sister I'm thinking of, not you. Tell me, is it true that you are being threatened with the Marshalsea?'

Victor nodded.

'And your bills and debts. Where are they? Who owns them now?'

'They're over there, on my desk. Waldheim's have bought the lot, damn them. It's they who are threatening me with the Marshalsea if I can't pay.'

Alan let go of him. 'Waldheim's, you say? There might be hope there.'

'You make me laugh, Dilhorne. You're green. Hope with Waldheim's? Not a hope! They're the hardest of the lot.'

'Shut up, and let me look at them.'

Victor grinned madly. 'Look away. They'll tell you nothing.'

'For God's sake, Victor, I'm a businessman.'

'Yes, but you're not a money-lender.'

Alan ignored him for a moment and began to examine the pile of bills.

'You mistake, Victor. Your cousin Hester married a man who, among other things, is the biggest money-lender in Sydney. I ran that side of the business for him for two years.'

Victor sneered. 'I always knew that you weren't a gentleman.'

'I never claimed to be one,' returned Alan equably.

He sat down, found an unused sheet of soiled paper and began listing the dog-eared bills before him. Occasionally he asked Victor about rates of interest—to receive grudging replies. Victor watched him, fascinated against his will, until presently Alan looked up.

'Is this all?'

'Yes,' replied Victor, dropping his eyes.

'You're lying. Where are the rest? Damn you, Loring, I won't help you if you don't come clean.'

Loring, is it now? thought Victor resentfully, but said, 'The rest are in the right-hand drawer, and that's the lot, as God is my witness.'

'Well, he isn't. And God can't give evidence, particularly not in a mess like this. Shut up, man, I want to finish this, and I'm tired. I've done a day's work already.'

He wrote in silence for several more minutes before he said, 'What with the interest and all, there's a small fortune owing here. You do know that if they send you to the Marshalsea there's not the faintest hope that you'll ever get out again? I suppose that's why you're in here with a pistol. Only you're too weak to pull the trigger.'

Victor's answer was an anguished nod.

'I'll do what I can to clear matters up, but I can't promise that I shall be able to—only try.'

'Oh, God,' wailed Victor. 'I want to be saved, but to be saved by you is the worst thing of all.'

'Don't you ever listen to me? I keep telling you that I'm trying to save Clara and Caroline. If it weren't for them you could rot in the Marshalsea for ever for all I care.'

'Noble swine, aren't you?' sneered Victor.

'You're all the family I've got,' said Alan simply. 'My father has none, so you are, in some strange way, my responsibility, particularly since mine was the final blow which drove you to this. That's all.'

He picked up the pile of papers.

'You'll do two things for me in return. You'll not leave this house until I order you to, and you'll not bully poor Caroline for coming to tell me of your predicament. Now give me the pistol. You never intended to use it—other than to bully your wretched women. Try to comfort them a little, instead.'

Eleanor found Alan a trifle *distrait* that evening. They were at Lady Templestowe's ball, and during a brief interval while they queued for supper Eleanor said, 'You're not with us tonight, Alan.'

'No, I'm sorry. I've been thinking.'

She laughed up at him. 'It's not usual at a ball.'

'I know, but I've work to do tomorrow.'

'And that's not usual, either.'

They walked on for a little in silence. Then Alan said, 'Eleanor, I have a favour to ask of you.'

'And it is?' she replied swiftly.

'That's nice,' said Alan, laughing. 'No querying, no coyness. I like that.' His eyes stroked her which made her shiver. 'It's this. Be kind to my cousin Caroline and her mother. Life is very hard for them just now. I know it will be difficult for you, considering everything.'

'Yes,' agreed Eleanor, 'but that's not Caro's fault, is it?'

'Victor is in a bad way, too. Note that I do not ask you to be kind to *him*.'

'I should think not! But, yes, I'm sorry for Caro and I have been avoiding her. I thought that she would be here tonight. I know that she arranged to meet Anthony Beauchamp, but he told me just now that she must have cried off. Poor Caro, I know that she likes him, but she stands to lose him to other girls who are more determined.'

Alan took her small hand and pressed it gently. He looked at her as affectionately as he dared before the eyes of several hundred people and her great-aunt Almeria.

'Are you a determined girl, Eleanor?'

Her smile was wry. 'Mother thinks that I'm too determined, and so does Sir Hart.' Greatly daring, she added, 'What do you think, Alan?'

'That I like a girl who knows her own mind. I've never admired doormats.'

This set her laughing. 'And I like a man who says clever things. I shall miss you when you go home again.'

His eyes caressed her again. 'I've not yet made up my mind where home is, Eleanor. Perhaps you can help me.'

She had no notion of how to reply to that. It was the most direct statement he had yet made of any interest in her. So she smiled and said, 'Knowing you, I think that when the time comes you'll do exactly what you ought.'

Alan nodded, regretting that he had to leave early. He had, he told her, urgent business to do in the morning, and he needed a clear head. She watched him go, wondering how many other men in the vast assembly took their duties as seriously as Alan Dilhorne did.

He was up at dawn. He put on his finest togs, as Ned called them, and went off into the rabbit warrens of the City where the greatest names in money had their offices.

He ended up at Rothschild's, where his name took him into an imposing office where he talked to a youngish man of smooth appearance. They were closeted together for an hour and a half, which was a long time for the smooth man to spend with an unknown who was under thirty.

At the end of it sherry was brought in, and biscuits, on a silver salver. The two men drank to the fact that if matters went in a certain direction they might do business together immediately. If not, however, and the smooth man fully understood that this was problematical, there would be business done between them in the long, rather than, the short run.

When Alan had gone the smooth man entered an office where a slightly younger version of himself sat, who asked, 'Well, brother Lionel?'

The smooth man laughed. 'Very well, brother. I've just met the wariest young devil since father Nathan came to London, and if he doesn't take the City by storm some time soon, then I've lost my talent for judging men!'

Alan was consequently late in arriving at Dilhorne's—much to his staff's surprise. He went straight to Johnstone's office to ask him a question whose answer he thought that he already knew.

Alan was abrupt. 'What percentage of our bills are brokered through Waldheim's?'

'All our continental business, which is substantial, as you know. For once my predecessor worked out a good deal: good for them and good for us. Sebastian Waldheim is a tight-fisted swine, but honest. No kickbacks—unlike Simpson's.'

'And who is the senior partner there?'

'Mr Sebastian is the senior and Mr Julian is the junior—but Mr Sebastian never sees clients. Everything is done through Mr Julian.'

'He'll see me, I think,' said Alan, grinning at Johnstone's dubious face. 'Now, ask Phipps to give me as much detail about it as he can in the next half-hour, there's a good fellow. Tell him it's urgent.'

He missed luncheon to read through what Phipps had prepared for him, before walking to the dirty alley off Cheapside where Waldheim's offices were. He was stopped at the door by a porter who asked him his business while looking askance at his splendid clothes.

'I've come about some debts,' said Alan cheerfully.

'Have you, indeed?' sneered the porter, jumping to all the wrong conclusions. 'Just go through there.'

'There' proved to be a grimy cubby-hole with a hard-faced clerk standing before an old-fashioned tall desk. He turned at Alan's entrance and pointed to a chair with his quill, saying repressively, 'Wait.'

'Sorry,' said Alan cheerfully. 'Can't. I'm a busy man.'

'If you've come to settle debts, or pay interest, or to announce a default for that matter, you'll wait,' said the clerk severely.

'I am not the principal,' said Alan. 'I represent the debtor.'

'You represent the debtor?' The clerk's stare took in Alan's gentlemanly clothes. 'No matter. It's all one.'

'Not to me it isn't.'

'And pray who may you be?' The clerk's sneer was a work of art.

'Nemo. You may call me Nemo.'

The clerk's stare grew. He knew that Nemo, translated, meant Nobody, but decided not to let that trouble him.

'Well, Mr Nemo, whom do you represent?'

'I'm tired of exchanging chit-chat with underlings,' said Alan. His accompanying smile was so agreeable it almost took the sting out of his words. 'I'll speak to your superior—or nobody.'

The clerk ignored this and repeated, 'Whom do you represent?'

'His name is Victor. Loring. But any bargaining I do will be with Mr Sebastian.'

The clerk gave a short laugh. 'Him! There's nothing to represent. He can't pay; he's for the Marshalsea.'

'I've come to ask for time and consideration for him—of Mr Sebastian, if you please.'

'Mr Sebastian speaks to nobody. Everyone in the City

knows that. In any case, he'll get neither. In a fortnight we shall send in the bailiffs and the tipstaff.'

Alan said, 'If Mr Sebastian speaks to nobody then he must speak to me, seeing that I am Nemo, or nobody.'

'By no means—' began the clerk.

Alan raised his voice to a powerful bellow. 'I *demand* to speak to Mr Sebastian, since you are losing him business.'

He waved Victor's bills in one hand and some accounts and invoices in the other.

'The answer's the same.'

'Ah, but what about these?' His voice had now reached its best quarterdeck shout, learned on the Macao run. 'I don't think that Mr Sebastian will like losing all these contracts with Dilhorne and Sons, as well as a good settlement with Victor Loring.'

In the wall against which the clerk's desk stood was a door, divided in two at the middle. At this last statement the top half flew open and a testy middle-aged gentleman looked out.

'What the devil is all this noise about Dilhorne's and Loring? What's going on? I can't work in this din, young man. Can't you satisfy, Mr Needham?'

Alan spoke before the clerk could answer. 'No, because I wish to speak to Mr Sebastian.'

'Who the devil are you to speak to me?'

'His name's Mr Nemo,' said the clerk, hastily putting his oar in.

'Mr Nemo? Mr Nobody? Bah! He's pulling your leg.'

Alan gave Mr Sebastian the present of his most brilliant smile. 'Well, to be truthful, it's Dilhorne, actually. Alan—one of the principals in Dilhorne and Sons. I was told that Mr Sebastian spoke to nobody, so I called myself Nemo so that you might speak to me. You follow my logic, sir, I trust? I'm troubled that you might lose all your business with us, Mr Sebastian. You wouldn't like that, would you?' He was all ingenuous charm.

'Damn your impudence, boy. But it's possibly easier to talk to you than argue with you. Though I'm dam'd if I can see why you shouldn't talk to Needham.'

'Only talk to principals,' smiled Alan, 'being one myself.'

Mr Sebastian rolled his eyes to heaven. 'Oh, very well, time is money, I suppose. Come in and have done.'

Mr Sebastian's office was little grander and little cleaner than his clerk's cubby-hole.

'Now, what is all this?' he barked. Be dam'd if the young puppy didn't look more like a pugilist than a businessman.

Alan sat down. 'I've come to ask you to be a little easier over Mr Victor Loring's debts—me being his agent in this matter. Oh, I know that he's in deep, but you'll get little out of him if you throw him into the Marshalsea.'

'And little out of him if he isn't!' Mr Sebastian's bark was more savage than ever.

'Agreed. But I am in a position to exercise pressure on him and put him where he might be able to earn a little and pay it back slowly.'

'No, no, and no again. That's not how I do business. I write off my losses.'

'Oh, I do so agree with you,' exclaimed Alan earnestly. 'And that's how I do business in New South Wales. But Victor, worthless though he is, is my cousin, and I'm honour-bound to try to save him. Don't refuse me, Mr Sebastian, I beg of you. Just think of all those beautiful contracts you have with Dilhorne and Sons which are coming up for renewal soon.'

His smile was angelic.

'By God, I do believe that you're blackmailing me, you dam'd young puppy!'

'Oh, yes, sir, I am. In a dreadful cause, too, but I really

mean what I say. Very wrong of me, I know—but you leave me with no alternative.'

'If you don't renew I'll see that others won't deal with you, either.'

'Oh, dear. I thought that you might say that. But it's too late, sir. I've already shaken hands with Rothschild's on the possibility of a better deal than you can offer me. They are quite aware that I wish to renew with you, seeing how well we have dealt together, but if you feel unable to do so—for whatever reason—they will take over our business at once.'

Sebastian Waldheim stared at the smiling young devil opposite to him, who added, 'Think how well you'll be doing if you close with me. You keep all the Dilhorne contracts and get some return from worthless Victor Loring, too. It beggars belief, don't it?'

'By God, *you* beggar belief, boy! Your contracts are too good to lose, I admit. Particularly if Rothschild's want them. Good payers, Dilhorne's. You're not lying to me, I trust?'

Alan bowed at this tribute.

'Never. Before I left Mr Lionel he gave me this.' He fetched from his pocket the letter which Lionel had written earlier, promising to take over Dilhorne's business if he failed to make terms with Waldheim's.

'What's in it for them, if I do renew?'

'Well, there are other inducements, sir, as we begin to expand now that I'm running the English end of the business. We spoke at length of them—I can't tell you any more than that, naturally.'

'Naturally!' snorted Mr Sebastian. 'By God, boy, you'll go far—if you don't hang first, that is. I'll tell Needham to call off the bailiffs. I'll want some cash down, mind, as earnest of your good faith. We'll settle a reduced interest before you go so that Mr Victor Loring won't be a dead loss.'

'I thought that you might want some money first,' said Alan. 'That's why I've brought a banker's draft for £2,500 with me.'

'And your money, not his or Dilhorne's, I'll be bound,' said Mr Sebastian shrewdly. 'What are you getting out of this? Apart from the joy of coercing me, that is?'

'Not much,' Alan admitted. 'But indirectly I've lost Victor and his family infinitely more than £2,500. I owe him something and I intend to try to make him see the light a little in future.'

'The hopefulness of youth,' said Mr Sebastian wryly. 'Well, young man, you seem to know what you're doing, even if you don't know quite why you're doing it! I'll see you again when we sign the renewals, both for Loring's debts and your business.'

He paused before adding, 'And you may buy me a dinner worth eating straight away—it's not often anyone bests me, so the occasion is worth celebrating!'

Alan knew that his really difficult task lay in persuading Victor to co-operate with his plans for him. Common sense told him that Victor would refuse, and if he did then the agreement with Sebastian Waldheim would fail. Victor would be unable to pay the money-lender and would inevitably end up in the Marshalsea.

His cousin Clara was waiting for him in her pretty, shabby drawing room. Caroline was with her. He was dressed to drive out to the Star and Garter for supper with Frank Gresham and a few friends so he hoped that his business would not take long.

He raised his brows involuntarily when he saw that Victor was absent. Clara interpreted his look correctly. 'Oh, he's come downstairs, cousin Alan,' she said nervously.

'He's in the study. He's been there all day, except for meals. I'll take you there.'

She led him to the study, where he found Victor standing by the window, his back to the door. He turned on hearing Alan enter. His face was yellow, but he had shaved and was well turned-out.

'So, the Golden Boy is back,' he said derisively. 'Did they put the red carpet out for you at Waldheim's?'

Alan was unruffled. 'Of course. I dined with Mr Sebastian in the early evening and drank sherry with Lionel Rothschild this morning.'

Victor's smile was ugly. 'No need to bam me, Alan. I'm your cousin, remember?'

'No bamming,' returned Alan equably. 'Both my statements were true. Sebastian Waldheim and I reached an agreement over your debts. You'll not go to the Marshalsea, but there are conditions.'

Victor stared at him. 'You spoke to Sebastian Waldheim? No one speaks to Sebastian Waldheim. How in God's name did you do that?'

'God had nothing to do with it,' offered Alan. 'We struck a business deal, Sebastian and I. But it depends on you. You might not like the conditions.'

Victor sat down suddenly. 'What conditions?' What did you bind me to? Where's the catch?'

'Well, I gave Sebastian a sweetener in the shape of a banker's draft for £2,500, which cleared some of what you owed him straight away. After that we decided on a low rate of interest for you, to be paid six-monthly, not quarterly. So, all being well, the Marshalsea is not a prospect for you.'

Victor was fascinated. 'You know I've nothing left. How do I pay his low rate of interest? Or pay you for your banker's draft, for that matter?'

'Well, that's the difficult bit, I do admit. I am, however,

prepared to take you on as a junior clerk at Dilhorne's under Phipps. You'll get a salary, which won't be large, but if you reform yourself and stop drinking and gambling it will help you and my cousins to live—if frugally.

'Part of your salary will be commuted, so that Phipps can pay Waldheim's interest for you each six months until you are fit to manage your own affairs. The draft I'm prepared to write off. I think that my mother will agree that it's a fair portion of the estate to be gifted to you, seeing that Sir John encouraged you to live beyond your means, and then disinherited you for doing so.'

'Become one of your clerks! I'm a gentleman. I'd die rather.'

'If that's what you wish,' returned Alan indifferently. 'But you'll do so in the Marshalsea sooner or later if you refuse my offer. As for being a gentleman, I suppose that a gentleman can let his women starve. My gentlemanly grandfather, Fred, was perfectly prepared to leave my mother destitute, even if my common father wasn't. It's your choice.'

'To work for you!'

'No,' said Alan. 'You won't see much of me. You'll be a junior clerk, remember. It's Dilhorne and Sons you'll work for.'

'It's all one.'

'It's as you please,' said Alan indifferently. 'I can do no more. Rot in the Marshalsea or work in the City. Your choice, always your choice.'

He swung round to leave. Before he could reach the door Victor spoke.

'Alan,' he said. His voice had changed. His eyes dropped when he met Alan's direct gaze.

He walked across the room and put out his hand. 'I'm a swine,' he said stiffly, 'and ungrateful, too. I suppose that you've spent all day on this, and never a word of thanks from me for that. You had no call. Sir John left your mother the money fair and square—the lawyers said so.'

'He played you a rotten trick, though,' said Alan soberly.

'Other people seem to have it so easy,' said Victor. He could not stop himself from adding, 'You, for instance.'

'I?' Alan said. 'You mistake again. When did you stand before the mast in a typhoon in the China Seas? Or hump loads for ten hours a day on the wharf at Sydney, as I did? I'd say that you'd had it easy and don't know it, and that's your trouble, all of you.'

Victor stared at him again. 'So that was where the shoulders came from,' he said involuntarily. 'No wonder that you're not really like Ned. Well, I'll try it your way. I can't say more—I'm afraid of making promises I can't keep. Go ahead with the deal. I suppose that we'll have to sell up and leave here?'

'Yes,' said Alan. 'I trust you to go to Waldheim's first thing in the morning, and report to Phipps when you've finished there.'

'Tomorrow?' said Victor, paling. 'So soon?'

'What better day?' asked Alan cheerfully. 'Wear something sober. It wouldn't do to begin by offending the other clerks on the first day. Who knows? You might even like working.'

He pulled out his watch. 'That's all. Try not to let Clara and Caroline down—they depend on you. I have to go now. If anything troubles you about the deal you may contact me through Phipps.'

He was at the door again before Victor said slowly. 'I'll do my best, cousin Alan, but it will be a hard row for me to hoe, you know that, don't you?'

'Yes, I do know that, but try to remember that many men have been given even harder ones and come through in the end.'

He nearly added, My father for one, but thought that Victor had had enough sermons for one day, and Gurney would be growing impatient.

Besides, Gresham and the rest would be waiting for him.

Chapter Seven

'Goodness! What have you all being doing to make you look so cheerful?'

Ned had returned home to discover a lively tea-party taking place in Almeria's usually sedate drawing room.

Alan had arrived shortly after luncheon—he had a standing invitation from Eleanor's great-aunt to visit whenever he wished—and had proposed a trip to the Zoological Gardens at Regent's Park. Charles had wanted to see the rhinoceros and the hippopotamus—he had talked enthusiastically about them to Alan on a previous visit.

Off they all had gone: Eleanor, Charles, Charles's tutor, Mr Dudley, and Alan, who had arranged the visit as much to be with Eleanor and away from the formality of high society as to satisfy his and Charles's curiosity. If he had enjoyed the opportunity of allowing her to take his arm while they walked around the Zoo, Eleanor had taken delight in Alan's grave pleasure in the animals. She could not help contrasting it with Ned's boredom whenever he was asked to do something to entertain his young cousin.

As for Victor Loring! Well, the mere idea that he should occupy himself by amusing a small boy was ludicrous in the extreme. Alan, however, had not only admired the animals but had found a small kiosk where they sold coffee, tea, lemonade and ices, which they'd eaten and drunk at a table in the shade of some trees. After that, to Charles's delight, they had thrown buns to the bears, who had climbed their poles to reach them.

Not only had Charles been on his highest ropes, but his tutor, who had never before been allowed out with the family—other than his charge—had rapidly lost his awe of Alan sufficiently to ask him about the plants and animals of New South Wales.

Alan and Eleanor hadn't walked hand in hand—it would not have been proper. They had reached the early stage of attraction when simply to be with the relatively unknown other was exciting in itself—or that was Eleanor's condition.

Alan's reactions to being with Eleanor were more complex. She was beginning to present a real temptation to him: a temptation which was increased by her charming artlessness and inexperience. She had no notion of the effect which her smiles—and her mere presence—had on him, and the conventions of the society in which they were living meant that they could never be alone together. All in all, he thought ruefully, that was probably a good thing: merely to be with her was becoming sufficient to rouse him. He had always prided himself on his ability to control his love life, and to find himself vulnerable to passion was a new—and salutary—thing for him.

Their happy afternoon had flown by so rapidly that they had barely arrived in time for tea with Almeria, as they had promised. Alan had taken the tutor by the arm when he'd been about to start upstairs and steered him into the drawing room. Fortunately Beastly Beverley was absent, for once, and Almeria was now gracious enough to pass Mr Dudley his tea while being favoured by Charles with a lengthy description of his happy afternoon.

Ned listened to this nursery conversation with a smile and, on being informed that Alan and Eleanor had formed part of the party—Alan taking the afternoon off, for once—exclaimed, 'What next! After the news about Victor, though, one supposes little that one hears these days could shock.'

'What news is that?' asked Almeria, who disliked Victor.

'Oh, Alan is a sly one, isn't he, to say nothing? How did you get Victor to agree to keep quiet?'

Both Almeria and Eleanor said exasperatedly, 'Goodness, Ned, for once tell a story straight!'

'Well, then,' said Ned, rolling his eyes at them, 'old slyboots, Alan here, fails to tell us that Victor Loring, totally strapped for cash, has taken up a clerkship at Dilhorne's. The word is that the Lorings are selling the white elephant in Russell Square and are buying a little place in Chelsea—I ask you—since Anthony Beauchamp has offered for Caroline. Did you know all this, Alan?'

'No, not all of it. Only that he's coming to Dilhorne's. He needed money and an occupation and he had neither.'

'I can't see Victor reformed,' commented Ned dubiously. 'But with Caroline off their hands they might have enough to live on, I suppose. I'm surprised that you wanted him, Alan.'

'Really, Ned,' said Eleanor angrily, 'I know that you don't like Victor these days, but he is Alan's cousin, after all, and poor Clara Loring deserves more than to be thrown to the wolves.'

Alan was wryly amused at Ned's cheerful heartlessness. Freed, temporarily, from his own money worries, he had little sympathy for the ruined Victor and his wretched family, although a fortnight ago he had been willing to sell Eleanor to him in order to clear his own debts. He put in a mild word.

'He has to be given a chance, Ned. Sir John did him a

bad turn, even if he was my great-uncle, leading him to expect money, encouraging him to believe that he didn't need to do anything but wait for the estate to fall into his open mouth—that's bad enough—and then disinheriting him when he was too old to learn a trade.'

'Learn a trade!' cried Ned, struck. 'But Victor's a gentleman.'

'Well, I learned several trades,' said Alan severely, 'so you'd better strike me off your list of friends, because I'm not a gentleman, either.'

'Oh, you, you're different,' said Ned cheerfully. 'You're a colonial; Victor isn't.'

Eleanor and Almeria exclaimed at this together, much to Alan's amusement.

'Oh, Ned, you are too bad,' said Almeria angrily. 'You have neither sense nor manners. I really think that Alan has the right of it. It's a pity you weren't put to anything.'

Charles listened to this, his mouth open. The idea of Ned working at anything beggared belief. He looked at his new friend Alan with some respect.

'Do you know any Latin, Mr Dilhorne?'

'Alan to you, Charles,' said Alan. 'A little, why?'

'Then you must be a gentleman, Alan,' said Charles earnestly. 'Mr Dudley says that only gentlemen know Latin.'

This also caused general amusement.

'*I* don't know much Latin,' said Ned.

'You don't know anything,' said Eleanor severely. 'Which is what Sir Hart complains of. I think Alan's right. A year at a desk in the City might do you some good.'

Alan caught the tutor's slightly satiric eye. 'Oh, I don't know,' he returned. 'A year on the China run might be better.'

Ned laughed at that, and said cheerfully, 'Well, I don't need to do either, thank God. Like it or not I'm Sir Hart's heir, and he isn't going to do a Sir John on me. No long-lost cousins in the Hatton family are going to pop up to take away the money and the title—'

He got no further. Alan was laughing, and Almeria and Eleanor began reprimanding him again.

'But Alan doesn't mind what I say, do you, old fellow?' he drawled when the noise died down. 'It isn't his fault that his mother appeared out of nowhere, is it?'

Uproar reigned once more. Almeria said, breathing heavily, 'If you were Charles's age, Ned, I'd send you to your room. As it is I can only thank God for my brother's long life. The thought of you inheriting as you are is too painful. You should really apologise to Alan for your discourtesy.'

'What for?' asked Ned, who honestly could not see why.

'No,' said Alan. He privately thought that despite his chronological age Ned was little older than Charles, and possessed a great deal less sense. Little ruffled him since he was too far gone to understand his own limitations.

Order finally reigned when Eleanor, who was daily learning more tact, turned the conversation in the direction of other matters—particularly about their move to Yorkshire once the season was over. This was something which Alan was beginning to regret: the more he saw of Eleanor, the more he was drawn to her. He did not wish to see her disappear just as the relationship between them was beginning to flower.

He wryly considered that although it was the brother who had introduced him to society, it was the sister who was now the one whose company he sought. Ned's attraction for him had rapidly palled; Eleanor's was growing equally rapidly.

Victor Loring's transition from idle and dissolute man about town to a clerk in a City office was a nine days' wonder, soon forgotten. Shortly after he had started work at Dilhorne and Sons Eleanor arrived home late one afternoon to find that Victor was in the drawing room waiting to see her.

'Tea?' she asked, once the formality of greetings was over.

He shook his head. He was wearing a plain and sober suit, and a modest cravat. He looked rather ill.

'It's not a social call. I asked permission to leave a little early to make it. I've come to say goodbye, Eleanor.'

His manner was so changed that she hardly knew him.

'I suppose you know that we've sold up. It's all gone: the house, the horses, everything, even the cottage in Surrey. There was little left at the end, when Mother's debts were paid. We're going to live in Chelsea. Caroline will be with us until she marries Beauchamp. I don't suppose that you'll want to know us now that Dilhorne has told you all about everything to do with us.'

'Oh, Victor, you know that's not true. He never mentioned your name or affairs to any of us until Ned raised the matter by telling us that you'd gone to Dilhorne's. Alan merely said then that you needed a steady income and that's why you'd gone into the City. He also said that Sir John had dealt hardly by you.'

'Well, leave that,' he said roughly. 'I don't know whether I shall last there. The days are long, the work is hard, and I miss my old life cruelly. The only reason I stick at it is so that *he* won't have an opportunity to jeer at me for failing.'

By 'he', he meant Alan. He paused, and said more gently, 'There's something I have to ask you. Was there ever any hope for me with you? Even without cousin Alan coming?'

'I can't lie to you, Victor. I thought once, when we first met, that there might be, but even before your cousin arrived in London I knew that we could never be more than friends. I know that won't comfort you, but, truly, it was not Alan's fault.'

He looked at the ground. 'In any case, I can't offer for you now, when I have nothing.'

'If I'd loved you, you could have had nothing or something, and we could have made a life together. Whether you are rich or poor has nothing to do with it. I don't care for you in that way.'

'At least you're honest, Eleanor. I never thought otherwise. I don't suppose that we shall meet again, although I hope that you will visit mother occasionally.'

He had been standing, having refused to sit down. He picked his hat and gloves up from a side-table and made for the door.

Eleanor stopped him. She put out her hand and said, 'At least let us part friends, Victor. You must know that I wish you well in your new life.'

His face lightened a little and he smiled at her. 'You're a good girl, Eleanor, quite unlike Ned. One would scarcely think you were related. I wish you happy, too, and if that means you take up with cousin Alan, then at least I know that he will look after you. He looks after everyone, damn him. Forgive me for saying that, but you look at me with such truthful eyes that I must tell *you* the truth.'

He took her hand, but did not shake it. In lieu of anything else he kissed the back of it, said, 'Adieu,' and was gone before she could answer him.

A part of her life was over, she thought, but the rest of it was still there to live.

Ned told Alan that once the season ended everyone would leave London. 'It never lasts much beyond the middle of August,' he said, 'and even before that many members of society return to their country homes. Town will be empty,' he added gloomily.

Alan laughed a little at this. Ned's 'everyone' was the few people at the top of society, and when they had gone, although their town-houses were closed and the rooms were shrouded in dust sheets, the rest of London scarcely noticed their going and went on with its work as usual. This year that included Victor Loring, who was still in his cubby-hole at Dilhorne's.

Ned and his family were leaving in early August, and Stanton House would be closed thereafter. One evening after dinner he said, as though the inspiration had just struck him, 'Why don't you pay a visit to us at Temple Hatton? Even you need a holiday, old fellow. You've been at it ever since you landed here. You know the saying—"All work and no play makes Jack a dull boy." Mustn't be a dull boy, Alan, wouldn't do.'

'I'll think about it,' replied Alan.

He duly did, and concluded that affairs at Dilhorne and Sons were so improved that he would be able to leave them for a few weeks. It might, in fact, be a good idea to demonstrate his trust in George by putting him in charge during his absence.

Consequently he told Ned that he would be delighted to take up his invitation. The real reason for his acceptance was Eleanor. He wanted to meet her mother, and her grandfather, Sir Hartley. Ned had told him that Sir Hart was Eleanor's guardian, and that it was to him he was to apply for her hand in marriage, not her mother.

He was still not sure whether Eleanor felt for him what he was beginning to feel for her. He believed that inside the decorous conventions which prevailed between young men and women Eleanor was showing an interest in him. She was, however, so innocent, and so unversed in the give and take of sexual interplay of even the most elementary kind, that he had, to some extent, to take her feelings for granted. In the weeks before she left for Temple Hatton he hoped to test these feelings further.

More than that, he was not sure whether Sir Hartley Hatton would find a brash young businessman, the son of a felon, however rich, to be a suitable husband for Eleanor. Ned, whose frank carelessness caused him to pour out everything he knew, had told him that Sir Hart favoured Stacy Trent, the son of a near neighbour, as a suitable husband for her.

Ned also told him of another man, the widowed Earl of Knaresborough, who had always shown great interest in Eleanor even though he was years older than she was. He was related to the Royal Family and was the catch of the season, or of many seasons.

'He rarely comes to London these days,' Ned had said, 'and whether he's a candidate for Eleanor's hand or not is a bit of a mystery. I do know that Sir Hart thinks highly of him. You're bound to meet him if you come to Yorkshire.'

Given all this, it might be no easy matter to persuade the old man to listen to his suit—let alone favour it. Charles, Almeria, Beastly Beverley and his mama would also be visiting Yorkshire after they had spent some time at the Stanton's place at Hollingbourne in Kent.

Charles liked his new friend, who treated him as an equal and who shared his enthusiasm for those matters which bored the rest of his family. Beastly Beverley, on the other hand, disliked Alan, and was annoyed when told he intended to visit Yorkshire. 'What does *he* want to go there for?' he exclaimed loudly. 'What would *he* do there? I don't want *him* there when I visit Temple Hatton.'

Almeria had closed her eyes at this rudeness, which had gone unchecked by his mother. She was not sure that she wished Alan to visit Yorkshire, either—and for a number of reasons about which she said nothing to anyone.

She was quite aware of Alan's attraction to Eleanor: sometimes this cheered her, sometimes it worried her. It cheered her because she liked and admired the young man and his steadiness of purpose. It worried her because his likeness to Ned, which at first had seemed a joke, had suddenly begun to trouble her greatly.

They had all been talking and laughing together at something idly said when Ned and Alan had come out together with the same phrase in the same voice, in a quick and unthinking reaction. They might have been the two halves of the same person: Ned all volatility and Alan all steadiness. For the first time, watching them, she could not believe that the likeness was a mere coincidence: an accident.

She considered writing to Sir Hartley about it—but what could she say? She was impatient with herself. It was irrational to be so worried. What could the son of a London felon—for Alan had let drop one day that his father had spoken familiarly of the London of over forty years ago—have to do with the Hattons?

She liked Alan too much to send him away, partly because he was so good for Ned, and for Charles, who was growing up in a house full of women whilst his parents were in India. She wondered how far matters had gone with Eleanor and whether she ought to discourage that.

Matters were going further than she thought.

Not long before Charles was to leave, Alan arranged for him, his tutor and Eleanor to see a railway, the Eastern Counties, being built. He had persuaded the foreman and works engineer to allow them on to the half-made track.

Ned cried off, even after Alan told him that the new railways would change their lives completely.

'No, thanks, old chap,' Ned drawled. 'They can change things without troubling me, I'm sure. Can't think why you're so interested.'

Alan smiled. 'Perhaps because I've invested some of my money in them. It's chancy, I know, but exciting.'

Charles could not resist staring at Ned and announcing, 'I want to be an engine-driver when I grow up.'

'Much your grandmother would like that,' said Alan, amused at the difference between the cousins.

Eleanor, listening to what Almeria called men's talk, said, 'I think that if I were a man I should want to have something to do with railways. I can understand what Alan means when he talks of excitement.'

Alan gave her a grateful smile, and it was this statement which made him add her to the expedition. Not only was she impressed by the scale of the lines, the bridges and the cuttings which were under construction, and the number of men employed, but it delighted her to watch the big boy and the little boy—which was how she thought of Alan and Charles—clambering about, clucking with admiration. Because he was so steady, and taken so seriously by his elders, it was easy to forget how young Alan was, not so much older than Ned, but, oh, so different.

Charles and Mr Dudley wanted to walk up the track, but Eleanor had to cry off. She was wearing light kid shoes, not suitable for such rough ground. Alan arranged for the foreman to guide them, and told Eleanor he would stay behind with her.

'I've already walked the line,' he said. 'We can admire some of the workings together.'

It was the first time that they had ever been quite alone, out of doors. Eleanor discovered that standing, unchaperoned, beside Alan made her knees feel weak, and what was worse—or better—she wasn't sure which—she suddenly became very conscious of the rest of her body. She had never been near enough before to a man in the open to discover that men gave off an aura quite different from that of women.

She had an impression of warmth, of the smell of clean linen, of the bay rum which Alan had rubbed into his hair, and something which was faintly musky, something which was uniquely Alan and neither Ned nor Victor.

He put his hand on her arm and they looked at one another. Eleanor had once read in a poem about lovers drowning in one another's eyes, and for the first time she knew what the poet had meant. Alan smiled at her and her heart wrenched.

'Come,' he said, and led her gently into a completed tunnel, where they were hidden not only from the workmen on the line but also from Mr Dudley, Charles, and the foreman, who were disappearing in the opposite direction.

He tipped her bonnet back, saying, 'Nice Eleanor,' before he kissed her on the cheek, and then on the tip of her nose. She found her mouth suddenly searching for his, and this time they kissed together, her eyes closing and her mouth opening under his like a flower in spring.

His hand on her shoulder tightened its grasp to pull her closer to him. The kiss, from being tentative, became urgent. His hand slipped from her shoulder and caught against her breast. An exquisite shock ran through Eleanor's body, and her right hand rose to catch at the back of his head to bring him ever nearer.

Alan suddenly pulled away, his eyes shining in the half-dark. Desire roared through him, rousing him so much that he was in pain. For her part, Eleanor felt the world spin about her as though she were going to fall. Swiftly, abruptly, she had become a woman, aware not only of the difference between the sexes, but that its existence created in men and women a pleasure between them so sweet that it was overwhelming in its demands on the body.

Alan took her arm and steadied her.

'No,' he said hoarsely. 'No more. Not now. I shouldn't

have done that, but I've wanted to kiss you for so long and I've never yet had the opportunity.'

Her heart was beating wildly. She leaned forward, her face questioning him, blindly seeking his nearness again.

'By God, Eleanor, you tempt me,' he exclaimed. 'Tell me, if I come to Yorkshire, as Ned wishes, may I speak to your grandfather?'

'Oh, yes, Alan, yes,' she said breathlessly. 'But I don't know what he'll say. I do know that he wishes me to marry my old friend, Stacy Trent, but I've never wanted to marry him. I thought that I never wanted to marry anyone, but now that I know you…'

She stopped, breathless, clinging to him, hiding her face in his broad chest so that he drew in his breath before giving her one last kiss: a chaste one on the cheek, almost brotherly.

'Well, we'll have to find out, shan't we?' he murmured. 'Now we must go outside, before anyone notices that we've hidden ourselves away.'

Eleanor feared that the whole world would be aware of the tumult inside her, but when they walked along the workmen stared indifferently at them. Charles came running up to them, excited by his own affairs, and the world seemed to be taking things pretty much as usual.

Except that young Mr Dudley, who had long worshipped her from afar, gave them a sorrowful, questioning look, so perhaps something of what had happened did show to keen eyes after all.

For Alan, his belief that his feelings were returned was confirmed in the best possible way. Holding Eleanor and kissing her had been difficult, for he did not want to do anything which would distress or frighten her. All the same he dearly wanted to go beyond what La Bencolin had derisively called nursery games, but there would be time enough for that later, in Yorkshire.

After he had escorted them home, tired and happy, he returned to the Albany to dress for a last dinner with Frank Gresham before Gresham left for the country.

Alan found, to his surprise, that he was Frank Gresham's only guest. He liked Frank, and thought that he was the best of all Ned's grand friends, and Frank liked him. His home, near Hyde Park, was small and beautiful, rather than grand and beautiful. The room in which they dined was also small, containing two exquisite Canalettos and a portrait of Frank's mother over the fireplace.

Alone with Alan before dinner, Frank became adult and serious, not at all the careless companion whom Ned Hatton knew. He held up his wine to the light before saying, 'I suppose you know that Eleanor Hatton has been promised to Stacy Trent these many years?'

Now, am I being warned off, or encouraged? Alan asked himself, amused.

He nodded a yes.

'I thought that you might know,' said Frank. 'You make it your business to know things, don't you?'

He said nothing more of a personal nature until the brandy arrived at the end of the meal and they sat before a crackling fire, even though it was early August.

'Going to Temple Hatton, are you? Do you think it wise?' He stared at Alan, hard, over the rim of his glass.

Alan swirled the fiery stuff around his mouth. He preferred it to port. 'What is wise?' he offered.

Frank laughed. 'Making you give yourself away is like cracking nuts, isn't it? I keep forgetting that you're God's gift to the City, not a loose-mouth like Ned. Yes, wise. No one in London is much troubled about the odd likeness, you know, since finding out that you're not at all like Ned in other ways. But going to Yorkshire, the Hattons' stamping ground, that's different. You're tempting fate, aren't you?'

His usually idle eyes were suddenly shrewd. 'Why not come to Greshamsbury with me, instead? I've a pretty sister there who don't like town. I can promise you a good time—and no complications.'

The next Prime Minister but three, thought Alan. He's changing before my eyes from an idler to someone impressive.

'Oh, I've already accepted Ned's invitation. I couldn't cry off without giving offence, could I? Besides, I might like to tempt fate.'

Frank gave a crack of laughter. 'You'd find it difficult to offend Ned, I think. Yes, I might have known you'd tempt fate, you're a devil of a fellow for taking a chance. I've heard about you in the City. Want it all, do you? Ned's pretty sister and check whether the likeness is a mere accident? Is that it? I suppose if I were you I'd feel the same. Forgive me for asking, but what in the world are the rest of your family like?'

Alan laughed. 'Like me, of course.'

'Of course,' said Frank. 'Thank God I don't live there, then. Fancy meeting the whole brood of you. Let's pray that they don't decide to settle here. Between you, you'd take London over!'

He paused before saying, 'If we're being honest with one another, and you're bound and determined to take a chance up north, then there's something you ought to know which isn't common knowledge. Something I know only through my mother's connections. It's about Eleanor Hatton. She isn't Ned's full sister, only his half-sister. When Ned's father became totally intolerable, and impotent as well, her mother had an affair with a sympathetic neighbour. Very brief, I understand, and out of pity on the man's side. I tell you so that the likeness need not stand in your way. If it's

Ned you're related to, and mind I'm not saying you are, then Eleanor is no blood relative of yours.

'The world thinks that she's a Hatton, but since I know that you're the closest-mouthed creature ever to visit these shores, I also know that you'll say nothing of this—to her or anyone else.'

'Of course,' said Alan coolly. 'No one's business but the Hattons.'

Frank raised his glass again at this, and said something which echoed an earlier thought of Alan's. 'If you'll settle here, and I hope you do, when I become Prime Minister I shall want you in my government—with or without Eleanor Hatton.'

After that they spoke of nothings, but Alan's visit to Temple Hatton had taken on quite a different colour.

Chapter Eight

Temple Hatton, near Brinkley, Yorkshire Moors and Dales

In their different ways both Eleanor and Ned missed Alan when they left London for Yorkshire.

For Ned, Alan was a jolly, if sometimes severe companion, who occasionally joined in the mindless games of Frank Gresham's set but always refused to go beyond a certain point of upper-class lunacy. He refused to tease and exploit working-class men and women whom many of the set, though not Frank, thought fair game. He considered manhandling cabbies and servants very much not the thing.

Ned and his friends put this mild eccentricity down to his being a colonial rather than the true reason, which was that Alan's own experiences as an underling had bred in him respect, as well as sympathy for those less fortunate than himself. Anyone less obviously masculine than Alan, who could ride, box, fence and shoot better than any of them, would have been dismissed as a prig.

Eleanor missed him dreadfully—her own word—even more than she had expected to: her body, as well as her mind, resented Alan's loss. After he had kissed and caressed her on the railway workings she had matured sexually and would never look at men again with uncaring, innocent eyes.

Sir Hart welcomed them, and by their first evening with him he knew at once that twenty-year-old Eleanor had grown up, and that twenty-four-year old Ned had not. He stifled a sigh. It was becoming increasingly obvious that Ned was a softer version of his father, George, Sir Hart's profligate elder son.

Eleanor's mother was only too happy to see her children again. To her loving but uncritical eyes both seemed unchanged. It was true that Eleanor was quieter, and would never let ferrets loose in the drawing room again, and that when she met Nat she looked away from him, embarrassed. Eve had eaten of the apple of knowledge.

Her changed manner made Nat savage. He took it out on the parlour maid he had been favouring since Eleanor had gone to London. He repeatedly told himself not to be a fool, that Eleanor was beyond him, but he still mooned after her whenever he saw her—which was not often.

Sir Hart recognised, even if her mother did not, that the old partnership of Ned and Nell was dissolving in the face of her growing maturity. Her mother would not even acknowledge that Ned was becoming more and more like the father who had treated her so badly.

Soon after his arrival Sir Hart called Ned into his study. 'Well, sir, I hope that your intentions are becoming fixed on some suitable young lady. It is high time that you thought of marriage, and even higher that Shotton—' Sir Hart's land agent '—should begin to teach you the running of the estate.'

Ned made a face. 'Must he, sir? I infinitely prefer city life to the country. Not that I dislike Temple Hatton, you understand, but London is better.'

'London does not provide you with rents. It is where you

spend them,' said his grandfather severely. 'You live an idle life there, and make idle friends.'

'Begging your pardon, sir, that is not strictly true,' said artful Ned. 'I have made a very serious friend, a little older than I am, who runs a great business in the City. He is from Australia and Great-Aunt Almeria approves of him. She thinks that he is a good influence on me.'

Fortunately he refrained from adding that Alan was sweet on Nell. Too much ought not to be thrown at the old man at once.

'An Australian and a businessman who is little older than you! I find that beggars belief. Why should he make a friend of an idler like you?'

This was a difficult question for Ned to answer, seeing that he wished to withhold from Sir Hart the true reason for the friendship—the chance meeting with his double.

'Oh, Frank Gresham introduced us,' he said vaguely.

Sir Hart's face was a picture. 'Frank Gresham, of all people, introduces you to someone of whom my sister approves. I really find that difficult to believe!'

'Well, sir, it's true.' Ned smiled. 'And, what's more, I've invited him here, and Great-Aunt approves of that, too.'

'Pray, sir, what is this prodigy's name?' said Sir Hart. 'For I take it that he has a name, and not a convict's number?'

'Oh, sir, Alan is a gentleman, even if he is from New South Wales. His mother is one of the Warings of Essendene and she has just inherited it. You will like him, I know. He is a partner in the business he runs with his father and his twin brother. His name is Dilhorne, and he even had sherry once with Lionel Rothschild when he was doing business there.'

The expression on Sir Hart's face was a strange one. 'Did you say Dilhorne, sir? His name is Dilhorne, you say?'

'Yes,' said Ned, a little puzzled. He usually found his

grandfather uncommonly quick on the uptake. Old age must be getting to him, though, for him not to grasp Alan's name when told it.

'His name is Alan Dilhorne. He has been managing the London end of the business since he arrived in England. George Johnstone, who works there, and the rest of his staff, think the world of him, too.'

'I see. And you have invited this Australian who drinks with the Rothschilds here? When does he arrive, may I ask?'

'In a fortnight, sir. He says that he cannot neglect his business, and may not stay too long. From what he has let drop I don't think that his father would approve of his idling.'

'Well, I wish that you would take a leaf from his book,' said Sir Hart slowly. 'I look forward to meeting this serious young man, who makes a friend of you and who actually takes note of his father.'

'Sir Hart was at his worst,' Ned confided gloomily to Eleanor later. 'Never a kind word from him, and I have to dance after Shotton while I am here. It is too bad. Fortunately he doesn't mind Alan coming, even if he did roast me a bit over him. D'you think that he dislikes Australians, Nell? I'd half a mind to confide in him how he saved me over Victor, but I thought better not.'

'Better not, indeed,' said Eleanor faintly. 'Unless you wish him to disinherit you on the spot.'

Really, Ned had no sense at all, and, with Alan's steadying influence gone, was back at his flightiest. The sooner Stacy and Alan arrived, the sooner she could enjoy some sensible conversation.

Stacy Trent came over from Culverwell Manor a week before Alan was due. He had changed, too. His time at university had conferred on him a maturity which Ned would never possess. It was Sir Hart's dearest wish to see Eleanor settled for life with such a steady and sensible young man. She would be free of Ned, and her vague mother, and he might die happy.

Stacy's first act was to invite Eleanor to walk with him in the Elizabethan knot garden at the back of the big house.

'I've met this girl,' he confided.

'Oh, Stacy, I'm so happy for you.'

'You may be happy,' he said ruefully. 'Sir Hart won't be. You know what he wants for us.'

'Yes,' said Eleanor, sparkling a little. 'But I've met someone I like, too.'

'Tell!' exclaimed Stacy, eyes glinting.

'No, you first.'

'Well, she's not like you. She's fair and small. She's not clever, but she's nice.'

'Oh, Stacy, you mean that I'm not nice,' said Eleanor, laughing at him.

'No, I mean she's not clever. You're clever *and* nice. She's…well, she thinks I'm marvellous. You don't think that because we're much of a muchness.'

'Both clever,' agreed Eleanor.

'She's pretty. You're beautiful, Eleanor, but you're not for me. You're my sister, not my lover. What's yours like?'

'Clever. Much, much cleverer than any of us—cleverer than anyone I've ever met. He's handsome, too. And he's… I can't explain. He's serious. He's capable. He does things. He almost frightens me sometimes. He's from Australia.'

'Australia! Does Sir Hart know?'

'I'm not sure. Oh, dear, I don't know what he'll say. Sir Hart is already suspicious because he's Ned's friend.'

'Now that *is* bad. Are you *sure* that he's clever and serious and Ned's friend?'

'Oh, dear, again. You sound just like Sir Hart. There's a

reason that he's Ned's friend, but I can't tell you why.
You'll see when you meet him.'

'That's mysterious. Does he like you?'

'I have reason to believe,' said Eleanor pompously, 'that
he does.'

'Then he's kissed you. I've kissed Jane. That's her name.
Allow me to kiss you.'

Eleanor offered her cheek. Stacy kissed it, then placed a
cold kiss on her mouth.

'That's not it at all,' he said dismally. 'Quite wrong—
dull, even. Sir Hart *will* be disappointed. Why can't life be
easy? It would have been so much more convenient if we'd
loved one another. Not just been friends.'

'I don't want life to be convenient,' said Eleanor. 'And
I don't think that Alan does. He likes solving things. He
sounds to have a really frightening father. Alan says his
father is cleverer than he is. His mama sounds nice,
though.'

'Jane's mama is a dragon,' said Stacy despondently.
'And she eats Jane's papa twice a day. He's like the manna
in the wilderness, renewed each morning. You may grasp
from this that he's a clergyman.'

Eleanor collapsed into laughter. 'I shall miss you,' she
said at last. 'You always make me laugh, but I want you
to be happy.'

'And I you. I warn you, I shall look this paragon over
very carefully. If he isn't good enough for you, I shall
throw him to Jane's mama.'

They walked back to the great house, golden in the evening sun, arm in arm and laughing, so that Sir Hart, watching them from his study window, wrongly had his hopes
raised. They would always be good friends, never lovers:
Stacy needed someone to care for and protect, and Eleanor
needed someone to stand up to her, and they had each, they
hoped, found their true mate.

* * *

The week crawled slowly towards Alan's visit. Ned, following Shotton about, fumed and fretted and yawned, staring uncomprehendingly at the estate's ledgers. He drank too much in the evening until Sir Hart banned liquor from the table temporarily, and then he yawned and groaned until bedtime.

The day on which Alan should have arrived came and went. Ned was even grumpier that night, and Eleanor played the piano vindictively until Sir Hart winced and retired to his room. The next day, a fine one, brought Alan in the afternoon in a hired chaise, Gurney driving.

He had intended to travel to Leeds on the new railway, the North Midland, he told them later, but the engine had broken down near Doncaster and he had spent the night at a dirty inn there before rejoining the train and then hiring a post-chaise for the journey from Leeds.

Ned greeted him as though he were an army come to lift a siege, running out on to the gravelled sweep and grasping him by the arm almost before he had alighted.

Eleanor, who was a little more reticent, stood in the porch beside Stacy, who was eager to see the man who had captured Eleanor's citadel and entranced Ned.

'You didn't say that he was big,' he murmured enviously, being a shortish, stocky man himself. 'He's as big as Sir Hart must have been.'

Then, as Alan turned towards Ned, Stacy's eyes widened. 'So, that's it. That's your mystery. He's Ned's double. Does Sir Hart know?'

Eleanor shook her head, ashamed. She should have had more common sense than to agree to Ned not telling their grandfather of the likeness. She had only done so because she felt that these days she was always refusing to fall in with his wishes. She ought to have remembered her own annoyance at being deceived.

'Then he should have been told,' said Stacy firmly. 'Par-

ticularly since he looks like Ned but is clever. Sir Hart...
is...clever.'

He shrugged his shoulders, looked at Eleanor, then at
Ned, and finally at Alan. Eleanor had called Stacy clever,
which was true. His mind was presenting him with possi-
bilities which had apparently never occurred to innocent
Eleanor or careless Ned.

'But he's from Australia,' he said at last, *àpropos* of
nothing, to a puzzled Eleanor. 'Despite that, Sir Hart ought
to have been told of the likeness.'

'Ned wanted him to be surprised,' said Eleanor, knowing
how feeble that would sound to sensible Stacy.

Oh, he'll be surprised right enough, thought Stacy, although what sort of surprise he'll feel, who can say? He
watched Ned and Alan walk arm in arm into the house,
following them with a grim expression on his face.

Alan was impressed by Stacy when introduced to him.
He shook hands with this solid, chunky young man, and
explained why he had been delayed. His manner was so
firm, yet so easy, that Stacy suddenly felt a violent prick
of jealousy. No man had the right to be so sure of himself
as Alan Dilhorne was. He made Stacy feel even more juvenile than usual.

Once in the house, in the magnificent Great Hall, now
used as a dining room, Ned had eagerly begun telling Stacy
of how Frank Gresham had found Alan when the door
opened and Sir Hart came in.

Alan had been occupying himself by smiling at Eleanor,
and admiring the hammer-beam ceiling with its gilded dec-
orations and its coats of arms hanging around the cornice.
The giant fireplace had a Hatton eagle flying over it. He
almost missed Sir Hart's entrance in his open admiration
of the beauty around him.

Sir Hart had heard the commotion of his visitor's arrival.
Eleanor's mama was out visiting friends and, seated alone

in his study, he had seen the chaise from its windows and had come downstairs to greet Ned's friend.

When he entered Alan was half turned away from him. He was inspecting an elaborate carving of fruit and flowers by Grinling Gibbons, and Sir Hart could only see that he was a big, sandy-haired man, as tall as Ned, but broader.

Ned said brightly, 'May I introduce my friend, Alan Dilhorne from Australia, to you, sir?'

Alan, on hearing this, swung round, and Sir Hart saw his face for the first time.

He had hoped to spring a surprise, but even Ned could not have anticipated the powerful effect which their meeting had on both his friend and his grandfather. Sir Hart's face turned grey. He staggered and put out his hand, as though to ward Alan off. For the first time he looked all of his nearly eighty years.

Stacy, who had been watching closely, almost fearfully, sprang forward and took the old man's arm. 'Lean on me, sir.'

Alan was equally affected. His face was as white as paper. He moved forward to help Stacy with Sir Hart.

Sir Hart stood erect again and waved them both away.

'I'm sorry, sir,' he said to Alan, with the punctilious courtesy which was so much a part of him. 'Forgive me for being so discomposed. Age sometimes has its penalties. I can only say that my home is always open to Ned's friends.'

He added, almost in a whisper, 'You are very like him. I hope to offer you a better welcome later.'

Uncharacteristically Alan did not speak, merely bowed. Sir Hart refused all offers to help him from the room. After the door had closed behind him Alan turned furiously on Ned.

'You did not inform him of the likeness! You are even

more stupidly tactless than I thought you were. I hope that you told him that I am from Australia.'

'No need to be huffy, old fellow!' began Ned.

Alan ignored him and rounded on Eleanor. 'I am surprised that you didn't think to forewarn the old man, but I suppose that Ned suborned you.'

Stacy's eyes widened. Had the occasion not been so serious he would have laughed. He could quite see why Eleanor's friend frightened her. He radiated a strength and power missing from most of the young men in their circle.

Ned continued to defend himself until the butler's arrival to arrange the disposal of Alan's belongings lightened the situation a little. Alan was taken upstairs to his room, leaving Ned to try to justify his failed prank to a shocked Stacy and a remorseful Eleanor.

When he had run down, Stacy said severely, 'Your friend was quite right, Ned. You should have warned Sir Hart. Tactless is a kind word. Do you never think what you are doing?'

'Oh, nobody's happy these days until they've had a go at me,' exclaimed Ned ungraciously. 'How was I to know that the old man would take it like that? He knows Alan comes from Australia, so there's nothing in it. Dead bores, the lot of you.'

He stalked away from them both to sulk in his room.

Alan had left London with all his affairs in order. He brought Gurney with him to be his valet, driver and friend.

The journey from the agrarian south to the harsh, industrial Midlands and the North had interested him profoundly. He'd wanted to leave the train and explore the exciting new world which ran alongside the track, but which his fellow passengers had dismissed without so much as a glance.

His passion for everything mechanical, which worked and moved, and which had taken him on to the railway line in London, had made him want to visit the clanging work-shops where the future was being forged. The half-formed desire to settle in England and become involved in these developments had been reinforced by every mile he trav-elled.

South Yorkshire was different again, once he had left Bradford and its mills behind. He'd made a mental note to explore them once he was settled at Temple Hatton, which he knew was in the wild country north of the new mill towns. Though Temple Hatton village, a mile or so beyond Brinkley—another new mill town—was tiny and untouched by time.

Temple Hatton House had been a shock. Its size and splendour were beyond his wildest expectations and its magnificence was enhanced by the untamed beauty of the moors among which it was set. It was quite different from his mother's inheritance of Essendene which was a charm-ingly small Palladian villa surrounded by manicured lawns and gardens. Temple Hatton had been built in the sixteenth century and obviously needed an army of servants to run it.

He had wondered that Ned could be so indifferent to its charms, and so reluctant to return to it from London. Eleanor's feelings were different. She had told him that she possessed no real wish to live permanently in London and had been longing to return home ever since she had left it two years earlier.

Not even her enthusiasm had prepared him for the reality of it. He could, for the first time, understand why Frank and his friends, for all their love of London, were tied to the country, and neglected the wider world of industry and commerce. If he possessed this, why would he ever want anything else?

In an odd way it had almost been like coming home to see it.

He had ordered Gurney to stop the chaise when the House came into view. He had alighted and stood for a time admiring it. The air was keener and sharper than in the South, and when he had re-entered the chaise he'd lowered the window panel to give him a better view of the changing beauty of the moors, bright under the golden sun.

This happy mood had stayed with him until he'd reached the house and seen Eleanor, who had never been out of his thoughts, standing by a sturdy young man who must be the Stacy Trent of whom she had spoken. Ned had run at him, pleasure at his arrival shining on his face. Eleanor had smiled a welcome and introduced the boy beside her. He had greeted Alan with wary eyes, but with genuine pleasure. They had gone arm-in-arm into the House, Gurney behind, carrying his luggage.

Once inside the House he had seen more glories. He had drawn in his breath at the splendour of it, from the great table to the glorious ceiling—and then everything had changed, and the day had darkened in a trice.

The big door at the far end of the room had opened to let in an old man. He had turned and seen the old man—and the old man had seen him.

He had known at once that his appearance had shocked the old man beyond belief—but that was not all. The old man had shocked him. For it was his father grown very old whom he saw before him. He possessed the same bright blue eyes, the same silver hair, and even the expression on Sir Hart's face, before shock changed it, had been his father's.

Had it not been for the presence of Eleanor and Stacy he would have struck Ned for not telling his grandfather of the likeness. His own shock was nothing: he was young and resilient. He had thought that his resemblance to Ned was a mere accident, but he could think that no longer.

There must be a link, but what that link might be he dared not conjecture.

Briefly he had remembered Frank Gresham's hidden warning of what a visit to Temple Hatton might bring. A warning which he had airily dismissed. He could no longer dismiss it.

Now he followed the butler upstairs, his mind whirling, his memory providing the possibility of a link. His own face looked down on him from the family portraits on the walls of the long gallery at the top of the stairs—and he knew why he had frequently found Almeria watching him closely, and he half wished that he had never come to this place of secrets—until he thought of Eleanor.

Sir Hart did not come down for tea. Before that Stacy and Eleanor took Alan on a tour of the House. Ned sulked in his room. Alan liked Stacy; he thought that he had sense. He obviously cared for Eleanor, but made it plain to Alan that his affections were fixed elsewhere.

'I have met this young lady,' he told him. 'Her name is Jane Chalmers and she will be visiting Temple Hatton shortly. I hope that you will still be here so that I may introduce you to her.'

Ned came in for tea. 'I've news for you,' he told Alan brightly, in a bid to mend bridges. 'Sir Hart has already assigned two of his best horses for your use. After tea we ought to visit the stables so that you can judge whether they are suitable.'

Eleanor's relief was plain. Alan took her arm when, tea over, Ned walked them to the stables, near to the forge where a blacksmith was working on a shoe. To Ned's surprise—and delight—Alan threw off his splendid coat, saying, 'I really need some exercise; I have been sitting too long at a desk.'

To the astonished smith he said, 'May I help?' before

borrowing a leather apron from him and finishing the shoe. Nat Swain glowered at him from the background: kitchen gossip already had it that this upstart from Australia was sweet on Miss Eleanor and that she was sweet on him.

'I worked for some months in the forge belonging to my father,' Alan explained, once he had finished with the shoe and was putting on his fine coat again. 'We had horses to care for, as well as bullocks which we used for draught.'

Stacy could see why he had captivated Eleanor: his mixture of intellect and athleticism was rare and exciting. There was also an unselfconsciousness about him, as though he cared little for what others thought of him so long as he was true to himself.

Sir Hart reappeared for dinner. Alan had already met Eleanor's mother. A large company sat down at table—which was commonplace for Temple Hatton, Sir Hart sat at the head, and, as well as the Hatton family, Robert Harshaw and two other Yorkshire landowners and their wives were present.

Robert Harshaw glared at Alan, partly because he had Ned's face and partly because he immediately sensed a rival for Eleanor, over whom he had long mooned.

The dinner table was as splendid as the Great Hall itself. Ned pointed out to Alan the initials of the Hall's builder, Sir Osgarthorpe Hatton, which appeared everywhere.

'We Hattons used to go in for the most splendid names,' he whispered. 'Mine's a bit of a comedown, I must say.'

The dinner service was matchless in green and gold. It had been made for Catherine the Great but had never been paid for, and had been purchased by Sir Beauchamp Hatton, Sir Hart's father, for a song—or a relative song, as Stacy would say later. The silver wine cooler was big enough to bath a small calf in.

Dinner began silently, until Sir Hart turned to Ned and said coldly, 'You at least had the grace, Ned, to tell me that your friend is of similar height and build to yourself. You also said that he was a good horseman and kind to his cattle. Meeting him, however, I find that he is broader and heavier than you are, and accordingly one of the two horses I have assigned to him is not suitable. I have therefore instructed Hargreaves to make Abdul ready for you, Mr Dilhorne, whenever you wish to use him—which I hope will be soon.'

When Sir Hart finished speaking everyone stopped eating to stare at him. Artless Ned exclaimed, 'Why, sir, no one rides Abdul—except yourself, of course!'

Sir Hart favoured Ned with a basilisk stare. 'Do I understand that you are instructing me in the disposal of my cattle, Ned? Any young man whom the blacksmith informs me can finish a shoe as well as, if not better than he can, is more than welcome to ride the pick of my stable.'

'Finish a shoe?' queried Robert Harshaw loftily. 'You mean that you are a blacksmith by trade, Dilhorne?' His sneer was palpable.

'Oh, I wouldn't make that claim,' replied Alan cheerfully. 'But I spent some time in the smithy when I cared for the horses which hauled my father's wagons in Sydney. It was expected of me, sir,' he explained to Sir Hart. 'My father made my twin brother and myself work through many of the junior positions in his various business ventures.'

'A wise decision,' said Sir Hart heavily. 'And a practice which I wish had followed with your father and yourself, Ned.'

'Well, I don't,' said Ned frankly. 'It's bad enough trying to follow Shotton about without trying to be a stable-hand and a smith as well. I don't know how you stood it, Alan, as I've said before.'

'Oh, with my father easier to stand it than not. Besides, I've often found the knowledge I gained useful. Few people can put you down if they know that you've been through the mill yourself. Better than that, it's harder to cheat someone who knows exactly what it is he's dealing with from practice rather than theory.'

Several of the older hands nodded at this. Ned's disbelief was palpable. Stacy, who was sitting beside Eleanor, said, 'I've decided to save your new friend from Jane's mama. He may look like Ned, but good gracious, he could not be more different!'

Eleanor rewarded him with a happy smile. Her delight that her grandfather, and the general company, approved of Alan made her feel warm all over. Sir Hart continued to draw Alan out. He had seldom before shown such interest in a guest.

'So, you are a man of action, sir, as I suppose your father was?'

'Well, as to that, Sir Hart, my father has many gifts. He is quite my despair in the variety of his interests, both of the mind and the body. My brother Tom and I decided long ago that while we might try to emulate him we could not equal him—but at least we could give him a run for his money.'

His smile embraced the table. 'The Patriarch is a great man,' he finished simply.

Sir Hart nodded and spoke of other things. After the women had left he called Alan over to sit by him, Stacy on his other side.

'Ned tells me that my sister Almeria thinks that you may be good for him, and, meeting you, I think that she may be right. He also tells me that your mother is the late Sir John Waring's niece. I knew him a little when we were both in government. I never knew your grandfather, Frederick, though. He lost his money, I understand, and took up a government clerkship in New South Wales, and died quite soon after that.'

Alan bowed. No need to tell Sir Hart of Fred Waring's dreadful end. 'A lesson in not letting drink take you by the throat,' his father had said once. He was amused that Sir Hart was being so delicate about his father, and who or what he had been.

The old man deserved to be told the truth—or a little of it. He must wish to know how a Waring of Essendene had come to be the wife and mother of Australian businessmen, and exactly who, and what, Mr Alan Dilhorne's father was—and had been.

He looked the assembled men in the eye, for they were listening avidly while Sir Hart questioned him.

'No need to temporise with you, Sir Hart. My father *was* a felon, long reformed. He saved my mother from destitution and worse after her parents died penniless. He has made a great fortune by his own honest efforts and I am here to run his business in England.'

Well, if Sir Hart didn't like that, then he could always turn him out.

Stacy Trent said, 'Bravo,' softly. Robert Harshaw looked down his nose at the convict's son.

'And your twin brother?' asked Sir Hart, not commenting on Alan's frank answer. 'Does he resemble you?'

'No,' said Alan. 'Had he come to England Ned would never have met him. Tom is like my uncle Rowland, who died in the Peninsular War when my mother was a girl. He is tall and dark and handsome, not at all like me.'

After this, talk became general again. Sir Hart decided that questioning his guest further would go beyond the bounds of politeness. He had learned a little of what he wanted to know, and over the weeks of Alan's visit he hoped to learn more.

Perhaps 'hoped' was the wrong word—'feared' might be

a better one for a man who was becoming increasingly aware that a past he had thought dead had returned to life and come back to haunt not only him but his innocent descendants.

Chapter Nine

'You are enjoying yourself, are you not, Alan? Sir Hart likes you, I know.'

'I like him, Eleanor—and the house. I had never thought to see anything quite so beautiful, lost among the moors.'

They had left the gardens which surrounded the house and were walking on a rough path which gave them a splendid view of the blue distance. They were rarely left alone together, but that afternoon they had tactfully slipped away in the middle of an argument between Sir Hart and Ned over his refusal to be instructed by Shotton.

'Ned does not like either Sir Hart or the house,' she said mournfully.

Alan stopped and turned to face her. 'But you do, Eleanor. You would make a better heir.'

She looked up at him sadly. 'I know. I would guard the heritage as the Hattons before have guarded it, but it's useless thinking like that. He *is* the heir, and he's my brother, whom I love, despite all.'

He put an arm about her to hold him to her in such away that although her nearness might tempt him, the temptation would not be overwhelming.

'I would guard you, Eleanor, you know that—if you gave me permission.'

It was not a declaration of marriage, but it was near enough. Eleanor was now grown up enough to understand that she must keep her distance from him a little in these early days, and that when he finally declared his love for her it would be after he had spoken to Sir Hart—and that would not be yet.

His next words confirmed her instinctive knowledge. 'I cannot offer for you yet, Eleanor. Not until Sir Hart has come to know me better and to believe that he may entrust you to me. He is resigned to Stacy marrying elsewhere, but he is a cautious man—and you are his treasure; the more so because of Ned's weaknesses.'

It was a mark of their growing rapport that he could speak so frankly. He bent down from his great height and kissed her, chastely, on the cheek. 'I dare not do more than that yet,' he said simply. 'You understand me?'

Eleanor nodded mutely.

'Time to go back,' he said.

They found a tea-party assembled on the lawn at the back of the house beneath a tree which Sir Hart had told them was centuries old. Sir Hart's armchair had been brought out. Alan reclined at Eleanor's feet and she fed him sandwiches, careless of what others thought. Her mother looked displeased, Sir Hart faintly amused.

At a lull in the conversation Alan sat up and spoke to the old man. 'With your permission, sir, I should like to spend a day or two in Bradford to inspect the mills and the town. Perhaps Ned would care to go with me.'

Before Sir Hart could answer, Ned said frankly, 'Not I, old fellow. Shouldn't care to peer into the innards of mills. Nasty places, mills.'

Eleanor winced at this confirmation of her earlier fears; Sir Hart looked severely at him. 'You are frivolous, Ned.

Of course you may visit Bradford, Mr Dilhorne. You may take Abdul with you, if you wish to ride there.'

'With due respect, I must refuse your kind offer, sir,' Alan replied. 'I would prefer one of his more workaday fellows. It would not do to come on too strong, as one of the nobs. A less wealthy image would be better.'

Sir Hart said, 'Since foolish Ned will not go with you, why not take Stacy?'

Alan looked at Stacy. 'I can think of nothing better. If it would please him, that is.'

'Of all things I should like to go,' said Stacy eagerly. He guessed, correctly, that the one person in the world whom Alan would have liked to take was Eleanor—but that was impossible.

'Good,' said Alan. 'The day after tomorrow, then. I must think on, as my father says.'

He fell back again and, smiling up at Eleanor, said, 'Madam, is the cake-mine empty that I receive only sandwiches?'

'Oh, you're insatiable,' she teased him, 'which is a polite word for greedy. All the same, you may have some good Yorkshire parkin with plenty of treacle in it to set you up for your journey.'

'I shan't be long,' he told her softly, 'seeing that it is you to whom I return.'

Two days later they rode to Bradford. Stacy, at Alan's request, also dressed down, so that he looked like a junior clerk. Before they left Alan took him into his room, wetted his hair, parted it down the middle and combed the sides flat again.

'Now for some fun,' said Alan cheerfully, 'and I want you to help me have it. I know you well enough to be sure that you won't refuse to do whatever I ask, however odd it might seem. I'll tell you the rest of it when we reach Bradford.'

They came back in three days, not the two Alan had told Sir Hart. They were red-eyed and kept bursting into wild laughter. Stacy said that he'd never had such a jolly time, despite his thick head from the previous night's drinking.

Sir Hart and Eleanor were both a little disappointed. Neither of them had thought that it was mere debauchery which had taken Alan to Bradford. Sir Hart sent for Stacy when his head was better and questioned him. What he learned, for Alan had told Stacy to tell him the truth, made him more thoughtful than ever. He looked at his guest with even greater respect.

Eleanor simply said to Alan in mock severity, 'I hope that you didn't lead Stacy into bad ways.'

'Indeed not,' he told her, grinning. 'But since what we did do is not quite finished we had better keep quiet. After that, Stacy may tell you as much of the truth as he thinks fit.'

The next day they all went over to Byethorpe, Robert Harshaw's place, for dinner. The manor house was nearly as old as Temple Hatton, but was dour and harsh, like Robert himself. The dinner was good, though.

Halfway through it Robert said to Alan, 'Ned tells me that you took young Stacy to Bradford with you. What were you doing there? Thinking of buying a woollen mill?'

He said this last in a jeering tone.

'No,' said Alan mildly. 'I'm not thinking of buying one.'

Stacy, despite himself, began to laugh. Robert looked suspiciously at him. 'I was not aware that I had made a joke, Stacy.'

'No, not you,' said Stacy, still laughing. 'Alan, it's Alan who makes the jokes.'

'Where is the joke in what you said, Dilhorne?' queried Robert, brows lowered.

'Why, as to that,' said Alan, 'I am not thinking of buying a woollen mill, for I have bought one.'

'You have bought one? Here? Now? What with?'

Robert was not the only one who was surprised, for the whole table was listening.

'With an advance in the form of a banker's draft,' said Alan, still cheerful. 'I lodged it with a house in Bradford as surety to be held in neutral hands until I am satisfied as to what I am buying. I have looked only cursorily at the books, but my man from London will be coming to examine them further. The lawyers must also have their say, and when all is done to my satisfaction, Outhwaite's shall be mine.'

'Outhwaite's! You have bought Outhwaite's,' exclaimed Robert. He jeered again. 'I suppose that your draft was drawn on Rothschild's!'

'Now how did you guess that,' said Alan innocently, looking Robert straight in the eye. 'But, yes. I dined with Mr Lionel before I left for Yorkshire. The talk was of this and that. That was mostly Yorkshire woollen mills.'

He ate his food with his usual appetite.

Sir Hart said, 'I see that you mix business with pleasure. I wish Ned had gone with you. It would have done him good.'

'I fear, sir, that he would not have enjoyed it. Stacy, I know, had a dam'd dull time. He made an excellent clerk.'

'Not I,' said Stacy, 'never had such fun in my life.' But neither Alan nor he would be drawn further to amplify on that.

'One does not enlarge on one's business deals, sir. That is one of my father's maxims,' Alan said to his companion at dinner, who also owned a mill or two, and tried to question him on how Outhwaite's had come to sell—and for what return.

Ned, listening to all this, put down his knife and fork and began to laugh.

'So, you have been at it again, Alan.' He looked around the table. 'I could tell you such tales of what he got up to in London. How—'

'But you will not,' said Alan, cutting across him. 'For that would be a breach of confidence, freely given.'

His voice was so cold and hard that Ned, for once, was overborne. He flushed, and picked up his knife and fork again.

'Yes,' he said, in a low voice. 'You are right.'

Sir Hart looked from one to the other: so alike and yet so different. Eleanor also, looking at them, thought that she loved Alan in spite of his having Ned's face and not because of it. It was his strength and his zest for life which drew her to him more than anything else about him.

Stacy whispered in Eleanor's ear, 'I think that I shall feed Jane's mama to *him*, after Bradford.'

Not even to Eleanor would he reveal all that they had done. He had told Sir Hart only the bare bones of their adventure, with few details.

On their first day in Bradford Alan had dressed Stacy's hair again, had made him wear a dirty neck-cloth and an ink-stained shirt with grimy cuffs. He had given him a notebook and a pencil and precise instructions.

'While they are talking look wise, and write any gibberish down in it. Walk behind me, be outwardly deferential, but make it plain that you are the clever young clerk and I am the rich young fool. That I am your charge.'

When they reached the mill Alan had turned into a dreadful parody of Ned, laughing, inconsequential and stupid, apparently taking heed of nothing. He'd clambered around, joking and asking people's pardon, had disappeared around corners, poked and prodded daftly at things.

The machines took his fancy. He asked questions of such

profound silliness that the contempt for him of the owners, their bookkeeper and their lawyers was undisguised.

'The stupid son of a rich, hard-working pa,' was their conclusion after he had left.

All the time he was there, though, his cold, scheming brain had been at work, while they gave themselves away. So it went on. Stacy obediently walked behind him, occasionally placed a hand on his apparently heedless arm, whispering at him when he was being particularly stupid.

Stacy wrote and wrote in his notebook. He filled it with The Lord's Prayer, The Twenty-third Psalm, great chunks of Caesar, Livy and Ovid's *Ars Amoris—The Art of Love—* particularly the more erotic bits—and all in Latin. After that he wrote down pages of Greek.

When they were left alone with Stacy, Alan having been taken away on his own, the owners were wariness itself, but before Alan no such thing.

Then, on the last afternoon, when he had found out what he wanted—that contrary to general belief Outhwaite's plant was out of date and they were nearly bankrupt—he changed before Stacy's eyes into someone so cold and hard that he was barely recognisable. After that they went back to Outhwaite's—that whited sepulchre—and the real business of the deal was done.

He changed from a clambering, eager, silly boy into a mocking man. He took the notebook from Stacy more than once, opened it and put his forefinger on a meaningless page, saying, 'But my man here noted at this point that you said quite otherwise yesterday. Is not that so?'

To which Stacy nodded, looked wise, replying helpfully, 'Indeed, Mr Alan, sir. I quite recollect, and so noted at the time.'

On the last night, with the deal well done, Alan took Stacy off to celebrate. The usual uproar was going on at Outhwaite's after he had left, with the usual recriminations about a bastard boy who had got the business for far less than he could have paid or they had hoped to get. Who in the world would have guessed that he knew so much—and so quickly—and had picked up so much more while he was behaving like a tumbler at a fair?

It was while they were drinking themselves stupid back at the inn where they had been staying that Alan picked up Stacy's notebook and solemnly began to read from it.

'''The Lord is my shepherd, Mr Outhwaite, sir'',' he intoned, '''as Stacy Trent has so noted, and my love has breasts of such magnitude, Ovid says, that even you, Mr Outhwaite, sir, might be astonished at them''.'

He threw the notebook into the fire, to Stacy's disappointment, because he'd wanted to keep it in memory of having had fun with Alan. Alan, only half-drunk at this point, looked him in the eye and said, 'The best evidence in such cases is no evidence—another of the Patriarch's maxims. Carry away with you the memory that they were so busy watching you that they quite forgot to check what I was doing.

'Now, drink up, Stacy, I want you unconscious before morning.'

Although Alan was generally popular with those who frequented Temple Hatton House, Robert Harshaw hated him, and Nat, the stable hand, glared at him whenever he visited the stables to watch and to help with the schooling and management of the horses.

One of the estate workers had been a pugilist, and early in the morning Alan, stripped to the waist, made a habit of sparring with him as a change from Gurney. Nat, unlike the other staff, hated him for this, too. Such a brute, he was, to care for Miss Eleanor and have his care returned.

The day after Alan had come back from Bradford Eleanor went to the stables before breakfast. Snowflake, the old pony whom she had ridden when she was younger and smaller, was ill, and she had come to see how he was.

She met Nat on entering the yard. He was carrying a bucket of water which he put down when he saw her. Eleanor gave him a brief, almost unseeing, nod, her attention fixed on the animal she had come to see. It stung him by its difference from their old camaraderie. Nat thought that he knew the cause.

'A word with you, Miss Eleanor, if you please.'

At last he had her full attention. 'Yes, Nat.' She smiled at him. He had been her old friend, after all. 'What is it?'

Despite her politeness, her manner to him was so different that rage built up inside him. He controlled himself with difficulty.

His voice hoarse, he began. 'Begging your pardon, the word is that you are taken with this young man from Australia Master Ned has brought here.'

Eleanor's face froze. 'I can't talk to you about him, Nat.'

She started to move away from him. Greatly daring, he caught her by the arm. Eyes widening, she looked down at his intrusive hand. He drew it away and stepped back.

'Don't look at him, Miss Eleanor, don't. He's not for a lady like you. I've seen him sparring with Ralf. He's a coarse brute, a great bruiser. They say that his father's a convict, too. He's not for you,' he repeated, moving towards her again.

'No,' she said. No more, Nat. Please go. You've already said too much. If you go at once I'll forget what you said.'

'No,' he said, 'not until I've finished.' He was very near to her now, and he put both hands out to grasp her by the shoulders this time.

Frightened by his hands, and by the wild look in his eye, Eleanor pulled away. A new voice behind her suddenly said, 'What is all this, Swain? You forget yourself, I think.'

They both turned to see Alan. It was not the Alan whom

Eleanor knew. He was lightly dressed in tan cotton trousers, and was wearing an open-necked white cotton shirt and shoes so light and soft that they looked like slippers. His hair was wet, and clung to his skull. He had a towel slung around his shoulders. But his face was the most changed, so cold and stern it was.

He did not look at all like Ned, more like the great Gainsborough portrait of Sir Beauchamp, Sir Hart's father. He was stiff with anger. She shivered.

Nat stepped back. 'I meant no harm.'

'Nor shall you do any,' said Alan. 'Apologise to Miss Hatton at once.'

'No,' said Nat, his voice cracking. 'I meant her no harm. You may beat and bully me, for you're twice my size. I knew her long before you came here. You don't deserve her; she should marry a gentleman—which you aren't.'

Alan froze on the last words and let out a long sigh. 'Like that, is it?'

He looked at Eleanor. 'Do I tell Sir Hart? Is he to be turned off? Can he be trusted not to do this again.'

He swung suddenly towards Nat, who flinched away from him.

'You're right,' he said. 'I'll not beat you. You're too small for me.'

'My fault,' said Eleanor painfully. 'We were playmates once.'

'Yes,' said Alan gently. 'I gathered that. But not any more. He can't stay here after this, you know.'

Nat was reckless. 'So, I'm to lose Miss Eleanor and my work too?'

'No,' said Alan. 'I'll find you work—but not here.'

'Oh, yes,' said Nat bitterly. 'You fix everything, don't you? I've heard your man talking. It's Mr Alan does this, Mr Alan does that. You'll not fix me.'

'I think I will,' said Alan, his voice as hard as granite

again. 'Your choice,' he told Nat, as he had told Victor. 'If I inform Sir Hartley of your behaviour to Miss Eleanor you'll be turned away without a character. On the other hand you can let me find a place for you and your girl. You do have a girl, Gurney tells me.'

'Know everything, don't you?'

'No, but I know that. Well?'

'Now? You'll make me choose now?'

'You brought yourself to this, not I.'

'Must he go?' asked Eleanor, her face white. 'He's always lived here. He loves the country.'

Her eyes dropped beneath Alan's steady stare. 'Yes, you're right. Oh, dear, Nat, I'm so sorry.'

'No you're not!' Nat flung at her. 'You stopped being sorry for me long ago. I've no choice,' he said. 'I'll go.'

'Then pack today,' said Alan. 'Tell the girl to pack, too—if that is what you want. You'll leave tomorrow. Come to me after breakfast and I'll tell you where to go.'

'Tomorrow! So soon… Sir Hartley…' Nat stopped, his head hanging.

'He'll let you go if I ask him,' said Alan.

Nat gave him one last look, then walked away, picking up the bucket as he went.

'Be ready to leave by twelve o'clock, sharp,' said Alan to his back.

Eleanor said nothing, merely stared at Alan. He put out his hand, touched her shoulder gently and steered her out of the yard to the small herb garden nearby, where they were screened from the house. He helped her to a bench and sat down beside her.

'Where are you sending them?' she asked numbly, still shocked.

'Outhwaite's. They're undermanned. They need someone in the yard to help with the horses and the wagons. He'll be paid more than he is here, and there are prospects for a likely lad. Hargreaves says that he is a good worker.'

'Oh, Alan, he'll hate Bradford. He loves the country so. Oh, it's my fault, all my fault.' She began to cry.

'Eleanor, look at me. I've known what was wrong with him ever since I first came here. I've seen him watching you, and the way in which he watches you. He watches me, too. His girl is expecting his child—it's better that they go.'

'How do you know such things?' she cried passionately into her handkerchief. 'You frighten me at times.'

'Eleanor, I often don't know how I know. But I notice and think.'

'And I don't—or not enough—although I'm getting better. It's my fault. I wouldn't give him up when the boys left. Sir Hart warned me about him, and so did Mother. I never heeded them then, I was so blind. When I came back I knew that I'd been unfair to him, but I had no notion that he… Believe me, I have never encouraged him in any way at any time—although he must have thought that I did.'

'I know that, dear Eleanor. It's not your fault,' he told her, his voice kind.

She had been so unawakened then, but not now, Alan thought, not now.

To comfort her he put a brotherly arm around her. She wailed into his chest, 'Oh, I have made such mistakes…'

'We all do,' he told her. 'If it's any comfort I've made dreadful mistakes because I take dreadful risks.'

Her sobbing gradually grew less. Finally, when the noise from the House signalled that the day there was beginning, she said soberly, 'Oh, Alan, I'm so sorry. I've kept you from your sparring with Ralf this morning.'

He smiled at her. 'So you know about that?'

'Nat told me,' she said. 'It's one of the things you do

which he seems to dislike most. You will be careful, won't you?'

Alan debated what to say. He had no desire to tell her the truth, that when he was about eighteen a boxer, an ex-champion transported for theft, had told his father that he could make a champion of him.

'Brains and strength, Mester Dilhorne, and cunning, too. What more could you want? Let me train him.'

'Only for pleasure,' his father had said. 'I'm not having his brains knocked out.'

He had never really wanted to be a pugilist, and to tell her of this would simply add one more page to the tale of his oddity in England. As he so often did, he came out with a half-truth.

'Oh, no fear of my getting hurt. I'm only a gentleman amateur and Ralf is a real bruiser who once fought for money. He knows how to treat me so that he doesn't spoil my pretty face. I only spar to keep myself in trim. I'm big, you see, and I like my food. I don't want to end up fat and heavy; that would never do.'

Ned will get fat, Eleanor thought suddenly. He's soft, eats and drinks too much and is already putting on weight. The thought depressed her and she began to shiver again.

Alan thought that she needed comforting. Perhaps a few gentle kisses would help, if he could keep them gentle. He began experimenting—to find Eleanor responding so enthusiastically that the kisses became more and more ardent.

Fortunately—or unfortunately—they heard footsteps approaching and broke away. By the time that Ned appeared they were sitting decorously side by side.

'So this is where you've got to, Alan.' He looked severely at Eleanor. 'I went to see him spar with Ralf, and instead I find him sitting mooning about with you.'

Alan rose to his feet. 'No sparring today, Ned, I'm hungry.' He helped Eleanor to rise and they walked back to breakfast together, Ned still complaining about his lost entertainment.

Sir Hart was waiting in his study for young Dilhorne. The young man had asked to speak to him after breakfast on a matter of business. The study was next door to and opened out of the library, which was one of the glories of the House. Above the thousands of books ranged behind gold lattices there was a Van Dyck painting of the first Baronet, Sir Beverley Hatton, and his family, surrounded by dogs and horses: Temple Hatton House and the moorland beyond it were dim in the background. Opposite to it was a Tudor fireplace ornately decorated with the arms of all the noble families in the district.

The study, however, was a small jewel, not a large one. No family portraits hung there, and the books were all severely practical, relating to the running of the estate and Sir Hart's time in Parliament. Only a Turner oil of the House, done when he had come North, glowed against the dark, oak-panelled wall.

Sir Hart was wondering what young Dilhorne wanted. There was an estate ledger on the desk before him, an old one of sixty years before, open at a page which he had stared at a thousand times until thirty years ago he had closed it and put it away for ever.

On the night of Alan's arrival he had fetched it out and stared at it again.

Sir Hart closed the book, but left it on his desk, for once irresolute. There was a knock on the door. He called, 'Enter,' and the young man came in. His handsome face, so apparently open and innocent, but which was no mirror of the devious mind behind it, bore the stamp of worry. He looked briefly around the room, his eye caught by the Turner, before he spoke.

'I am sorry to trouble you, sir, but I have a favour to ask of you.'

Sir Hart made a slight movement of his right hand which Alan took as a signal to continue.

'It is about the young stable hand, Sir Hartley, Nat Swain. He seems to be a good worker and I have an opening for such a one at Outhwaite's. I am sure that he would do well there, but I should not like to invite him to leave here without asking your permission first.'

Sir Hart looked sharply at him. 'It is he whom you particularly want?'

'Indeed—and I need him immediately. I would wish him to leave tomorrow, if possible.'

'Tomorrow? You are sure that it is necessary for him to go from here?'

Alan looked the old man full in the eye. 'Most necessary, I do assure you.' He hesitated. 'I told him that you would not stand in his way.'

'I understand you fully, sir. I wish that I did not. Yes, he may go to Outhwaite's. That is, if he consents. Does he consent?'

'Oh, yes, indeed. I took the liberty of speaking to him first, but said that it depended on you.'

Sir Hart sighed. His right hand reached out and stroked the old ledger. 'You are devious, young man.'

'So I believe, sir. I cannot help it. I am like my father.'

'And Ned is like his,' sighed Sir Hart. 'You admire my room, sir?'

'I admire the whole House. We have nothing like it at home, although my father's home is exceptional in its own way. His treasures are all from the Far East, however.'

'Indeed. He sounds an interesting man.'

'Yes, but devious, sir. We all are. It is our nature.'

'We cannot help our natures,' said Sir Hart heavily, 'but we can control them if we are so minded.'

'That is true. I may speak to Nat Swain, then?'

'By all means. The thing is done. I shall speak to Hargreaves immediately. He will need to train another lad.' He sighed again. 'I have been remiss in doing nothing about young Swain. You have done my work for me.'

Before Alan could answer him he said, 'You are enjoying your stay in Yorkshire, I believe?'

'Very much. The wild beauty of the countryside appeals to me. But I like Bradford, too. That is where the future lies.'

'And here we are living in the past. I take your meaning, sir.' Sir Hart looked out of the window. 'It may be beautiful now, but it is grim in winter on the moors. Wild and desolate. I would have liked Turner to see it then.' He waved a hand at the landscape which had caught Alan's eye.

'A strange man, the painter. I suspect that my father would not have had him in the House. But then, there were many whom Sir Beauchamp would not have admitted to his company.'

There was an odd, bitter note in his voice. He looked away and said, 'We are not all fortunate in our fathers sir. Ned, for example. But perhaps we're not all fortunate in our sons, either.'

He moved his hand dismissively. 'Well, I am pleased that you are happy here. Ned said that you were good for him, and for once he is right. I wish that he had gone with you.'

'He would not have enjoyed himself, I fear.'

'True, true.' Sir Hart looked at the young man before him and did not wish to send him away.

'You have seen the picture gallery, Mr Dilhorne?'

Alan wondered why the old man had suddenly spoken his name. He had so far avoided doing so.

'Only in passing, sir, not in detail.'

'And Ned knows nothing of it, I fear. Come.'

Together they walked the long gallery, whose windows opened on to the moors. The facing wall was hung with a collection of works which would have graced a palace. Prominent among them were the Hatton family portraits, nearly all painted by the great names of their day.

'Here is Sir Berkeley Hatton, our founder. He built most of the Tudor part of the House. He was a nobody, although the family claims that he was related to Sir Christopher Hatton, Queen Bess's minister. His name was not Berkeley, it was William. It wasn't Hatton either: it was Clark. I suppose that his real name wasn't grand enough for such a thruster. Another devious gentleman, Berkeley.'

Berkeley Hatton had the sandy hair and the brilliant blue eyes which appeared and reappeared in the painted faces of the male Hattons.

'Here is another thruster, the first Baronet, Beverley. You see, we go in for pompous names. He made us uncommonly rich—he was even more devious than Berkeley, and bought his title from James I. Blacks and molasses, drink and corruption were what he dealt in. We were not always gentlemen.

'Here, sir, is our Titian, the glory of the collection. Sir Beverley acquired it. They say that when his agent brought it from Venice he stared at it and said, ''My God, it's a deal of money for a bit of spoiled canvas, but a gentleman has to have his toys to show the world his worth''.'

Alan laughed. 'My father would enjoy that.'

Together they admired Titian's *Venus*, naked in a golden sunset, an adoring boy at her feet, cherubs hovering overhead, before passing on to a giant canvas, central to the room.

A cold, proud man who shared his face with Sir Hart, Ned and Alan, gazed impersonally at them. His bright blue eyes were inimical. The star flashed on his shoulder and the Garter's blue around his knee rivalled his eyes. He was in white Court dress, one hand on his sword. A storm gathered behind his head. Gainsborough had painted him and, despite the elegance of the feathery brushwork, he had been unable to soften the grim scorn with which Sir Beauchamp surveyed his world.

'My father, Sir Beauchamp, frightened everyone,' said Sir Hart. 'He was such a hard man. He was in Government, too. When the French Revolution broke out in '89 he rose in the Commons and said, ''I told you nearly fourteen years ago when the Americans revolted that the old order was doomed. You would not listen then and you will not listen now, and the world is ending—even as I said it would.'''

'They shouted at him, and he walked out and never returned. I did not like, nor love, my father, but he was true to his own harsh principles, which is more than you can say of many.'

The tour ended at the far door. Sir Hart bowed to Alan and left him.

Alan walked thoughtfully away, disturbed by what he had seen, and the old man's showing of it to him in such detail. The repetition of the word devious, which had been earlier applied to himself, and then the showpiece painting of Sir Beauchamp had frightened him. Was Sir Hart trying to tell him something about himself?

The morning had disappeared while he walked with Sir Hart. Ned met him on the stairs.

'The old man kept you long enough,' he grumbled. 'And here is a fine to-do. Great-Aunt is already here, with Charles. I am to tell Sir Hart.' He hurried along to the gallery, shouting, 'Wait for me, Alan.'

Alan stood, irresolute, until Ned reappeared with Sir Hart and they walked down the stairs together.

Charles ran at him when they entered the drawing room, saying excitedly, 'Oh, splendid, Alan, you are still here. I persuaded Grandmama to come early so that we should not miss you. Have you been doing famous things in Yorkshire? There are no railways here yet, but I should like of all things to visit a mill.'

'So you shall, Charles. You shall visit my mill,' said Alan.

'Your mill? Even more famous. Perhaps you could buy a railway and then I could drive one of the trains.'

'That, I fear, is a little beyond me.'

'Now, Charles,' said Almeria severely, 'you must not trouble Mr Dilhorne too much. Besides, you forget your manners. Make your bow to your great-uncle.'

An amused Sir Hart welcomed Charles, who exclaimed, 'Forgive me, sir, but so few people like railways and machines. You don't, do you?'

'Not much,' said Sir Hart, 'but I do not boast of it, like some.' And he looked at Ned as he spoke.

'Oh, I prefer horses,' said Ned.

'Horses are all very well, but they don't possess interesting things like pistons,' said Charles, throwing the whole company into laughter.

Eleanor had been standing to one side, and when the Stanton party were led away to their various rooms Alan took the opportunity to speak to her. She was still a little in shock and her eyes were brilliant in her white face.

She answered his unspoken question. 'Oh, yes, I am quite recovered. Ned tells me that you have spent the whole. morning with Sir Hart. Was it very difficult for you?'

'Not at all. He quite understood.'

'You did not tell him…?'

'I told him nothing. Sir Hart misses little, you know. I was so long because he wished to show me the picture gallery.'

'It is beautiful, is it not? He showed you his favourites, I'll be bound.'

Alan smiled. 'Yes, he showed me the Titian. The *Venus*

is beautiful, but I prefer the living lady, Eleanor, to the painted one.'

Her face grew rosy instantly, but she was not coy with him, did not simper.

'I thank you, sir,' she said, and then, 'What did you think of Sir Beauchamp?'

'That although I might like to have met him, I am glad that I did not. We are too alike.'

Eleanor was aghast. 'Oh, no! You are not at all alike. He was hateful, for all his splendid looks. Great-Aunt says that he treated Sir Hart cruelly when he was a boy—right from being born, and then later on. For some imaginary misdemeanour—although it is difficult to imagine Sir Hart committing one—he beat him dreadfully and exiled him to France. You are not like that, Alan.'

'No, but I share his ruthlessness as well as his face, Eleanor, and you must accept that. I would not hurt people, as he did, but I understand him.'

'I'm glad that you only share your face with him, and not your ancestry. You are pleased that Charles has come?'

Alan nodded. 'Very much. With Charles and Stacy to join us we shall have some splendid times.'

Eleanor noted ruefully that Ned's name was missing from this list. Since reaching Yorkshire the difference between the two, from being a slight one, had developed into a gulf. Other than their face they had nothing in common. Ned was becoming impatient with Alan's seriousness, and Alan privately deplored Ned's frivolity, more open here because he was bored.

The afternoon brought further surprises. Seated at tea in the green drawing room, among the Canalettos and the Guardis and the Louis Quinze furniture, the enlarged company became aware of further bustle outside. The Honourable Henrietta Hatton and Beastly Beverley had arrived.

Beverley entered the room like a mannerless whirlwind.

On seeing Alan, he blurted out, before greeting or being greeted by his grandfather, 'So! *You* are still here! I hoped that you would be gone before we arrived.'

'Beverley, please,' bleated his mother. 'Bow to Sir Hart—and you must not say such things.'

'Why not? Why shouldn't I? I don't like him. I don't like the way he looks at me. When I told my uncle Harry that he had Ned's face, Uncle Harry laughed and said—'

Before Beverley could say the unsayable Sir Hart broke into his tirade. 'Master Hatton!' he barked.

For once Beverley stopped speaking, his grandfather's voice was so fearsome.

'Master Hatton, you will go to your room at once and remain there until I give you permission to return. That will be when you have learned the art of civilised intercourse. Remove him at once, Henrietta.'

'I shan't go,' screamed Beverley, purple in the face. 'She can't make me.'

'Yes, Sir Hart, that is true,' said Henrietta pleadingly, nearly in tears. 'He is too strong for me. Please relent: he does not know what he is saying.'

'Oh, but I do,' roared Beverley, 'and I will not go.'

Sir Hart put his hand on the bell-pull. 'I shall ring for two footmen to remove you, sir, seeing that your mother has lost control over you.'

Beverley struggled between his desire to repeat what his uncle had said of Alan and the possible humiliation of being removed by two strapping footmen who would laugh about him in the servants' hall afterwards.

'Oh, very well,' he exclaimed ungraciously. He made for the door, plunging by and treading on the toes of a horrified Charles on the way. 'But I shall tell you what Uncle Harry said of him another day.'

Sir Hart said severely to Henrietta when she flew after him, 'Once Beverley is settled in his rooms with his tutor, who, judging by this behaviour, is a remarkably incompetent young man, you will return here at once. You are not to remain with him.'

'But, Sir Hart…' wailed Henrietta.

'Unless you wish to leave tomorrow, taking your ill-conditioned cub with you, you will do as I ask.'

Later, Stacy, talking to Alan of Charles's passion for machinery, said suddenly, 'I am bound to tell you, Alan—and do not take this amiss—that others besides Beverley's uncle Harry will comment on your likeness to Ned and the reason for it. I must say that I am surprised by Ned and Eleanor's apparent innocence over the matter.'

Alan smiled. 'That is because I come from New South Wales, and my father sprang from the gutter in London, and they know that there is no possible connection between us.'

He looked Stacy straight in the face while he told him this thundering lie—or rather half-truth. Try though he might, deviousness was a fundamental part of him and came without effort.

He had told no one the little he knew of his father's origins, of his grandmother and the possible link there. He had come to Yorkshire partly for that reason, and he was troubled by the portraits and Sir Hart's commentary which had pointedly linked him with the Hatton deviousness—so sadly lacking in Ned and Beverley. He had been even further troubled on hearing of Sir Hart's disgrace as a very young man.

But surely that could have nothing to do with his grandmother? Sir Beauchamp would not have exercised himself over his son's putting a servant in the family way: it was what gentlemen's sons did to peasant girls. They should consider themselves flattered. No, the disgrace must have been for something else.

When Alan was troubled, or disturbed, he did what he

always did: he worked to take his mind off what worried him. The next day he rode to Brinkley. He told Sir Hart that he had business there, and would be back in time for dinner. They were all processing into the Great Hall when he returned.

He was filthy. His face and hands were greasy, his linen was soiled, his fine coat was torn and there was a heavy bruise on one cheek. He had obviously been drinking, and although he was not drunk he had taken enough to lose the hard edge of his self-control. He spoke cheerfully to Sir Hart.

'You pardon, Sir Hart, for my ruined appearance and my lateness for dinner. I have been doing business with hard-headed Yorkshiremen, and I had to follow their ways or be bested. I think that they may be feeling worse than I am. I must ask you to allow me to miss dinner this evening. As you see, I am not fit.'

'I forgive you, young man, if you have been working, but I shall not let you off dinner. Repair yourself, and come down later. Food will help, not harm your condition.'

He had scarcely finished speaking when Charles said eagerly, 'Have you bought another mill, Alan?'

'A little one, old fellow, and some workshops. Now, forgive me, I must obey Sir Hart.'

He took the stairs two at a time. He thrust his spinning head into a bucket of water and Gurney helped him into clean clothes. His hair dark from its ducking, he returned, and ate his dinner under Sir Hart's sardonic gaze.

The old man does not treat me so when *I* overdo it, thought Ned resentfully—something which the other dinner guests had already noticed, Eleanor among them.

The house-party grew in numbers. Sir Hart had given up his dream of a marriage between Stacy and Eleanor and had invited Jane Chalmers and her mother to Temple Hatton.

'Chalmers of Biddenden,' he said approvingly. 'I think that I knew her grandfather, Anthony, at Oxford. The clergyman father is a younger son, I suppose.'

So Mrs Chalmers—the Dragon Queen, as Stacy had nicknamed her—duly arrived, with Jane in tow. Jane, charming, shy and submissive, was soon on as good terms with Eleanor as Mrs Chalmers was with Eleanor's mother.

The biggest joke of all, though, was that Mrs Chalmers, far from eating Alan, or being eaten, was completely taken by him. Stacy she respected, because he was a tremendous catch for Jane, but Alan Dilhorne!

She positively simpered at him from the first tea-time when he helped her to cake and turned his brilliant blue eyes on her.

'They all love you,' said Ned. There was almost a snarl in his voice, for he was jealous of the friend he had to share with others. 'You don't trouble yourself about me these days.'

'Now you know that is not true,' replied Alan. 'You were the first person I asked to go on the Brinkley expedition.'

'Oh, that!' said Ned. 'You know I don't care for such things.'

'Well, then,' said Alan with his usual—to Ned—exasperating common sense.

The Brinkley expedition was to be arranged for those who wished to see the small mill and the workshops which Alan was in process of acquiring. Stacy had discovered that he had won them in a drinking session-cum-trial of strength with their owner, Jack Thorpe, on the day when he had been late for dinner.

Thorpe had barely been making a profit, and when he had heard that Alan had bought Outhwaite's and was in process of turning it round, he had offered Alan a deal dependent on Alan's being able to overcome Yorkshire strength in an arm-wrestling competition with him.

When Alan had won the contest, Thorpe had suddenly gripped him and demanded further payment if, in a real wrestling bout, he could overcome Alan by beating him two falls to nothing. If Alan won Thorpe would accept Alan's original terms—hence his ripped coat and his dirty appearance, since much of the wrestling had been done on the inn floor.

The heavy drinking had been done before the contest—'Ale before work,' Thorpe had said. Stacy's delight had to be solitary, seeing that Alan kept silent about it—the devious dog—and it was Ralf who had told him what had happened.

The expedition to Brinkley consisted of all the young people: Alan, Eleanor, Jane, Stacy, Charles and Mr Dudley. They went off in two carriages with hampers of picnic food, wine, china, plate and silver cutlery.

'We must eat in the open,' Alan told them, 'for there is nowhere in the mill or shops fit for ladies to eat. And you must all wear your oldest clothes.'

They accordingly put on their drabs—Eleanor's word—and walked around the village. They inspected the workshops swaying through the noisy, dusty rooms where dull-eyed girls looked enviously at them—their drabs being princely here.

Eleanor and Jane were both subdued afterwards, never having seen the world of industrial work before, merely driving, riding or walking through the village with little idea of what went on behind walls and windows.

After they left the workshops Eleanor questioned Alan about the girls, some barely more than children. Jane clung to Stacy's arm and said quietly, 'I am glad that I am not a mill girl.'

Consequently their picnic in a field outside Brinkley was

a quiet one, since their ample food and drink, as Stacy said, seemed to mock the haggard faces which they had seen. Only Charles, who had taken paper and pencil with him to draw the machinery, was untouched, for he was too young to see what troubled his elders.

'We are so fortunate and we do not know it,' said Eleanor to Alan, who was driving her on the way home.

'Yes,' agreed Alan, who had taken them to Brinkley for that very purpose, since none of them ever thought of the lost lives which sustained them in their idleness.

'You would not have liked it,' said Eleanor to Ned at dinner, 'but it would have done you good to go there.'

'Now, why is that?' drawled Ned.

'All those wretched people working such long hours for a mere pittance—especially the poor girls,' Eleanor told him. 'Compared with our lives it is quite dreadful.'

Ned raised his brows. 'Why compare them to us? They are nothing to do with us. They need not work if they do not like the mills nor the pay.'

'They work because they need the money,' exclaimed Eleanor, exasperated.

'Oh,' said Ned, 'I see. Then why do they not go where the pay is better?'

He offered this imaginary insight to the table with a triumphant smile.

'Because the pay is not better at any other mill,' said Alan.

'And you should know, old fellow, because you employ them. If it makes you unhappy—and damme you look sour about it—why don't you pay them more?'

Alan spoke in the voice of one instructing a child. 'Because if my competitors pay their girls low wages—which they do—and I pay mine high ones, their prices will be lower than mine and I shall not be able to compete with them in the open market.

'The consequence would be that I should not be able to sell my goods. My factories and workshops would close and the girls would lose even the pittance they earn now. If you can instruct me on a way out of this impasse, Ned, then I shall be happy to adopt it, but, until then, matters must remain as they are.'

'Don't ask me, old fellow,' returned Ned happily, quite unrebuked by this explanation, 'I know nothing of it. Can't help you, I'm afraid.'

Eleanor looked shocked at this idle reply. Sir Hart sighed again on hearing Ned's frivolity. To Alan he said, 'I see that you have thought deeply about this painful matter.'

'Oh, my father and I have discussed it frequently. "Think on," he used to say, when I came up with noble but useless ideas of reform.'

'Ah, an old Yorkshire phrase,' said Sir Hart quickly. 'I thought that your father came from London?'

'So he did, but he had friends from Yorkshire,' Alan explained. He regretted having spoken without considering his words, and his explanation, while not untruthful, was not the whole truth and had been designed to deceive.

'Are you saying that you have no choice?' Eleanor asked him.

'None, and, begging your pardon, we all live on the backs of the mill girls, so if they lose, we lose, too.'

'Well, I'm dam'd if I do,' exclaimed Ned. 'I don't know any, don't employ any, and they don't do it for me.'

Sir Hart closed his eyes.

Jane's mother said admiringly, 'You are so clever, Mr Dilhorne, you are positively frightening. We poor women can only admire and wonder!'

Alan tried not to catch Eleanor's eye.

Charles, who had been eating his dinner quietly, said, 'Shall you manage Outhwaite's and the Brinkley mill, Alan?'

'No,' he said. 'They cannot afford me. When I have straightened matters out I shall put in managers, or overseers, who will report to me.'

'I am sick of mills,' said Ned pettishly. 'Had I wanted to know about them I would have gone with you today. A boring outing you had of it, I must say.'

'I found it interesting,' said Jane Chalmers gently. 'It was so different from anything I know—and I believe Stacy thought so, too.'

'Stacy would enjoy himself reading the Lord's Prayer,' replied Ned rudely, 'so that is no matter. Let us talk of something interesting—like the York Races.'

Alan thought that there were times when Ned was little more than a nicer version of Beastly Beverley.

Sir Hart looked weary unto death. He tried not to remember that Ned was his heir, and that the care and future of the House, the land, the servants and the tenants would fall on him soon, and he so ill-qualified for any responsibility.

Chapter Ten

Jane, Stacy and Eleanor found Alan waiting for them in the entrance hall when they met to take their usual pre-breakfast walk. He was not wearing the clothes in which he sparred with Ralf.

'I thought that I might join you,' he said. 'If you will have me.'

'Always welcome,' remarked Stacy. 'You're not working out with Ralf today, then?'

'He's off on an errand for Sir Hart. I thought that Eleanor might like the use of my arm.'

Jane and Stacy smiled at the speed with which Eleanor attached herself to Alan—matched only by Jane's with Stacy. They set off towards Brant's Wood, named after a Hatton heir who had died young, Stacy told them.

'I had a letter this morning from Caroline Loring,' Eleanor said to Alan. They were walking a little behind Stacy and Jane. 'She tells me that she is now happily married to Anthony Beauchamp—so that's one worry solved—and that Victor is still working at Dilhorne's—to everyone's surprise.'

'Good,' replied Alan absently. He had recently received a report from George telling him the same thing and that their deal with Rothschild's had gone through. His more immediate concern was to try to manoeuvre matters so that he and Eleanor might spend a few moments alone.

His chance came when Jane had to stop on the edge of the wood to remove a stone from her shoe. Stacy gallantly went down on one knee to help her, saying over his shoulder to Alan, 'No need for you two to hang about. We'll catch you up later when this major operation is over.'

'Do you think,' said Alan mischievously to Eleanor once they were well into the wood, 'that Stacy is as pleased for an excuse to be alone with Jane as I am to be with you?'

'Oh, I expect so,' she said, laughing up at him. 'Fortunately there is no one about to say to me, "Now, Eleanor, it is neither proper nor safe for you to be alone with Mr Dilhorne without a chaperon." Is that true, Alan? Am I not safe with you?'

'Do you want a polite answer, or a truthful one?' he asked her, equally mischievously.

'Oh, a truthful one, of course. One is always supposed to tell the truth.'

'Then the answer is that I am not sure. Of course, I intend to behave like a perfect gentleman now that I am alone with you, but although the spirit may be willing, the flesh is weak.'

They had stopped walking and the eyes he turned on Eleanor were flashing a message at her which was unmistakable. She remembered what had happened the last time when they were alone together in the railway tunnel and she shivered with delight.

'What does your weak flesh wish you to do, Alan?'

She could not help herself; the wanton words had flown out of her as though she were once again the wild Eleanor of old and not the decorous creature she had become. She was aware that she was tempting him, but the desire to challenge him was so strong in her that she was unable to resist it.

'This,' he said, and bent his head and kissed her tenderly on the mouth. He knew that they would not have long alone together, that Stacy would give them only a short respite from shared frustration.

Her arms crept round his neck, but he resisted the temptation to do more than caress her gently. She gave a little cry when his kiss deepened and he felt her whole body vibrate in response to his lovemaking, gentle though it was.

Stacy could be heard speaking to Jane, 'I wonder how far they have got?' he was saying, undoubtedly to warn them of his approach. 'They're probably almost through the wood by now.'

Alan gave a short laugh, seized Eleanor's hand and ran her gently along the path until they could see broad daylight again. Some minutes later Stacy and Jane joined them. Jane was slightly flushed and Stacy looked happy. They also had obviously used their short time together to great advantage.

Breakfast called them when they had walked a little way beyond the wood, laughing and talking together.

Ned stopped Alan in the Entrance Hall.

'Robert and I intend to make a day of it. There is to be a prize-fight in the fields outside Bingley this afternoon. A bruiser from London is meeting a lad from Brinkley. And after that we shall join a group of the fellows for some fun. You will come, won't you?'

Alan debated with himself. He had neglected Ned lately, through no fault of his own, but the idea of a day spent in drinking and ending in more drinking and possibly riot in the evening did not appeal.

Besides, he had promised to see his new workers at Thorpe's that day, and it would be too bad to send word that he could not come if they found out that he had neglected them to visit a prize-fight.

'I'm sorry, Ned. I'm already engaged to visit Brinkley. Had I known earlier I could have called it off. As it is...' And he shrugged.

'That is too bad! Why can you not come? You could go there another day.'

'I have given my word. You must not tempt me to break it, Ned.'

'Your word! Break it! You sound like Stacy these days—or a parson. Even Eleanor has become dull. Well, I see that there is no moving you. It will be a great day, and you will be sorry that you have missed it.'

I doubt that, thought Alan, watching Ned stamp off in a temper. Eleanor, who had been listening to them, put her small hand on Alan's strong arm. 'Oh, dear—I see that Ned is upset again.'

'Yes, and there is no help for it. I have my duty.'

'And Ned has none,' said Eleanor sadly, so sadly that Alan said impulsively, 'I promise not to be too late back, and then we may go riding together this afternoon—if that would please you.'

'Oh, Alan, of course it would. I shall be waiting for you, but do not hurry back if your business should overrun.'

She was changing, Eleanor knew, slowly but surely. Such a consideration would not have occurred to her once. But, like a kitten's, her eyes were slowly opening to a world far removed from the easy one in which she had lived since birth.

If Alan should offer for me, she thought, and I am half certain that he will, shall I be brave enough to go to live with him on the other side of the world—if that is what he wishes?

She answered her own question with a fierce, Indeed, I will. I cannot face the notion of a life without him. Like Ruth in the Bible I shall say, 'Whither thou goest, I will go...thy people shall be my people... 'But if he wishes to stay in England, I shall accept that, too. If he does not offer I must be brave, however much I might suffer.

She took these thoughts with her into the dining room, where Alan and Stacy began to help her and Jane to choose their breakfast dishes. It was pleasant, Alan thought, to sit in the beautiful room, talking idly, the servants endlessly providing for them, replacing food which had grown cold in the silver dishes on the sideboard. Their every whim was catered for without thought. Such a life explained Ned, Victor and Beverly. Charles was obviously strong-minded, but could even he fail to be affected? Would he, too, fall into idleness and frivolity—become like Ned?

He made his mind up. If he married Eleanor he would do his best to rescue Charles—if he could. For the moment he laughed and talked with Eleanor, and later she walked with him to the stables before he took horse for Brinkley.

Bereft, Eleanor walked slowly back into the House to find Sir Hart had come down to breakfast. Seated there alone he looked very old and tired, and it struck her that one day, quite soon, she would lose him—and that was another new thought. She walked over to him and kissed him on the cheek.

'Why, Granddaughter, you honour me,' he said kindly.

'You deserve it, sir.'

'Sit with me for a moment, Eleanor. You care for Ned's Australian friend, do you not?'

'Yes,' she said simply, where once she might have been effusive.

'Enough to marry him—and leave all this?'

He might have been reading her mind this question was so *àpropos*.

'Yes, I think so, but most of all I don't want to lose you.'

'You will lose me quite soon, I think. My time cannot be long now; I am well past the common age of man.'

She threw her arms around him. 'Do not say so, Grand-father.'

'I must, my dear. I fear that I can do nothing for Ned and Beverley, but I would like to see you settled before I die. Once I would have wanted you to marry Stacy. I know now that I was wrong. This stern young man from Austra-lia, Eleanor, is he what you want?'

Eleanor was puzzled. 'Stern, Grandfather?'

'Yes, it is the right word for him, Eleanor. Do not mis-take him, I beg of you. He is charm on the surface, steel below. I know him, Eleanor. I have met him before, long ago. Except that he is kind and the other was not.'

She had no idea of whom he spoke. She simply put her young hand on his old one and told him, 'Yes, I love him, Grandfather. Perhaps because he is so different from every-one I know—and in spite of his having Ned's face, not because.' Eleanor felt that she had to say this.

Sir Hart's face twisted in pain. 'Yes, indeed, he is not at all like Ned—and I believe that he has not spoken to you yet?'

'No, Grandfather, but he will—I think.'

'Eleanor, I must warn you. Nothing is sure in this life. It may be that his duty might prevent him from doing so.'

She was puzzled again. 'His duty? Do you mean that his world and mine might not fit? I do hope not.'

It was not what Sir Hart meant, but he allowed her to think so. He must speak to the boy before he offered for Eleanor—and tell him the truth. Matters could not go on as they were. The young man was devious, but so was he. Sir Hart saw his guest's evasions and was certain that he knew more of his father's origins than he cared to give away.

Besides, there was the unknown father to be consid-ered… Sir Hart tried not to think of him.

He put his hand on Eleanor's head. 'My only wish is for

you to be happy, Eleanor. Remember that. You are a good girl and you are growing up rapidly.'

To himself he added, You are not silly, like your mother and Ned, and for that I must thank your true father, whom you are beginning to resemble in character.

As if to confirm this unspoken judgement, Eleanor's mother came in, exclaiming, 'Oh, they have all gone, I see. Only fancy, Ned's guest is neglecting him again. Ned wanted him to go to the prize-fight at Brinkley and he refused. Some nonsense about work. I am not sure that he is quite the gentleman.'

'Fortunately for him, probably not,' said Sir Hart, noting Eleanor's indignant face. He rose. 'I shall leave you both; I am very tired. Eleanor, pray remember what I said to you.'

'What did he say?' asked her mother eagerly when Sir Hart had gone.

'Why, nothing,' answered Eleanor, unconsciously imitating Alan when he was being devious. 'Only that he grows old.'

'Oh, that!' said her mother, disappointed. 'I was wondering what splendid marriage he had in mind for you now that Stacy has not come up to scratch.'

Eleanor made no answer when she called Alan 'Ned's barbarian', as though he had arrived dressed in skins and carrying a battle-axe. The picture this conjured up set Eleanor laughing.

Unfortunately, that remark symbolised her mother's ignorance over what was going on around her, she thought sadly. Mother is quite blind to all the signals which Alan and I are giving off! She is also completely unaware that Sir Hart might favour Alan—for that surely was what he had been hinting in their *tête-à-tête*.

Next it was Ned who came in to reproach her when he found her smiling.

'At least someone is happy,' he said sourly. 'Alan has gone already, I collect.'

'Yes, he was eager to start work.'

'Work! He must be light in the attic. Well, I'm off. Do not expect me before night. Tell Sir Hart that—if you wish.'

He had never seemed more frivolous, she thought, watching him ride off. The dreadful thing was that the real point of the excursion was drink, not the fight. Sir Hart was still rationing him and Ned had complained bitterly of it in private. Well, he and Robert could drink themselves stupid for all she cared—except that it was hard on Sir Hart— and, like Sir Hart, she feared for the future of the House and the estate.

Midway through the afternoon Alan returned. He had spent the journey back dreaming of a ride with Eleanor where they might, after a little time, walk across the moor and he could favour her with a few more gentle kisses.

Unfortunately when he entered the House she came towards him, still in her afternoon dress, her face lacking all its usual joy at the sight of him.

'Oh, Alan, I am so sorry to disappoint you, but we have a grand visitor. Sir Hart wants you to meet him as soon as possible, so I fear that we must lose our ride—but I am sure that you will understand that his wishes come first.'

Before he could answer the hovering butler bowed. 'Ahem, Miss Eleanor. Sir Hartley was most urgent that Mr Alan should change as soon as he returned and take tea with him in the Gallery.'

In clean clothes, fresh from Gurney's ministrations, Alan made his way with Eleanor to the Picture Gallery. Tea had been laid on a long table where solander boxes containing water-colour paintings usually lay.

Sir Hart was sitting in his high-backed seventeenth-century chair. A tall man was standing before Sir Beauchamp's portrait, holding a glass of brandy.

He was dark, saturnine, with curling black hair touched with silver. He was wearing rough country clothing with gaiters—almost like a gamekeeper. Despite this he was formidable: authority radiated from him.

He turned to Alan when he entered, and before Sir Hart could introduce him put out the large hand which was not holding the brandy glass and said, 'I am William FitzUrse, called Knaresborough, and you, Sir Hart tells me, are Alan Dilhorne, from Sydney, New South Wales.'

'Indeed, m'lord,' said Alan, taking the hand which crushed his and looking into the black eyes which were on a level with his own. So this was the cousin of the Queen, known as the Belted Earl, descended from Charles II and a god in these parts.

'Big bruiser, aren't you?' Knaresborough was judicial. 'Spar with Ralf, I hear. I should like to see that.'

'I am not his equal, m'lord.' Alan smiled, avoiding Eleanor's eye—he always seemed to be doing that these days. He wondered what she made of the man—and why he was here.

'Don't serve me gammon,' said Knaresborough roughly. 'Deceive others, if you please, but not me. Servants talk, you know. I hear you buy mills and cozen Rothschild's— or so Hart tells me. What convict sired you, sir? I should like to meet him.'

He was so superb that it was impossible to take offence.

'My father is anyone's equal, m'lord.'

'So I should suppose. You bought Outhwaite's after you bammed him, and won those shops in Brinkley by drinking and wrestling. My agent told me that story.'

'You didn't tell me about Brinkley, Alan,' said Sir Hart reproachfully.

'Close-mouthed, too,' said Knaresborough. He stared

hard at Alan. 'I heard that you looked like Ned. God knows why anyone should think so. It's Sir Beauchamp, here, that you're the image of. I remember him, just. Oh, you have his look, boy—now how did you get that? No, don't answer me. I don't want to know—yet. Except that if you *are* like Sir Beauchamp, God help us all. You shoot, sir?'

'Yes,' said Alan, fascinated. This time he looked at Eleanor, who was smiling at him. The smile said, He likes you.

'Then you shall shoot with me and tell me of your wickednesses in London.'

'I have to return there fairly soon, m'lord.'

'None of that, boy. You must come to Castle Ashcourt. London will not go away and the world does not need your guiding hand on it all the time. Let fools have their folly for a little… You laugh, sir?' he added, seeing Alan begin to smile at this bravado. 'Pour me some tea, young man; I'm tired of brandy—and where is Ned? At the prize-fight, I suppose. Why are you not there, young man?'

'Work called, I fear.'

'And you answered. Tell me of Sydney. I had a friend there once, Lachlan Macquarie. You have heard of him?'

'He was my father's friend.'

The heavy brows rose. 'He would be, I'll be bound.' He rounded on Eleanor. 'Do we bore you, young lady?'

She smiled up at him, nothing daunted. 'No, indeed, m'lord. Not one of the three of you bores me—I have much to learn from you.'

'Well said.' He rounded on Alan again, and began to question him about Sydney and his home. He was indecently well-informed, but wore his learning lightly. Something about his frank manner seemed familiar, tweaked at Alan's consciousness.

Personal matters over, Knaresborough began to talk politics. 'I'm glad I'm not in the Cabinet now,' he told them largely, pouring fresh tea for himself. 'And so should you be, Hart. No true gentlemen left.'

He swung on Alan. 'By gentlemen, young man, I mean those with a proper feeling for their country, be they Earls, mill- owners—or adventurers like yourself.'

Eleanor laughed and Alan smiled.

'I am not an adventurer, m'lord.'

'If you are not, I never saw one. There are too few like you left here. England will fail without them. Enough for now. I suppose that I have my usual room, Hart? I will see you at dinner, young man, and you, too, Miss Eleanor, where we shall talk nonsense before the ladies retire. Afterwards we shall drink glass for glass, Master Alan, and see who is the better man.'

He bowed to Sir Hart and strode from the Gallery.

'Well said.' Sir Hart smiled, amused at Alan's expression.

'Very well,' returned Alan. 'Is he always like that?'

'Always.'

'Does he really expect me to drink with him? I am not usually a drinking man.'

'You must. His head is as hard as his heart—but he is a *nonpareil*. Do not be surprised if he asks you to spar with Ralf for him.'

'Not after a night's drinking, I hope.'

Eleanor laughed ruefully at that. Like Alan, she could see that Sir Hart was tired. She rose, and said gently, 'Grandfather, if you are to endure Knaresborough at dinner, you must rest for a little. With your permission, Alan and I will leave you. '

He waved them away. On the stairs, Alan said abruptly to Eleanor, 'Do you like him?'

'Knaresborough?' She considered. 'I don't think liking comes into it. He's always kind to me—and to mother— but he is usually abominable to Ned. He and our father were enemies, I think. It's odd, he frightens many people, but he doesn't frighten me.'

Later, in his room, pondering over the meeting with the Belted Earl, and what Eleanor had said to him afterwards, he wondered whether Eleanor knew, without knowing, as it were, that Knaresborough was not her suitor but her father.

Later that night, after the women had left, the men sat drinking as Knaresborough had promised. Midnight came and went, and the cloth was covered with dead men—empty bottles left by their carousal. Stacy had collapsed long ago, his head on the table, sleeping happily. The two local landowners who were also guests were upright still, but glassy-eyed. Sir Hart, excused from drinking by virtue of his age, sat there watching them.

Knaresborough, steady still, had his eyes on Alan, who was lying back in his chair, his face ashen, his eyes glittering, upright only by an effort of will, but refusing to satisfy the monstrous Knaresborough by collapsing before he did.

M'lord, smiling grimly, pushed the bottle over to him again.

'Another,' he ordered, watching the elaborate care with which Alan poured the liquid into his empty glass. The door opened and Robert Harshaw entered, Ned hanging on his arm.

'He would come in,' said Robert ruefully. 'There was no gainsaying him. We have made a day of it,' he added unnecessarily.

Ned lifted his head and stared at the littered table and the ruined company. He was still conscious, just. The ride home through the night had revived him a little.

'Well, well,' he said, nastily for him, pointing at Alan. 'So, the paragon is drunk, I see. The bottle is not kept from him. Tell me, Grandfather, what should I do to be so favoured?'

'Holding your tongue might help,' answered Knaresborough calmly before Sir Hart could speak.

Ned's laugh was short and ugly. 'You have my face, Alan, and you take my place, I see. Where is your reprimand for what I have been doing, Alan? Is Sir Beauchamp not with us tonight?'

'Leave it, Ned,' said Alan, his articulation over-perfect.

'No, I will not. Why did I bring you here?'

'Leave it,' said Alan again. 'It was your wish—and you will be sorry for what you have said in the morning.'

'He will not remember in the morning,' prophesied Knaresborough. 'I know him.'

Ned swayed away from Robert. 'Oh, you play God, too, Knaresborough. What ill wind brought you here?'

'I might have wished to see your face on another more worthy of it,' said Knaresborough, never loath to stir the pot. Sir Hart winced, and Alan closed his eyes at the sight of Ned's face, a mask of agony as all his shortcomings rose before him to reproach him.

'I did not have his advantages,' he said hoarsely, pointing at Alan. 'No harsh father. Nor his either,' he added, pointing at the sleeping Stacy. 'I have no brains, and no steadiness either.'

His mood changed suddenly, he was careless Ned again. 'I am sorry that you did not come with us, Alan. It was a good fight and the Brinkley boy beat the London bruiser— and I won good money on it.'

'Come, Ned,' urged Robert. 'To bed, old fellow. I am tired myself,' he said apologetically to the table.

'No,' said Ned, 'I shall be comfortable here.' He sat by Stacy, put his head on the table and fell asleep on the instant.

'We must all go to bed,' said Knaresborough suddenly

looking at Alan's sad face. 'For the cub has spoilt the party. I shall let you off, sir,' he said to Alan. 'You do not deserve my mock as well as his.'

He walked Alan to his room, where an anxious Gurney helped him to bed. Ned and Stacy remained sleeping at the table below.

Knaresborough was right. Ned did not remember in the morning, but Alan would have left for London had not Sir Hart begged him to stay. Because of Eleanor he agreed, although with a heavy heart: a heart which grew no lighter for although Ned's manner to him was as cheerful and friendly as ever, he knew that beneath it, hidden from Ned when he was sober, lay black resentment.

Chapter Eleven

On the morning after the drinking bout Eleanor took Alan for a walk on the moor immediately outside the grounds of Temple Hatton. She was troubled because she had overheard one of the servants talking about Ned's reproaches to Alan the night before. She was also angry because she knew that Knaresborough had coerced Alan into the drinking bout which had preceded it.

These days she was becoming more and more aware of the undercurrents in the world in which she lived. Consequently she said nothing to Alan about either event, but he was immediately aware that something was troubling her.

Their walk ended on a wide plateau at the edge of a cliff which gave them a superb view across that part of Yorkshire. Eleanor stopped beside a flat-topped boulder and invited him to sit beside her.

She thought that he looked tired and sad, but Alan's first words showed that he had lost nothing of his acute understanding of her.

'What is worrying you, Eleanor?' he asked.

'Nothing and everything,' she told him, giving him an odd little smile and an answer which he might have made himself to a difficult question.

He took her hand. 'I know that it's wrong of me to be curious, but…'

'No,' she said, interrupting him. 'I will give you a straight answer. It's Lord Knaresborough. I think that he brings trouble with him. He's not like Sir Hart…although Sir Hart values him. He uses people, I think, although he can be kind. He's always been kind to me,' she added a trifle inconsequentially.

Alan thought that he knew the reason why Knaresborough was kind to her—but that was not a story for him to tell.

'I admire him,' he said, 'but that does not mean that I like him. He would be a good friend, but a dreadful enemy. He likes to test people.'

He began to stroke her hand. 'You are not to worry about him—or me. I can look after myself.'

She then said something which he was to remember later. 'Where he is concerned, no one is safe. Be careful, Alan.'

He kissed the hand he held, and then leaned over a little to kiss her cheek. The scent of her roused him; it was so sweet that he was again in danger of forgetting himself. She turned willingly into his arms, and there, alone, overlooking the wild beauty below them, he made gentle love to her, kissing and stroking her so that she might feel pleasure but not be frightened.

It was sweet torment for both of them, until he was the one to break away. Eleanor, in the first throes of active love, was unable to deny him anything, and the time for them to progress beyond nursery matters was not yet.

Soon, he told himself when they walked back, hand in hand, I shall ask for her hand in marriage—but he knew that before he could there were mysteries to be solved, and ghosts from the past to be laid.

Eleanor was right: Knaresborough *was* dangerous. Two mornings later Alan found himself fighting Ralf, not sparring with him. Knaresborough had said that he wished to see a real bout, so he engineered one by deceiving Ralf when he met him in the stables after he had watched him sparring with Alan.

'I hear that the Australian boy is your master,' he said, jeering at him a little, 'and spares you when you spar with him.'

Now this was true, but Alan had said nothing of it to anyone. Wounded to the quick, Ralf denied the accusation fiercely.

Knaresborough shook his head at him. 'Easy to prove it,' he said. 'I'll give you good money if you can persuade him to engage in a real fight with you tomorrow morning. And if you beat him fair and square I'll treble your reward.'

'Fair and square, then. I'll tell him I want a real fight,' said Ralf, and so he informed Alan—to have Alan refuse him until he understood that he would have to agree in order to soothe Ralf's feelings, so casually plundered by Knaresborough.

He said nothing to anyone of his dismay. He knew that once in a real fight he would be unable to restrain himself, and would go for Ralf with all his strength and all his cunning—which was why he only ever sparred. But there was no way in which he could gainsay either Ralf or Knaresborough, so the next day he dressed himself for the fight and went to the moor beyond the House—to discover an eager crowd was waiting for him.

Besides the estate workers and the servants from the House there were gentlemen and labourers from Brinkley and other local villages come to see the fun—but the news had been kept from the women, he later found.

Everything was to be done in proper form: Knaresborough had seen to that. It was he who had arranged for the crowd to be present, and for betting to be organised.

Alan knew, even before the bout began, that, however

much he had promised himself to spare Ralf, once he was in the ring with him he would have only one idea in his head—to win it. Quite early on he knew that Ralf was his for the taking—he was older and slow; his fine edge had gone. Alan also knew that the pugilist who had taught him in Sydney had been right—he possessed the hard malevolence needed to be a champion, as well as the strength and the skill.

But when he turned Ralf for the last time, readying him for the final knock-out blow, Knaresborough's face came into view, and he saw that Knaresborough knew it, too, and could scarcely wait for the final blow which would defeat and humiliate Ralf—and complete his pleasure.

The killing rage against Ralf which he had built up during the bout was in an instant directed against himself and Knaresborough. He would not be manipulated in order to provide a Roman holiday for an unprincipled patrician by humiliating Ralf, whose last remaining and only pride was in his skill.

Coldly and deliberately he turned the rage on himself, and so that no one should suspect that he was throwing the fight he changed it, so that he was exposed to Ralf's most punishing blows.

Suddenly he was lying, half-fuddled, on the ground, supported by someone's strong arms which did not belong to either Ned or Stacy, his seconds. The same strong arms were lifting him on to a bench and were beginning to sponge his face. His senses steadied and he knew that it was Knaresborough who was ministering to him and holding the others back.

'No,' said Alan feebly, trying to push him away, but failing. 'No, not you. I don't want you.'

'Yes,' retorted Knaresborough, his voice low, so that the others surrounding them should not hear. 'I know what you did, if no one else does. You will not be managed, I see.

You are Sir Beauchamp's best. Be still, that I may help you.'

'No,' said Alan, turning his head away from him. 'Not you nor any man shall pull my strings. Ralf is not a toy for me to maul and break for your pleasure. Fight him yourself—or leave him alone. I'll not do your dirty work for you.'

'He has not addled your wits, I see,' said Knaresborough, still sponging Alan's face. 'And you are right to try to shame me. Must I apologise to you, then?'

'Apologise to Ralf, not to me.'

'Oh, Ralf does not need apologies. He will be well rewarded now that you have thrown the fight.'

The killing rage swept through Alan again, despite his weakness.

'That is a vile thing to say. Mind me. When I recover I shall strike you down for that, Earl though you are.'

Knaresborough stared at him. 'I believe you would. I will tell him that I was wrong to pit you at one another—not to escape your blows but because I see that Ralf is a man, too, in your mind. Let me help you up.'

Despite himself weakness had him taking Knaresborough's arm to rise. He found he was facing Ralf.

Ralf glared at Knaresborough, his face set. 'I shall not take your money, m'lord. I did not win the fight—he gave it to me most cunningly. Why, I don't know, only that he did. Until then he had me for the asking. He was never mine to beat, not now, nor when I was in my prime.'

'Do not say so,' returned Alan. 'You won fair and square and I shall spar with you when I am fit again. No, do not argue with me. I was wrong to agree to fight you. Take his money—as much as you can get of it. He owes you more than that.'

'Yes,' said Knaresborough, 'and I was wrong to set you at each other for my pleasure. Had I asked you both straight

that would have been different, but I did not. I ask your
pardon, Ralf.'

'That is nobly said, m'lord,' said Ralf.

Knaresborough put his hand in his pocket and pulled out
a purse of guineas. 'You shall get drunk for both of us,
Ralf. Now let us get him to the House.'

Alan did not come down from his room until the afternoon. By then the news of the fight was known to everyone.
Eleanor met him in the garden and exclaimed at his black
eye, swollen face, split lip and damaged hands.

'Oh, Alan, I was angry when we missed our ride this
morning. You told me once that you could not equal Ralf
in a fight, so why did you try?'

They had been riding together the previous day and they
had made gentle love again. Each time the power of what
they were doing struck Eleanor anew, and each time it was
stronger. Being in love was hard, not easy, she found. She
had a curious desire to *be* Alan. She wanted to be lost in
him, but did not know how, only that after a time mere
kissing became unsatisfactory—more than that was needed,
but the possible nature of the more frightened her.

'You will not be fit to ride with me tomorrow,' she said
sorrowfully.

Alan tried to smile at her, but smiling hurt, so he stopped.
'Never mind,' he said. 'It will not be long before I am fit
again.'

Since nothing else was possible, he allowed his eyes to
caress her to make up for his hands not being available.
Knaresborough, watching them together—the party was as-
sembling for tea on the lawn—said to Sir Hart, 'So that is
why he came here—against his better judgement, no doubt.
For he must suspect the meaning of the likeness.'

'Yes,' said Sir Hart painfully. 'I am sure that, but for
Eleanor, he would never have visited Temple Hatton. Now,

with Ned's hidden resentment revealed, he stays only for her. And me, a little, I think.'

'The sooner you tell him the truth, the better. My care is for Eleanor, as well as for him, as you must know. She deserves him, and must not lose him to his sense of honour—which is strong.'

'Yes—but you must understand that I have asked him nothing of his origins, and until then all must be supposition. I fear that he might tell me nothing. I also fear that he may believe Eleanor to be his cousin—with all the consequences which might flow from that.'

'In that case I shall smoke him out for you, since matters must not remain as they are. He must know the truth about Eleanor's parentage, as well.'

When Sir Hart began to protest he said gently, with none of his usual brutal panache, 'No, trust me. I shall use no bravado. The young man is of a metal which deserves our respect. He is gold through and through—Sir Beauchamp with a heart that feels for others. What could be stronger than that?'

Eleanor persuaded Stacy to rescue Alan from the unwanted attentions of the rest of the party, particularly Jane's mother. He took Alan to the upstairs drawing room, ostensibly to show him something he had found in the library that morning. Eleanor, joining them a little later, came in to find him sound asleep on the yellow brocade sofa. Stacy, quietly reading opposite to him, put his finger to his lips when he saw her.

Knaresborough had come to her at the end of the tea party and had walked her through the rose garden, chatting of this and that, until she had said, quite calmly, 'Tell me, m'lord. Is it true that you were responsible for setting Mr Dilhorne and Ralf at one another?'

'So,' he had said, equally calm, 'the gossip has reached you already. Yes, I must confess to that.'

Surprised at her own daring, for he had always seemed like a capricious God to her, someone so powerful and mighty that he was not to be questioned or criticised, she had said, 'The other day I told him to be careful, that you were dangerous. I did not think that you would prove me correct so soon. It was not well done, m'lord.'

'Oh, I quite agree with you, Miss Eleanor. It was not. I am delighted to discover that you have such a fund of good sense as to appreciate that.'

At first she had thought he was mocking her, but when he saw her anxious face, he'd added, 'The same good sense that has made you choose him from all the shallow fools who have courted you here and in London. I can only trust that he has the good sense to offer for you soon, and so I have told Sir Hart. Now may we talk nonsense—which is all that men and women are supposed to do, sense being usually employed only with one's own sex?'

This was so truly Knaresborough that Eleanor had begun to laugh. She wondered how often he ever made confession of a fault, and decided that it was rare. She was thinking of this when Alan woke up and put out a hand for her to hold. Stacy, seeing that he was awake, began to read to them until it was time to dress for dinner.

Alan and Knaresborough were playing piquet. Knaresborough was naughty, and cheated wildly. He had warned Alan that he would before the game began, since they would be playing for counters, not money.

'No holds barred, Master Alan. Anything goes for both of us when we're not playing for money.'

Alan's face was almost healed. That afternoon he had ridden out on the moors with Eleanor. For the first time he had unbuttoned her riding habit to reveal the silk beneath it. He had kissed her neck and shoulders and stroked her breasts through the silk. She had shivered her delight while he did so.

Eleanor had not known what to do with her hands, but she had caressed his face, running them down his strong jaw. Her body had been on fire, and her eyes had questioned him.

Alan had contained himself with difficulty, saying inwardly, A seasoned man has only so much self-restraint; there must be no more than this until I offer. He had imagined Knaresborough's grin if he had heard him.

He'd seen Jane and Stacy, whom they had outpaced, coming towards them, and rebuttoned Eleanor's habit rapidly. They had been decorously admiring the view by the time the other pair of lovers arrived.

Stacy, taking in Eleanor's brilliantly roused eyes and her flushed face, had said nothing, but thought a lot. He was taking great care not to frighten Jane and thought how strange it was that everything was allowed to young men and nothing to women, who consequently came ignorant to the marriage bed.

Now he was watching Alan and Knaresborough; their voices were low so that none could overhear them.

'You play well, young sir.'

Alan laughed at him. 'Oh, there is nothing to that. If one man marks the cards, the other may use them—if he knows how.'

'Yes, you are a fox among the chickens. I must not forget that.'

They played on a little in silence before Knaresborough said idly, 'You speak proudly of your father—but give little of him away.'

'Nothing to give away, m'lord.'

'Knaresborough. I am Knaresborough to you. I suppose that he was sent as a felon to New South Wales instead of being hanged in England?'

'You suppose correctly…Knaresborough.'

Knaresborough laughed. 'You did not mind me saying that?'

'He would not mind if he heard you, so why should I?'

'Why indeed? And from London, I hear. Pass the bottle, boy, you have nursed it long enough. Mark you, though, I note how little you actually drink. No Yorkshire connections at all?'

His voice was idle when he came out with this last.

Alan suddenly tired of both the games they were playing; tired of the half-truths and the evasions. He remembered Sir Hart's anxious face, Ned's angry one on the night of the fight, his father's likeness to Sir Hart—and, above all, his own to Sir Beauchamp. It was time to end it.

'Oh, yes, Knaresborough, there was a Yorkshire connection. However did you guess?' His voice was mocking.

'I am sure that Sir Beauchamp did not live for nothing.'

'Well, as to that, I don't know. They are your points this time, Knaresborough, but you have not won enough to help you.'

'I distracted you,' said Knaresborough mildly. 'Have you told Sir Hart of the connection?'

'No, nor has he asked me if there were one—but I am tired of being devious. Nothing but the truth will satisfy me now—for there is Eleanor to think of.'

Knaresborough made no immediate answer. At last he said, 'I think that I may have won my first hand.'

Alan's answering laugh had no mirth in it. 'I think not. You are rubiconed as the game has it, I fear, and have lost it.' He watched Knaresborough stare in disbelief at the cards before saying, 'My father, as you have doubtless guessed, had no acknowledged father, but you could not disturb him by calling him bastard.'

'Oh, I could believe anything of a father of such as you. But your father had a mother, I suppose?'

'Oh, yes, and I know that she was from Yorkshire. It is your turn to play.'

'Indeed, and you have beaten me again. Are there cards up *your* sleeve, too?'

'You must ponder that, Knaresborough, for I shall not tell you. What I *can* say is that she worked in a big house on the edge of the moors.'

More counters on Knaresborough's side passed to Alan. They played on.

'It was the old story, I suppose. The son of the house and the pretty servant, no doubt.'

'No doubt.'

Alan was short, for the game was nearly over.

'I can tell you that my father was born at a farm on the moors, but the moors are wide and there are many farms and many big houses on them.'

'Indeed, young man. But not many by-blow's sons have Sir Beauchamp's brass face, I assure you. You are too good for me again.'

Alan made him no direct answer, said instead, 'You would have done better to have played without marked cards and sleight of hand. My father taught me how to use them against the cheat, long ago.'

'So, you have beaten me; I give you best. You know that I shall tell Sir Hart all this?'

'Of course—else I should not have told *you*.'

Ned, seeing that the game had ended, walked over to them. 'So you have won, Alan, and against Knaresborough of all people. He always wins, for he plays dirty, you know, when he does not play for money.'

'Yes, I guessed that, Ned.'

Ned said sorrowfully, 'But you play dirty, too, Alan.'

'Yes, and did so for you, Ned.' Alan had not meant to remind Ned of the debt he owed him, but Ned's tone had stung.

'You shall both drink with me,' Knaresborough told them, 'to celebrate my defeat, for I rarely lose.'

Ned drank down one bumper and then left them. Knaresborough said dryly to Alan, 'You are sorry for Ned, I see. Why? He is most fortunate, being the Hatton heir.'

'He would have been happier in a cottage.'

'There is nothing to that. He is heir here, and that's an end to it. When you visit me at Castle Ashcourt leave him behind. He bores me.'

'You are frank, Knaresborough, but unkind.'

Knaresborough's laugh was humourless. 'There is no point in being able to call the Queen cousin if I may not say and do as I please. And it will not be long before me and mine will not be able to please themselves. For as my friend Alexander Baring says, "The field of coal will outstrip the field of barley", and you and yours will sit where I am sitting now—but until then I will do as I please. What was your grandmother's name?'

'The same as mine, only Mary. I know little of her beyond that. My father has never spoken to me of her, or of his English past.'

'As is natural. Well, I like you, and not only because you remind me of a man whom I feared and respected. I hope that you may be successful with Miss Eleanor. She deserves better than she may find here.'

Alan looked Knaresborough square in the face.

'I understand your concern for her, Knaresborough. It is most natural, given everything, and if we marry I shall try to make her as happy as her father might wish.'

Knaresborough whistled. 'You know, boy. How do you know? That was, and is, a well-kept secret.'

'Now, that I shall not tell you, nor will the secret ever be revealed by me. You may be sure of that.'

'The only thing that I am sure of is that Temple Hatton deserves one like you, and not like Ned.'

'That is as may be, Knaresborough.'

Alan bowed—and left him. For once the Belted Earl had been given his congé by an inferior, and had accepted it.

Eleanor motioned for Alan to sit beside her. She had been reading—or pretending to. 'He's splendid, isn't he?' she said. 'I ought to tell you that Ned hates him.'

'I'm not surprised. If he does not like you, or consider you worthy of his interest, he could be cruel.'

'Sir Hart says that he is a splendid relic. They were all like that when he was a boy.'

They thought together of that distant, different, world, so far removed from the one which they inhabited. Eleanor was restless: she was becoming aware of the body's demands.

'Ned says that you could have beaten Ralf. Is that true?'

'Half true,' he said, not wishing to hurt Ralf, but not wishing to lie, either.

'Ned is sometimes right,' she offered.

'We are all of us sometimes right, Ned included, only the sometimes is greater for one than for another.'

Eleanor said doubtfully, 'That does not seem fair.'

'Life is not fair, Eleanor, or we should not be sitting here in comfort while they half starve in Brinkley.'

She shivered. 'You live in the real world, Alan.'

'A little—but all worlds are real to those who live in them.'

He laughed, and added wryly, 'We are sober tonight.'

'Yes. Stacy is sober, too. He is playing chess with Jane in the library to get her away from her mama. My mama is teasing me about making a great marriage now that Stacy and I are no longer a pair.'

'Is that what *you* want, Eleanor?'

'You know it is not, Alan.'

She did not add, It is you I want—for that would not be

the act of a properly brought up young lady—but her face told him what she thought.

'Yes,' he said. 'I know.'

He also knew that he could not offer yet. Knaresborough must tell Sir Hart what he had learned, and then Sir Hart would speak to him of it. He knew that as surely as he knew each new day would bring the dawn.

'I'm afraid that we must prepare ourselves for tomorrow,' Eleanor said, trying to lighten the conversation, 'for Sir Hart has decreed that Beverley may join us again.'

'Poor Charles,' said Alan, and he was not speaking lightly.

'Poor all of us,' riposted Eleanor. 'But I think that if he misbehaves again Sir Hart will have him beaten, or sent away.'

She shivered, although the evening was warm. 'I often wonder why Sir Hart, who is goodness itself, should be plagued by such unworthy children and grandchildren as we are. You must know that my father and uncle were such disappointments as a man could scarcely bear to have for sons.

'I sometimes think that Mama and Ned are so flighty because that was the only way in which they could manage to live with Papa. Ned, though, is more good-hearted than Papa ever was. They say that Beverley is exactly like my father was when he was that age. I only know that I was glad when he was absent when I was a child. Such scenes here were. Such hate. Me, he particularly disliked, but then, he liked nobody but himself.'

She thought that Alan ought to know all this before he offered for her: it was only right.

'When he died I felt unworthy because I was not sorry. He would never beat Mama nor Ned again. It was strange— he never touched me. I sometimes think that Ned is as he is because of our father's treatment of him as a boy. Sir

Hart would not tell us how he died, but I fear that it was disgraceful, like Uncle John's death on the day that Beverley was born. Only Uncle John was kind, but silly, and Father was neither.'

Alan could see that telling him this pained her, but he could only admire her honesty. What was he to say to her? That we cannot choose our parents, or our children, only accept them as they are? The father of whom she had spoken so sadly must have been well aware that Eleanor was not his child—and fearful of what Knaresborough might do to him if he mistreated her.

Thinking of Eleanor's timid and frightened mother made him wonder how exactly she had come to have an affair with Knaresborough, of all people. But that was no business of his. Only that she had, and the result was Eleanor, who had inherited the bottom of sound common sense which lay beneath Knaresborough's theatrics.

After that they spoke of lighter things. She was to attend a friend's wedding in York soon, with Ned, and they would be away for a few days. 'I know that you must be fretting for London and occupation,' she said, 'but I hope that you will not leave until after we have returned. Sir Hart likes you, I know, and he has little enough to comfort him.'

Alan did not think that he comforted Sir Hart, but he did not tell Eleanor so.

Alan sparred with Ralf again in the early morning, but it was not the same. Knaresborough, in his careless arrogance, had spoiled it for them. He would have given up this much-needed exercise, but he needed it, not only to keep himself in trim, but to provide him with something to look forward to and to do.

Eleanor was right: he was missing occupation. That is why they are so unsatisfactory, if beautiful, these great ones, he had decided, for everything is done for them and they live only to please themselves, which they cannot do, for they have no lives to live; their servants do it for them.

Well, if Eleanor married him she would find that she would have occupation, for he did not intend his wife to be a mere decoration, a toy, but that she would take her part in his life, as his mother had done in his father's.

Sir Hart did not come down to breakfast on the morning after Alan had told Knaresborough of his grandmother's past, but Knaresborough did. A messenger from Castle Ashcourt brought him letters, and he sprawled in his chair, eating and drinking and exclaiming as he read them.

'I have to leave sooner than I intended,' he told them. 'Matters call me home—but my business here is ended— for the time being, at least.'

He took Alan on one side before he left that afternoon.

'I told the old man last night of your father's mother, and he took it hard, I know. Very hard, although he said nothing. I hope that you fix yourself with Eleanor. You have my blessing, and if you marry her in London she shall be sent off from my palace there. I ought to marry myself; my life is lonely since my poor Jenny died. Why should all I own go to the little Queen when *I* die? She has enough already. Mind you visit me before you return to London, else I shall follow you there and persecute you.'

The House seemed empty when he had gone. I do not like him, Alan thought, but he does not want to be liked, and I shall visit him because I admire such splendid arrogance.

He had thought that Sir Hart might have sent for him straight away, but he stayed in his room that day, sending word that he had a megrim and was unfit for company.

'Which is very unlike Sir Hart,' Eleanor told Alan.

Stacy agreed. 'He is seldom ill.'

Stacy consequently proposed that it was such a fine day

they should all ride over to his home, Culverwell Manor, which was not far distant. They could take food with them for a picnic there, leaving the House quiet for its owner.

'We will all win that way,' said Stacy cheerfully to Alan. 'In the afternoon the mamas will want to sit on the lawn in the sun and we can take the girls for a walk, unchaperoned, if we promise not to roam too far away.'

'I can see a successful career for you as a diplomat,' Alan told him gravely. 'Such an ability to please everyone should ensure that you rapidly become an ambassador.'

He shared the joke with Eleanor when, mounted on Abdul, he rode alongside the landau in which she sat beside Jane.

'It is nonsensical, is it not,' Eleanor remarked, 'that we should have to go such lengths to be alone together? Particularly now that I have discovered that it is an open secret that Lord Knaresborough and Mrs Lorimer have what is known as an ''understanding'', and that her husband is quite happy to turn a blind eye to it because he has one with another man's wife. Her daughter, Polly, on the other hand, is kept in what the Turks call purdah, and is barely allowed to speak to a young man. Mrs Lorimer thinks me horribly forward because I chat with you and Stacy.'

Jane nodded her head in agreement. Eleanor said eagerly, 'I have read that in America women are allowed to become doctors. Do you think that could ever happen here?'

'Would either of you like to be a doctor?' Alan asked them.

Jane shook her head, but Eleanor said thoughtfully, 'I am not sure whether or not I should wish to be a doctor, but I would like to think that if I wanted to I might be allowed to try.'

Alan thought that Eleanor was becoming more like her unknown father every day—and less like Ned and Beverley.

'Would you object to me becoming a doctor?' she asked him suddenly.

'I might not,' he said, 'but many men would.'

'Because they think it would be indelicate, I suppose,' Jane said.

Later, when she and Alan were walking in the little wilderness of shrubs and plants at the back of the Manor, Eleanor raised the matter again.

'It does seem odd to me,' she told him, 'that while it is not considered indelicate for women to work alongside the men down the pits in the Yorkshire coalfieds, it should be considered wrong for them to be doctors—or lawyers, for that matter—for that very reason.'

'Ah, but the world is not a reasonable place,' was Alan's answer. 'For example, as you rightly pointed out, married women may take lovers, if they so wish, so long as their husbands do not object, but the behaviour of young girls is regulated so that they must not be alone with young men lest the young men do this to them.'

He turned towards Eleanor, put his arms around her and kissed her gently on the lips.

They were quite alone in the warm and balmy afternoon among the scents of the flowers and plants. In the distance they could hear Jane and Stacy. Hidden from them by the trees, Mrs Hatton and Mrs Chalmers sat half-dozing in the sun. Ned had cried off from such a ladylike expedition, preferring to be roistering somewhere else with Robert Harshaw.

Eleanor, not to be outdone, kissed him back. 'I may not be allowed to become a doctor,' she murmured, 'but I can do this—so long as no one is about.'

'Much more fun for me,' agreed Alan. 'It wouldn't heal a broken arm, though!' He kissed her again.

There was a rustic bench in a little bower. They sank on it together.

'I shouldn't be doing this,' murmured Alan, giving her a third kiss.

'No, you shouldn't,' agreed Eleanor, blushing. She did not add, But I like it, for common sense was telling her not to allow him overmuch licence—who knew where such pleasant self-indulgence might end? It was not so much that she distrusted Alan, but rather that she distrusted herself. Her mind was telling her one thing and her body was telling her another.

For the first time she was beginning to understand how girls could allow themselves to be betrayed—to put it politely. It was not, she was slowly grasping, entirely the man's fault. Every time Alan started to make gentle love to her she found herself responding with greater enthusiasm—and consequently each time their lovemaking grew a little less gentle.

Perhaps, after all, there was some sense in the etiquette which forbade unmarried men and women to be alone together!

Alan must have thought so, too, for he suddenly drew away from her. He was rapidly becoming roused. The warmth of the day, the beauty of their surroundings, the beauty who had been briefly in his arms, were eroding the self-control on which he prided himself.

'We must be good,' he said.

The Eleanor she had once been might have said or done something to weaken his resolve, but the new woman who had learned responsibility moved sadly away from him so that they were no longer touching—since it was touching him which was doing the damage.

If he truly loved her, he would offer marriage, she thought, but so far, although Alan had shown her how much he felt for her, he had never said anything which could be construed as an offer. On the other hand she was now sure that she was the real reason why he had come to Yorkshire

Oh, how difficult life and love were for a poor girl, since in them the final initiative was always left to the man.

Alan had some inkling of what Eleanor was thinking but he also knew that it was imperative that he speak to Sir Hart before he offered for Eleanor—and that Sir Hart knew that too. If his delay was hard on Eleanor, it was also hard on himself: the strange likeness stood in their way and needed to be explained.

After their brief interlude together they continued to enjoy themselves, but for both of them the bright day had darkened a little. They privately comforted themselves with the thought that the unknown future might prove their friend.

Alas, the immediate future brought more delay. They arrived back at Temple Hatton to find a messenger from Bradford waiting for Alan.

'Maister Wilkinson bids me tell you that you mun come at once to Bradford or he cannot answer for the consequences. The hands are threatening to strike if their wages are not raised.'

'I will do as he asks,' Alan told the man, who was staring warily around at the magnificence which was Temple Hatton, 'but when I leave for London what will Wilkinson do then? Wait for me? He must learn to manage the mill himself. Go to the stables, find my man, Gurney, and tell him that I need my horse and my kit packed for a short stay in Bradford.'

Before he left Temple Hatton he walked with Eleanor in the long gallery upstairs.

'I'm sorry to have to leave you again so soon,' he said. They were standing before the great painting of Venus. 'It's my own fault, of course. I would get involved in the affairs of the district. You will forgive me, I hope—and Ned, too. Present my apologies to him when he comes down for lunch.'

'I think that he's reconciled to the fact that you have other duties which claim you,' said Eleanor gently.

Alan made a wry face. 'Nevertheless, I think that when he invited me here he thought that my visit was going to be one long bout of fun.'

'Then he didn't know you very well,' she said, her voice brisk.

'But you don't resent that?'

'Not at all. I only wish that Ned were more like you. You will be careful, though. Robert Harshaw was saying last night that the mood among the workmen in the Riding is ugly and that violence has been threatened.'

'I promise to be careful,' he said, knowing that he was not quite telling the truth.

They kissed goodbye beneath the great portrait of Sir Beauchamp and he left, but not before Sir Hart had sent for him.

The old man, looking white and ill, said, 'I had hoped to speak to you before now on most urgent matters, but I have been unwell and you must do your duty. I shall send for you when you return, that I promise.'

On the way out he ignored Beverley, who bellowed questions at him. 'Where are you off to now, hey? I hope that you do not come back!'

Charles said sadly, 'I wish that I could come with you, Alan.' He feared that Beverley, released again, would torment him cruelly once Alan, his protector, had gone.

'Not today, Charles. It would not be suitable, I fear. I shall try not to be gone too long.'

The fuss made on the sweep outside when he set out amused him. Sir Hart watched him go from the big window in his bedroom, and could not help thinking that the arrival of this one young man had caused more excitement at Temple Hatton than it had known for many a long year.

Eleanor also watched Alan leave with a heavy heart. If

Paula Marshall   221

she were to marry him their life would consist of many
such partings while he followed his star, and she would
have to learn to accept it. She shivered, remembering Sir
Hart's warning—that Alan's duty might prevent him from
marrying her. For she knew that with him duty would always come first.

Ned came towards her and echoed her thoughts. 'So, he
has gone. His duty again, I suppose. But it is really his
pleasure, you know.'

This was perceptive for Ned.

'I thought that you liked him,' Eleanor said gently, disturbed by his tone.

'Oh, I did, I did, but he is not the man I thought he was.
He will be a good companion, I thought, and that is true—
but he frightens me.'

'He saved you from ruin, Ned. I would have thought that
he had earned your gratitude for that, even if he has lost
your friendship.'

'He has not lost my friendship,' said Ned restlessly. 'I
hardly know how I feel about him. Respect, perhaps, a
little. I used to think his having my face was a joke, but
now I don't. It has begun to trouble me. Partly because he
is so much Sir Hart's favourite.'

Eleanor began to protest, but he said wearily, 'You must
know that is true. I suppose it may be because Alan is like
the grandson he always wanted. Someone who is serious—
and worried about his duty.'

He almost spat the last words out.

Eleanor looked at him. Ned might know what he ought
to be doing, but he would not do it. He was too stiff-necked
to try to please others.

'Do you intend to marry him, Eleanor?'

'If he asks me. I know that I love him—but he has said
nothing yet. Sir Hart warned me that he might not. Why?'

'I don't know. I almost wish that you would marry him,

and then…no. He's like my dam'd conscience, Eleanor—
and he's so hard. Do I want him around? To remind me of
what I am not?'

He flung himself down on the sofa, stretching his booted
legs before him. 'I want to enjoy myself with jolly good
fellows like Robert Harshaw, and Alan will always want
more than that from me. And you, Eleanor, do you really
want to be Golden Boy's tireless wife?'

'Golden Boy?' repeated Eleanor, bewildered.

Ned laughed. 'That's what Gurney calls him from what
he's done in London, let alone here. The other servants
have taken it up. Fits him, don't it? What a joke, eh? Sir
Beauchamp back on earth as a businessman.'

His change of mood was rapid. 'Oh, Eleanor, if you want
him, have him. He'll lead you a merry dance—though not
with other women. But you're energetic, too, I suppose,
and can join him in his duty.'

Well, that was the coda to his tune, thought Eleanor, as
Ned rose and walked away, whistling a melancholy song.
If Alan asks me, I shall certainly say yes, but, oh, he hasn't
and now I am fearful that he never will.

On the way to Bradford Alan thought about his last conversation with Sir Hart and Eleanor. They had both understood that he had to do his duty.

He shook his head ruefully. Duty! The word seemed to
follow him about. He rode into Bradford to find the trouble
there was worse than the recent small outbreak at Thorpe's
in Brinkley. Outhwaite's was bigger and the men were an-
grier. They ran a little Chartist newspaper which urged
them to action. It was edited by one of the union leaders
named Brough.

Alan was an outsider and was resented for that. It was
thought that he had cheated Outhwaite out of the mill, and
although Outhwaite had been hard, it was said that the new

owner was harder. He had stood up to Ralf, even though he had been beaten, and had been ruthless with the hands at Brinkley when they had tried to strike.

But they were hard, too, and more was at stake at Outhwaite's, for the men had a bargaining counter which the Brinkley hands had not possessed. Outhwaite's, whilst not remarkably so, was reasonably prosperous and was returning a small profit. That profit, though, would disappear if wages were raised, and Alan himself had more capital at stake here, unlike at Thorpe's, which he had gained for a song.

Men carrying home-made banners and shouting slogans stood in the mean street outside the mill. When they saw him they called after him, 'No foreign maisters wanted here!'

Those from outside the district were surprised by his size and strength and the hard indifference with which he pushed through them.

Wilkinson was waiting for him in his office on the first floor. It was a small dark room with unclean windows; one overlooked the shop floor, the other on to the men assembled in the yard outside. With him was a stocky, muscular man with a strong pushed-in face and coarse black hair, typical of the district, resembling many Alan had seen about the moors, less elegant versions of Stacy.

'Bob Sutcliffe,' said Wilkinson briefly. 'He threatens me with a strike and mischief if we do not raise our wages.'

'Does he so?' said Alan. 'Has he a voice? Can he speak for himself?'

'Aye, I can that, Maister Dilhorne. I use it to tell you that if you do not heed us I shall call all out. Men, women and children, too. We have had enough of starvation wages here before you came, and you are no better than those you kicked out of the mill.'

'I pay you a fair wage according to the practice of this part of the world.'

'But the practice is wrong.'

'So you say, sir.'

'I do say so. There were Luddites in this part of the world once. Armed.'

'Do you threaten me, then?'

'But you have threatened us. We cannot live decently on what you pay us. You merely lose a little of your profits if you give way to us.'

Alan changed tack a little. Useless to argue economics with a determined man. Instead he came out with, 'Our profits—when we have any, and we have little enough now—pay your wages. Do you think it wise that we should be at stand-off? Should not master and men work together as partners?'

'Strange partners where one has all and the other nothing.'

Alan sighed. 'That may be true, but I warn you, the mill is barely in profit. To raise your wages would destroy even that. Tell me, what shall I do? For it is your choice. Will you carry out your threat to withdraw your labour? If you do I shall turn all the hands away. The mill will be stripped and the building sold as soon as can be arranged. Withdraw your demands and work will continue as before.'

Sutcliffe glared at him. 'I've met hard men before, but I never thought to meet one as hard as you.'

'This is idle talk. I do not wish to close, sir. It is you who brings on all. Choose what I shall do—and quickly. I am a busy man.'

'Aye, busy at the big house. We all know that. They do not know what busy is. Soft, the lot of them.'

They stared at one another, neither giving way.

Sutcliffe said at last, 'It is a pity Brough cannot be here today. He would have made you sing a different tune.'

'No doubt—but he is not, and the choice is yours. Choose, and quickly. Strike and closure—or resume work at the same pay.'

'I choose—not to choose, Maister.'

'Good, you have chosen after all, Wilkinson, assemble the hands in the yard and tell them that they are turned away. Lock the doors behind you. Have the overseers fetch hammers and begin to smash the machinery. It is out of date and none would wish to buy it. Tell the clerk to pay the hands for work done before today. Inform the local auctioneers that the buildings are to go up for sale before Saturday. Any price is better than none. If no auctioneers are available before then I shall conduct the sale myself.'

He swung on Sutcliffe, whose face was grey, before finishing, 'I always cut my losses, sir.'

'You would not dare.'

'Indeed, I would. Remember the choice was yours—not mine.'

Wilkinson said harshly, 'I know him, Bob. I know how he got the mill and the shops. You do not know how hard he is.'

'Wilkinson, do as I bid you,' Alan ordered.

'No,' howled Sutcliffe. 'I change my choice. The men will return.'

'You are wise to choose so.'

'Oh, the power is yours, now,' said Sutcliffe bitterly, 'but we shall see who wins in the end.'

'Why, no one wins in the end,' said Alan, 'for we all die in the end, masters and men alike. I shall stay until tomorrow, Wilkinson, to see my orders carried out.'

That following morning, though, he found the hands in the street again, and many from the town and the surrounding district with them. They hurled curses at him, but made no attempt to harm him, although one spat on his boots—to be reprimanded by one of his fellows, who told him severely, 'You know what Brough said about violence, Jem.'

So Brough was back, and all was doubtless to do again. For Brough's reputation as a bargainer was known to everyone in the Riding, both gentle and simple. Alan found him in Wilkinson's office, with Sutcliffe and two other men at his back.

Brough was as he might have expected, dressed better than a mill hand, worse than a clerk. He had a hard shrewd face, and began to speak the moment Alan entered without waiting for an introduction.

'Come, come, Mr Dilhorne. Let us talk sense. You know that you really cannot wish to close the mill down if the men continue to make their legitimate demands. That is the idle threat of a blackmailer designed to get what he wants.'

'Interesting,' murmured Alan, showing his teeth. 'But if the men threaten to strike if I do not agree to their demands is not that also blackmail? It seems to me that we are at stand-off again if, through you, they renew their demands. They made another choice yesterday.'

Brough thought for a moment, but before he could speak again Alan continued with, 'My decision to close down if the men refused to return to work was not a threat, it was a promise. To concede what they ask would result in ruin and closure in the short run. Nothing has changed since yesterday afternoon. Like Sutcliffe, you must choose.'

The look Brough gave him was one of hate, mixed with respect. Report had not lied. He was as hard as the devil and did not waste words.

'Is there nothing you can offer us? For I warn you, if you carry out this threat we shall call out all the hands in the Bradford mills—and then you would have to contend with the anger of every mill-owner in the town. Think on, young man.'

Alan sat down before Wilkinson's disorderly desk and

picked up the papers on it. 'These tell me that there is little I can offer you. Make no mistakes, if I cut my losses here and close down I shall not lose much. Indeed, in the long run I will gain by losing a millstone.'

Brough leaned forward and said hoarsely, 'There you sit in your over-fed pride, disposing of us all. Does the thought of starving men and their families mean nothing to you? For starve they will; these are hard times in the North.'

'Hard times everywhere,' said Alan. He picked up the papers again. 'I will look at these and see whether I can make you any sort of offer, however small. I am not hopeful.'

He had no wish to see those for whom he was responsible suffer because he had not sufficiently considered every possible way by which he could agree to meet at least some of their demands—but he did not tell Brough that. Nor would he appear to give way easily. But he must not behave like Sir Beauchamp.

'You may come back tomorrow, at noon, and what I decide will be final.'

Brough thought to argue with him, but changed his mind. 'Tomorrow,' he said, 'at noon.'

'So noted.' Alan smiled. 'And now you must all leave, and quickly. I dislike wasted time, and I have work to do before I decide whether to close or not to close—as I please. You cannot coerce me.'

'Oh, I think,' said Brough, smiling, 'that somehow you will come to terms with us.'

Alan's grin was like the teeth-baring of a predatory animal. 'Don't tell me what to do, Brough. This is my mill. I shall decide.'

Brough looked at him queerly. 'By God, boy, you need a lesson, and Bradford might give you one. A touch of hardship is what a pampered young devil like you needs. You might feel a little for your fellows then.'

Alan's answering laugh was a genuine one. 'Hardship, is it, Brough? You do not know me, I think. Be off with you all—until noon tomorrow.'

His determination, which they could not shake, enraged them. He heard them cursing all the way down the rickety stairs, and he laughed to himself when he sent Gurney, Wilkinson and the clerk away, refusing all offers of help.

He stripped off his fine coat and worked in his rolled-up shirtsleeves without eating or drinking. He thought, calculated, went to the window, stared through its grime, and pondered on whether he was hard enough to destroy the livelihood of all at Outhwaite's in order to save his pride.

Against this was the knowledge that to raise wages at Outhwaite's much further would drive it into bankruptcy. What he and the hands had half agreed before the news from Brinkley had reached them might have been possible. To fulfil all their demands meant ruin.

By half-past ten that night Alan had covered sheets of paper with his calculations and had arrived at a conclusion which might just bring agreement. He was bone-weary, and ready for bed at the inn where he had left Gurney.

It was only a short way away, and he walked slowly towards it. They might listen to reason tomorrow if he showed them his calculations, and the basis on which he had made them.

Tiredness, and the feeling of safety which living at Temple Hatton had given him, was his undoing. He kept his mind only on the morrow, so that when they took him at the end of the road—they had been waiting for him for hours—he was not ready for them, and he was their captive without a struggle.

Chapter Twelve

They were gentle with him—which surprised him. They
seized him by the arms from behind when they caught him,
put a knife to his throat and told him to obey them or worse
might befall. Their faces were covered in coal dust so that
he could not recognise them. Then they blindfolded him
and walked him rapidly for quite a long distance, before he
was led up a steep hill.

Part of Alan was exhilarated in a mad way—danger always affected him so. Another part, the stronger, was beginning to fall into the thrall of the berserker rage, although
what use that might be, outnumbered as he was, he did not
know. Nor could he imagine what they were going to do
with him—although he was sure that he would not like it!

Finally they spun him round and removed the blindfold.
He was on the moor, above the town. There were men
carrying flambeaux and the place was lit like day. There
was a mass of people assembled there, and they cheered
when he blinked at them in the light after enduring the
lengthy dark.

'A big bruiser,' shouted one. 'You had the right of it,
lads.'

Their leader came forward and thrust his dirty face into

Alan's. He thought that some of them were probably col-
liers, joining the mill hands in comradeship. The face opposite to him had shining teeth, and the whites of its eyes
glinted in the light of the flambeaux.

'So, you made Bob Sutcliffe choose again and again, my
fine young gentleman,' he said, his accent so strong that
Alan could barely understand him. 'Now it's *your* turn to
choose.'

A cheer went up then. 'Choose! Choose!'

Alan wrenched away from the men who were holding
him, still lightly, and he wondered why. He had expected
blows.

'Choose?' he said, and his voice surprised them. There
was neither fear nor anger in it, only a kind of savage joy
'Tell me what I must do, and I will gladly choose.'

'Oh, it's a hard choice,' said their leader. 'Either we give
you a good hiding to pay you back for trying to close the
mill, or you fight Jem to entertain us. A good choice, boy
A thrashing for you either way.'

The crowd shouted again. 'Choose, Maister Dilhorne
choose.'

Now Alan understood why they had held him so lightly
for they wanted their fun, and Jem was the Brinkley bruise
whom Ned and Robert had seen overcome the man from
London.

He came forward laughing, ready to fight, stripped to the
waist, saying, 'Choose, Mr Dilhorne, sir, choose.' And the
crowd cheered again and again.

At that Alan threw his head back and laughed with him
saying, 'There *is* no choice, and I'll not keep you waiting
like Bob Sutcliffe kept me. Since it's a beating either way
I'll have my fun if I fight—and I hope to make your hea
sing a little, too, Jem.'

Without more ado he peeled off his fine coat, cravat an
waistcoat. He sat down and pulled off his splendid boot

from Lobb's, which Ned had helped him to buy, and his silk socks. After that he stood ready when Jem came for him and the crowd roared at them both.

It was far harder than fighting Ralf, for Jem was his age, and savagely fit and ready, while Alan was hungry and tired. He had neither eaten nor rested since breakfast. He knew that he was bound to be beaten in the end, but he meant to make it as hard as he could for Jem to win.

He would be dam'd if he did anything to disgrace himself, or the gentry whom he was supposed to represent. Sparring and then fighting with Ralf had sharpened him, and he had the advantage that Jem probably thought that Ralf had had the easy beating of him. Alan had no illusions, though: he was facing a fighter at the top of his powers— and at the top of the tree.

Jem began by being a little careless with the gentleman amateur, and Alan swiftly caught him with two punishing lefts before Jem became more wary and the fight began in earnest. The berserker rage which had gripped Alan on the walk came to his aid while he held Jem off, laughing at the other man's frustration that he was not the easy meat he had expected.

The crowd, which had thought that he would be felled straight away, fell silent. Suddenly there were some who cheered him when Jem came in too soon and was caught again. After that there was uproar, with cheering and counter-cheering. The crowd was relishing the battle.

Nevertheless, for all his skill Alan knew that the end was simply a matter of time—and Jem knew it, too.

'I'll down you yet, Maister,' he whispered at Alan.

Alan grinned at him when they came together, and retorted, 'Not until I've marked *your* face for you, too.'

Salvation came suddenly, and saved him from a *coup de grâce* worse than the one he had received from Ralf when his tiring legs had begun to betray him. His damaged body was one vast ache. The cheering stopped. There was a noise and a roar. The Peelers had arrived, alerted by the inevitable informer.

The crowd scattered, and Jem, from being an enemy, became a friend.

He seized Alan's hand, pulled him along, and they and the men who had organised the kidnap ran down the hillside and into the town, the two bruisers still barefoot.

They stood, panting, under a dim lamp. Jem shook Alan's hand and said, 'You're game, Maister, I'll say that for you, bastard though you are. I doubt whether I could do for you if you were trained and fresh.'

'And that's a lie,' said Alan gaily. He had never felt more alive than he did then, half-naked, with his body damaged and aching. 'If only I had my purse I'd buy you a drink on it.'

His captors had changed towards him because of the way in which he had accepted the fight and his performance in it.

'Here's your purse, Maister,' said one. 'We are not thieves.'

Another handed him his coat, but his shirt and boots were gone. Yet another, regretfully, handed him his watch, and he slipped it in his pocket.

There was an inn nearby and he bought them ale, throwing his purse to the landlord and telling him to spend it all on drinks for the house.

Some twenty were with him, and one of them, as he had thought, was Brough, his face and hands black. Sitting there, his body burning with pain, shivering slightly when reaction set in, Alan caught Brough's eye on him as he drank, not sparing the liquor for once.

'You'll not blackmail me, Brough,' he said, smiling through his pain.

'No,' said Brough. 'You're a right bastard, Dilhorne, bu

you're a man for all that. What in God's name do they make of you at the Big House?'

'What you do, Brough. The Queen's cousin used your exact words.'

'Knaresborough, eh? You could have stayed and peached on us to the Peelers. You could still do so.'

'What—and spoil the fun?'

His laugh was painful, and the shivering grew worse. The day had been long and hard before the fight, and he could not remember when he had last eaten. The drink suddenly hit him, and, since pride did not matter any more, he laid his head on the table and fell asleep, exhausted.

Jem looked at him. 'Ralf could never have beaten him were he ready and fit,' he proclaimed drunkenly.

The rest of them stared at him in silence. Brough said, 'Do any know where he lodges?'

'Aye, at The Nag's Head,' said one.

'Then we'll get him there,' Brough said. 'You'd best help us, Jem.'

They hauled him to his feet and walked him down the ill-paved road, past the place where they had kidnapped him and upstairs to his room, where Gurney undressed him before he lay upon his bed, lost to everything, dreaming that he was back home in his room, a boy again and his mother calling.

Alan was waiting for Brough and his friends at noon the next day. He was carefully dressed. His body was still one vast ache. He had been unable to eat properly, and had drunk spirits to ease the pain. He had a dreadful desire to vomit and only pride kept him on his feet.

Gurney had shouted at him, been insubordinate, and had told him that he ought to rest.

'I won't answer for the consequences if you don't,' he had roared.

In short he had gone on, as Alan had finally complained, holding his head, 'as though you were my dam'd nanny'.

'God, are we?' Gurney had howled rudely, forgetting all differences between master and man while he eased Alan into his clothes. 'Life's your bloody chessboard, is it, sir?' And the 'sir' had come out as an insult. 'First you let Ralf knock you about instead of doing for him, and now this!'

He had refused to be silent and insisted on accompanying Alan into Wilkinson's office—'Because, sir, damn your eyes, sir, you need someone there to look after you, if you won't do it for yourself. Left to myself I'd see those bastards who kidnapped you last night hanged, and their heads where they belong—on Tower Hill.'

'Just get my clothes on, and spare me the sermon,' Alan had said wearily. 'My head hurts me enough as it is without you making it worse.'

Swearing and muttering, Gurney had pushed his way into the office, and now sat there glowering at Brough and his men when they arrived.

If they were surprised to see Alan at work, spruce and beautifully turned out, and apart from his bruised hands and face apparently normal, they were not to know that only his resolute will kept him upright at all. They, too, were respectable again. Brough particularly so. He was dressed like the superior clerk he was.

Alan began without preamble. 'I want this strike no more than you do, and we all know it. I see no point in pretence. Mind me. If you push me too far I shall close the works and sell up. By now you should know that I always keep my word. I spent yesterday going over the books and I saw the shop at work. If you change your practices a little on the floor, and work with Wilkinson—instead of against him—with what we save on that the books show that I can offer you something midway between what I wanted to give and you wanted to take. That is my last word. Wilkinson will keep me informed of your progress when I return to London.'

Brough stared at him and knew that he meant what he said. 'So, that is why you were late leaving last night. Well, something is better than nothing.'

He knew that if he refused the offer Alan would carry out his threat and close down. After last night Brough knew that this man was no puling gentleman.

'I think that the men will agree,' he replied cautiously.

Alan laughed, a dreadful mistake. The room half-disappeared before him. 'Don't cozen me, Brough. The men will agree to whatever you tell them. But have it your way. Count heads, if you must. I want an answer by six o'clock tonight, and all the men back at work first thing tomorrow. Pay starts from then.'

He rose. He knew that if he stayed any longer his tight control would fail. 'Wilkinson here will show you the terms; I assure you that they are fair.'

Somehow he reached the door and, straight-backed, walked out. Gurney, following, took him by the arm and steered him down the stairs to the courtyard at the back.

Speculation in his eyes, Brough watched him go. He turned to his second-in-command and whispered to him to take over. He ran lightly down the stairs and into the court-yard where Alan lay prone—Gurney holding his head—vomiting into a drain in the corner. Gurney glared malignantly at Brough.

Alan croaked between spasms, 'Come to gloat?'

'If he has, I'll kill him for you,' Gurney snarled.

'No,' said Brough slowly. 'No, I saw that you were out on your feet in the office.'

'And no wonder,' snorted Gurney. 'It's more'n twenty-four hours since he's eaten. He came straight over t'other morning to save your dam'd mill for you, and then, after you'd made sure that he was knocked nearly senseless last night, he got up early to finish his sums so that you bastards needn't starve.'

'Give over, Gurney, do,' said Alan, who was feeling a little better after heaving up his heart. 'I've told you once already today, you're not my nanny.'

Brough walked over and looked down at him where he lay against the wall, 'Is that true?'

'What? Be plain. I'm in no condition to solve riddles.'

'That you came to save the mill?'

'I'm no dam'd philanthropist, Brough. Save it or sell it, whichever was best for business.'

Brough knew that he'd get nothing from him. He hesitated. Gurney suddenly roared at him, 'Help me to get him to his feet, man. He's too big for me to do it on my own.'

'Two dam'd nannies, then,' said Alan pleasantly when he hung between them. 'Get me to the inn, Gurney, and you can satisfy your passion to be my nursemaid. I don't think that my legs will carry me any further.'

Without warning he gave way at last, and fell against them, unconscious, Gurney cursing until they got him to the inn and finally to bed.

Eleanor was lonely and bored when Alan had gone. Stacy and Jane had each other—she was an extra wheel on their coach. The chatter of her mother, her aunt Hetta and Mrs Chalmers was scarcely bearable. The only amusing episode had been the quarrel between her mother and Mrs Chalmers. Her mother had expressed her disapproval of Alan, and Mrs Chalmers had immediately gushed back at her, 'But he's so handsome, and possesses such charm— one wonders if all young men from New South Wales are the same!'

Beastly Beverley had to be evaded, too, although Charles's tutor helped his charge to escape the worst of him by increasing his hours of tuition. This was no hardship for Charles, who was eager to learn and, insofar as such a good-natured child was capable of it, hated Beverley. His grandmother had left for a visit to friends in Northumbria.

Eleanor joined Charles when she could, although the Triumvirate, as she nicknamed them to herself, disapproved acutely.

'How can you wish to be shut away there?' wailed her mother sorrowfully. 'What use is it? We could be visiting the Lorimers. Polly Lorimer was saying only last week that she has not seen you since the Flood.'

Eleanor restrained herself from saying acidly that Polly Lorimer, her mother and brother Fred were all hearty boors, if not to say bores, whose brains were in their seats on their horses, and that she and they had little in common.

'I like helping Charles,' she said, 'he's lonely.'

'He needn't be, said her aunt Hetta indignantly. 'He has Beverley to play with.'

As well play with a scorpion, thought Eleanor, whose private thoughts grew nastier the longer Alan was away. She had seen the satiric twist to his lips whenever Beverley rampaged through the House—Beverley was rapidly recovering from the effect of his enforced exile to the nursery by Sir Hart, and was now nearly as rudely headstrong as he had been when he had arrived.

Sir Hart was absent, too. He had rarely left his room while Alan was visiting Bradford and only came down for dinner, leaving as soon as it was over. Ned was often away as well. He had made a good friend of Robert Harshaw and they roistered around the Riding, drinking together.

Eleanor had been in the library one afternoon after Charles and Mr Dudley had gone fishing—a new amusement for Charles. She'd had no mind to go with them. She had pulled out one of the great folios of Sir Joseph Banks's original journey to the South Seas in order to look at the plants and animals he had seen in Alan's homeland.

Mr Rivers, the librarian was having a protracted tea in the housekeeper's room, when Sir Hart arrived, to find her studying the folio which was propped on huge oak lecterns.

'I thought that I heard you, Granddaughter.' He came over to see what she was studying.

'Oh, Grandfather,' she exclaimed. 'It is very wrong of me to be so bored and so lonely when, as Alan says, I have everything. But there is nothing for me to do, nothing. I don't know how Mother and the others bear it. When I try to find occupation they look at me as though I have run mad. I cannot chatter, and embroider and unpick it and do it again, and listen to Aunt Hetta reading Mrs Gore's latest novel—or something even sillier—every day.

'Mother can at least pretend to instruct the house-keeper—who doesn't really need instructing. I thought that I might like to go into the garden and help with the plants, but Mother wailed at me that I should ruin my hands. When I try to study with Charles she comes in and chatters at us in order to pry me away. Then she takes me out to visit Polly Lorimer, who only cares about dogs and horses, which I suppose is something—but it is not enough.'

Her voice rose at the end and she thought that she might cry or throw herself about if she were not careful.

'You are missing him,' said Sir Hart gently. 'But, Grand-daughter, even so, were you never to have met him, you would still feel as you do.'

She began to cry at that. 'Oh, you do understand me. What am I to do? Why could not Ned have been like me and I like Ned? Then I could have chattered away to Mother and the rest and you would not have been disap-pointed in him. I should not be saying this, it is so wicked and disloyal, but it is true, and I cannot help my thoughts. Sometimes I feel like a changeling.'

Sir Hart gazed helplessly at her. He could not tell her that, in effect, she *was* a changeling. A changeling to whom her father, Knaresborough, had bequeathed his rare and challenging intelligence which sat so ill with what society thought a young woman of gentle birth ought to be. He tried to comfort her, but he had long ago decided that she should never know the truth—it would simply be one more burden for her to carry.

'It is painful for you, I know, and there is little I can do. If you marry, and your husband is kind, you may make your own life, and fix yourself on something which interests you.'

'And that is all,' she said sadly. 'To wait to be asked and then hope.'

If Alan asked her to marry him she knew that she would be able to share his life in a way that few women did. But suppose he were not to ask her. What then?

She did not speak to Sir Hart of that. Sir Hart must know how she felt about Alan, she had made no secret of it.

'I will not marry an old man or a man for whom I do not care in order to gain a position and a title,' she said. 'I had rather remain single—and be an aunt to Ned's children, if he has any.'

Sir Hart put an arm around her, he had never done so before. 'It is the lot of women at which you rail, Eleanor. Yet men's lives are bound by duty, too.'

'Oh, but they may choose their duty, and there is so much that men may do and so little for me. I am trained to nothing, yet my mind is as good as Charles's and a great deal better than Ned and Robert's. I would run Temple Hatton more carefully than either Ned or Beverley. It's such a waste. It's a pity that I am not more like Mother.'

'No,' he said sharply. 'Do not say that. Should you wish it I will ask Rivers to allow you to help him. He is cataloguing the books here and in London and needs an assistant. You could help him in the mornings. I will silence the complaints which your mother is sure to make. You must understand that once you have begun this work you will need to do it properly and continue it—even if you find it hard. I will not have Rivers played with.'

'Oh, yes, I understand that,' she cried passionately. 'But Mother will be sure to complain.'

'For once, your mother will do as I say.'

Eleanor had thought that there was a touch of Sir Beauchamp in his manner then, and, like Sir Beauchamp, he kept his word. He had been right to warn her that it might be difficult, for Mr Rivers was a hard, if just, taskmaster. She soon began to understand why Alan was so secretly contemptuous of them all, however much he tried to disguise it. For actually working and doing things correctly, as Sir Hart had warned, was quite different from playing.

Her mother was particularly annoyed by the brown Holland overall she wore when at her work, but that counted for nothing against the approval of both Mr Rivers and Sir Hart.

'She learns quickly, and retains what she learns,' Mr Rivers told Sir Hart. 'She is better than anyone we could hire, for she is learning to love the books and her interest is true and genuine.

'Excellent,' said Sir Hart, delighted to learn that he had made his granddaughter a gift which would last her all her life. She knocked at his door to tell him so that evening.

Her equals, though, apart from Jane and Stacy, who occasionally joined her, were not impressed at all, and her mother made her promise that she would not tell their friends.

'Such a strange thing for a young lady to wish to do with her time. I am surprised at Sir Hart for encouraging you.'

Secretly she thought that Eleanor was more like her true father than was comfortable. It would not do if her resemblance to him, already strong, were detected through this latest freak of conduct. Knaresborough was the subject of

gossip for being a bibliophile as well as a sportsman, and
spent a great deal of time in his library at Castle Ashcourt.

Eleanor longed to tell Alan of her new life, for he was
one of the few in the House, beside Jane and Stacy, who
enjoyed the library. She wondered what was happening in
Bradford which was keeping him so long.

Alan was staying away longer than he intended in order
to allow his face to heal before he returned to Temple Hatton. He saw the deal through with Brough and his men,
and spent part of his time mixing with the other mill-
owners. They invited him to dine in their brash new houses,
full of shining new furniture and dark brown paintings
which looked as though the gravy which they served in
such quantities had seeped on to the canvases.

The story of the fight on the moor had spread round the
district, but no one spoke of it to him, although the knowledge was canny in their hard faces. Some reproached him
for raising his hands' wages. He met that with, 'It's so
ordered that it doesn't touch our profits. Outhwaite's was
badly run, as you all know. I would have closed the mill
rather than give way to their original demand—I could not
carry a strike. A little rearrangement served to save all.'

They grunted dissent at him. Surrounded by new-won
wealth, they were aping the manners of the gentry in more
ways than one. For their sons—like Ned—were soft, and
were forgetting the hard work and industry which had created their fathers' fortunes. Life's patterns and cycles re-
created themselves, just as the old Greeks had said.

Eleanor was on her way to the library to do a voluntary
afternoon stint when she heard the noise of Alan's return.
She ran down the great staircase, wearing her Holland
apron, in order to be the first to greet him.

'Oh, I am so glad that you are back, Alan. Did all go well with you?'

She saw the fading bruises on his face, and later she would see the remnants of the fight written on his knuckles, but, smiling joyfully, she said nothing to him, other than 'Oh, I have such things to tell you—later, that is. Doubtless you have things to tell me. We can talk at tea.'

Her welcome of him was so frank and free that Alan was lifted by it, even when her mother said crossly, 'Miss Hatton, you forget yourself. And I wish that you would stay downstairs with us. Rivers must learn to do without you this afternoon.'

'Oh,' said Eleanor gaily, much to Alan's amusement, although he did not quite understand what they were talking about, 'it is not Mr Rivers who forces me to labour in the library, it is I who go there willingly, as I shall explain to you later, Alan.'

She ran lightly up the stairs, leaving him wondering at the apron, the reference to forced labour, and the Triumvirate's openly expressed annoyance at her behaviour when she had gone.

All three women felt that Eleanor's occupation and her interest in it was a vague threat to their pleasant, easy lives. 'For if,' as Aunt Hetta said, 'Sir Hart can compel Eleanor to do such strange things, what might he not ask of us?'

Alan gathered that Eleanor had found something to fill her idle days, and with Sir Hart's help, no doubt. He looked forward to seeing him again, although he half feared the revelations which might flow from him when he did.

Sir Hart did not come down to dinner that night, but sent word to Mr Dilhorne to be so good as to visit him in his study at ten-thirty the next morning.

'And that's a relief,' said Ned frankly to Alan. 'That he's not coming down. For much though I like the old man he's a bit of a death's head at the feast, you know. You see, I did learn something from those intolerably boring old men at Oxford, even if I've forgotten most of it. Now you may tell me of your adventures in Bradford, for I see by your face and hands that you have been fighting again.'

Eleanor raised internal eyebrows while Ned was speaking, and silently enjoyed watching Alan dodge Ned's questions. He was helped in this by the presence of Knaresborough, who was an unexpected visitor that night. He was on his way to London.

'Out of season,' Ned said. 'Wouldn't you know? Just like him to be different from everyone else.'

His splendid train of coaches, servants and wagons were being put up at Temple Hatton overnight—and all of it was going to be loaded on to a special train at Leeds. He was debating whether to stay in his coach on the train journey, or use an ordinary railway carriage, and gravely asked Alan's advice.

'I'm afraid that I may not entertain you at Castle Ashcourt after all, Master Alan, but you shall come to Knaresborough House in Piccadilly when you return to London. I'll brook no refusal from you, for if you do I shall get little Vic to put you into the Tower for contempt!'

Seated at dinner, and before Ned could quiz Alan again, Knaresborough said, 'So, you set Bradford by the ears, young man. It is all over the Riding that you fought with Jem Briggs on the moor above Bradford, until the Peelers broke it up. Now, how came that about?'

Eleanor turned white while Ned, Stacy and Charles said together, 'Oh, famous, Alan. How did you fare with him?'

'I narrowly missed a real beating,' Alan told them cheerfully, and gave them a highly edited version of his trip to Bradford. He did not tell them that Brough had visited him before he left to offer him his hand in friendship, and had told him that he was a true Yorkshireman for all that he came from the Antipodes.

'Your name's a give-away, young fellow,' he had told Alan. 'And you're as like the old man at the House as he must have been in youth to make more than one man think.'

'Don't think about it too hard,' Alan had replied. 'It wouldn't do to strain yourself overmuch. Your men need you.'

He avoided Knaresborough's satiric eye now, while he placated Ned, but he could not avoid Eleanor's tongue when they joined the ladies after the dinner.

'I thought that you had promised me not to run any unnecessary risks,' she said reproachfully, 'and there you were fighting the man Ned and Robert have been ranting about.'

Alan looked soulfully at her. 'I didn't intend to,' he said, 'but needs must when the devil drives.'

'I suppose that he was driving pretty hard around Bradford, judging by the state that you're in.'

'True—but you'll be happy to learn that we all became friends in the end, and drank together afterwards.'

Knaresborough, who had strolled up and was listening to them, drawled, 'Brough? Was it Brough you were dickering with? At least he's an honest rogue, unlike some.'

Both Eleanor and Alan stifled laughter at this typical pronouncement, and Alan wondered where and when Brough and Knaresborough had crossed swords and what they had made of one another. Fortunately the Belted Earl abandoned the topic of Alan's exploits and engaged the three of them in a discussion of Eleanor's new duties in the library, of which he heartily approved.

Ned and Robert remained in the dining room drinking, and did not emerge until after Alan had retired to bed. Once there he could not sleep for thinking about what Sir Har might have to tell him on the morrow.

Chapter Thirteen

Alan thought the next morning that even the weather was in tune with life. The sun of the last few weeks had disappeared, and it was raining hard. Sir Hart did not come down for breakfast: only Eleanor was present.

She had arrived early because she wished to speak to him before beginning her work in the library. They took a turn together in the large drawing room, where he told her more of his adventures in Bradford and his strange friendship with Brough.

She told him of her work with Mr Rivers and how much she was enjoying it and how much she was learning.

'The Latin and the little Greek I studied with Stacy and then with Charles have been so helpful, as well as the French which Mother insisted I learn.' She had found her *métier*, and Alan could only hope that, whether he married her or not, it would always be there for her.

Characteristically, while she was enthusing over the merits of various fine types and exquisite bookbinding, Alan found himself thinking that if she were to become his wife publishing was a business and book-collecting could be made one, and that might be something which they could develop together. She could learn about book-keeping and

business management. For if she could work so sensibly
with Mr Rivers, then there was little that she might not be
able to do.

But there was Sir Hart to see first, and when they walked
upstairs, she to the library and he to Sir Hart's study, he
wondered whether what Sir Hart would tell him might destroy that dream, too.

The old man did not look so ill this morning. He was
standing between his desk, on which lay an open ledger
and the windows.

They wound through the empty preliminary courtesies of
Sir Hart's world.

'Now, Mr Dilhorne, I must ask you a question, which
know that you are expecting. You may choose to answer
me or not, as you please.'

He wondered if Sir Hart had heard of what had happened
at Bradford, and was mocking him, but he thought not. This
was not the first time that he had heard echoes of himself
and his father in Sir Hart's speech.

'Why, sir, ask me, and I shall choose.'

'I wish to know if you will tell me of everything which
concerns your father's origins.'

'Willingly. I see no point in further evasions.'

'Nor do I.' The old man waited.

'I really know very little, and that at second-hand. My
father has never spoken of them to his children. Once
though, when my twin brother and I were made to do man-
ual work by him, we went to our mother. We told her that
he had no right to make our lives so hard, for we were
rich man's sons after all, and we asked her to intercede
with him for us.

'I shall never forget her reply. She had always been gentle with us, but not then. "Hard!" she said. "Hard! You
do not know what hard is. He asks nothing of you that you
are not able to give. I will tell you what hard is, for he wi

not. And you are not to speak to him of what I shall tell you. After that, if you still wish me to complain to him, you may go where you will, both of you, although you are my sons and I love you.

'''Your father's mother was a farmer's daughter, sent to work in a great house on the moors in Yorkshire. He never knew, or has forgotten, its name. She was seduced by the son of the house. The boy abandoned her when she was with child, and she was turned out. Her family abandoned her, too, and she became a servant on a farm. Your father was born there. Before your father was ten years old the farmer raped her before him, and made her his unwilling mistress. He was then compelled to turn her out by his wife's brothers.

'''They moved on to another farm where they were both cruelly ill-treated. One day the farmer began to beat your grandmother so brutally that your father feared that he would kill her. He was then about twelve years old. He took a knife and attacked the man with it. He never knew whether he had killed him or not, for they fled to London.

'''They walked there, and the journey killed his mother. She was ill with a lung disease before they fled. Your father was alone on the streets of London, without a home, a family, proper clothing or an education—that he got much later. He was trained for nothing and had nothing. He slept in the street and under bridges. He stole to live, for there was nothing else for him to do.'''

Alan's voice was cold and uninflected—as his mother's had been—and like her he looked away from his hearer, through the window towards the moors, grey under the driving rain.

Behind him Sir Hart, his face as grey as the landscape, listened as Alan had listened. Alan continued with his mother's story.

'''He became a thief and an organiser of thieves while

still young. He was too clever; his elders betrayed him to
the Runners. He was sentenced to death, but it was commuted to transportation for life. Do you still think that your
lives are hard?''

Alan turned to look at Sir Hart, as he had looked at his
mother. 'Neither Tom nor I knew what to say. We had often
speculated on his early life, but, careless boys though we
were then, what had happened to him, and to our grandmother, was too shocking for us to dwell on. We said nothing more, simply slunk out of the room. Neither of us spoke
to the other—or to him—about what we had heard. Lifting
loads at Campbell's Wharf seemed little enough after that.'

He fell silent. Sir Hart rose and walked to his desk.

'It is as I thought when I saw your face. When Ned told
me that he had invited someone named Dilhorne to stay at
Temple Hatton I was a little disturbed. The name is not
uncommon, but when you arrived and proved to be a Dilhorne who had my family's face, and was in every way so
like the Sir Beauchamp whom I remember—although without his cruelty—*that* was too much to be a coincidence.'

He beckoned Alan over to the desk and pushed the ledger
towards him, and invited him to read an entry in it. While
Alan studied the page, Sir Hart walked over to the window
and, as Alan had done, stared out at the rugged stretch of
landscape.

The entry was brief and uncompromising. 'Dismissed
this day, Mary Dilhorne, under-servant, for immorality. She
is expecting a bastard child.'

'My father.' Alan was suddenly filled with anger, and
was about to speak, to say he knew not what, but the old
man forestalled him. His voice was low, as though it came
from a great distance, and not from just behind Alan's back.

'The entry is wrong. The child was not a bastard. I had
married her.'

'You married her? In God's name, how? You were how old? Sixteen?'

'Nearly seventeen. She was very pretty. The same age as myself. Perhaps a little younger.' He paused. Alan could not bear to turn to look at him, or to question him. A marriage!

'I had an uncle.' Sir Hart's voice was stifled. 'They called him the Mad Parson. He had read Rousseau and believed in the equality of men and women. They gave him a little living, over in the Dales, without much of a congregation. She was a good girl. I told him that she'd never let me touch her until we were married—so he said that he'd marry us. He called the banns, quite legally and proper. Only some daft gaffers and gammers were there to hear him and to act as witnesses.'

Sir Hart paused again. This time Alan did turn to look at him. He was staring out of the window as though he saw something there. The ghost of a pretty girl long gone, perhaps.

'I shall never forget that summer with her. I dared not tell my father what I had done. We were all frightened of him—family, servants and friends. I never stopped to think what I ought to do after I had married her. I only knew that I wanted her and could not have her without it. But I feared him so. I started to tell him once, and then I looked at him and stopped. That was the great wrong which I did, for suddenly it was too late.'

'She became with child. I didn't know—she didn't tell me. I think now that she was frightened of him and what he might do to us. They were jealous of her, the other servants. They knew that she pleased me. One of them guessed and told the housekeeper. She told my father…'

This time his silence was a long one, and Alan did not interrupt it.

'I shall never forget that day, either. I'd been out shooting. I came in and my father was in the Hall. "To your room at once, sir! No questions." His face was… I started to argue. I suppose I realised that I had been found out. I tried to speak, but he roared at me, "No insolence, sir. To your room."'

Sir Hart stopped again. His head was bowed, resting on his hand. 'He came to my room with a whip. I had known him angry before, and I had endured many of his cold rages. He always thought me unworthy. "I've sent your whore and your bastard away," he said. "You could have tumbled as many as you pleased, but what you have done is unforgivable, if she was telling the truth."'

'He cut at me with his whip each time that he ended a sentence. "You have sent her away," I cried, aghast. "But you can't. She's my wife. Uncle Harry married us."'

'I thought that he would have killed me then. He beat me until I fell to the ground, half-conscious. "*That* is what is unforgivable: the marriage. And it didn't happen. Understand me, my boy. If you persist in claiming you married her, I'll break you as well as my parson brother, and send the girl to a brothel."'

'I said—I don't remember what I said. Only that I loved her. "You fool," he roared at me, "to think to waste yourself on a peasant. Any way, she's gone. I sent her away this morning. She's gone where you won't find her. Tomorrow you'll go to Cousin Jacques in France, and you'll stay there until you unlearn this folly that Harry has taught you. Equality. Marrying peasants. Fathering scum." And he struck at me with every word.'

Sir Hart paused for a moment, then said, 'I've no thought of this for over sixty years. I know that I was a coward. I have tried to forget how, in the end, I betrayed both her and our child. But what was I to do? I was locked in my room. For a week I spoke to nobody. The servant had orders not to speak to me. Two footmen were needed to carry me to the coach that took me away, because I refused to walk to it. I was exiled to France for the next five years. Years later, after Sir Beauchamp died, I tried to trace her, but the trail ended at the first farm of which you spoke.'

He stopped speaking with a groan.

Alan thought that this must be the end—but it was not.

Sir Hart continued. 'Do you know how old your father was when his mother died?'

It could not hurt to tell him the truth. The pain and the grief were the old man's, not his.

'He was twelve or thirteen, I think. He does not know exactly how old he is.'

'Twelve or thirteen.' Sir Hart's laugh was harsh and humourless. 'Ned's father was seven years younger than yours, God forgive me.'

This was almost too much. Alan said, stunned, 'You mean…?'

'You know what I mean. My wife, Mary Dilhorne, was still alive when I married again. And if you weren't the man I think that you are, I wouldn't have told you this. There's no proof now, beyond my word. My father took the living away from my uncle and destroyed the Parish Registers. My uncle died a broken drunkard in poverty. It was as though the marriage had never been. But it happened. What does that make of me, and my second so-called, wife, and my English children and grandchildren?'

'Why have you told me this?' demanded Alan. 'There was no need. You could have acknowledged my father as your bastard—you say that there is nothing to prove him otherwise.'

'Guilt. Guilt for the lie which I have lived. I never thought to hear anything of mother or child again. When I first saw you, and your name was Dilhorne, I could not believe it. When you told me, just now, that your grandmother's name was Mary, and how your father came to be born, and that she had worked in a great house in Yorkshire, then I knew, that after all these years the past had returned and I could not lie again.

'My life has been a living lie. Good Sir Hartley Hatton, who destroyed his wife and his child. I did not even know that I had a son.'

His face twisted again. 'He lied to me. Sir Beauchamp. When he wanted me to marry Priscilla Carhampton he said to me one night, as we drank after dinner, "You will be pleased to know that your whore is dead, and the bastard, too."

'Did I believe him—or was it an easy way out for me to pretend I did? He wanted me to marry and the girl was pretty, a great heiress because her worthless brothers killed themselves early in their folly—as my sons did. Later she became a faithless shrew. So I was well served for my cowardice. It was her sons and mine who were the bastards, not your father—and she who was, in effect, my mistress, not your grandmother.'

Alan scarcely knew what to say. He had not expected this. He had merely thought to hear some tale of a youthful peccadillo—a seduced and betrayed servant girl sent away. Instead he had discovered that the likeness was not a scandalous joke, but, because Sir Hart had married again—or rather had unknowingly committed bigamy, while his first wife was still alive—was more like a threat held over two generations of Hattons. A threat which—if it were revealed—would deprive them of legitimacy, land and title.

He thought of Ned's careless words to Almeria—that Sir Hart would not be presenting *him* with an unexpected cousin to claim the inheritance—and of the idle fashion in which he had dismissed the likeness and had brought Alan to Yorkshire. An act which had merely served to prove to his grandfather that the past is never over and that 'the whirligig of time brings in his revenges', as Shakespeare had so aptly put it.

'I ask you again,' he said, and he had no notion of how cold and stern he looked and sounded, so that his likeness to Sir Beauchamp was almost too much for Sir Hart. 'Why tell me now?'

'Perhaps…perhaps in order to call you grandson without insulting you.'

'Grandson?' Alan's voice was scathing. 'What of my father? What can you, or anyone, do for him and his early suffering. What of Ned?'

He did not say what of Eleanor, for she had none of the old man's blood in her.

'What would this do to your family if they knew of it? How many ruined lives are we speaking of, if the truth were known?'

He could not go on.

'I don't know,' said Sir Hart. His voice was low. 'When I think of you and Eleanor I am pleased, for the first time, that she is not a Hatton. You may marry her and not look at her and wonder whether she will give you sons like Ned and Beverley. Knaresborough tells me that you know that he is her father. On the other hand I felt that I could not leave you exposed to the world's conjectures over your striking likeness to Sir Beauchamp without telling you the truth. Knaresborough guessed who you must be the moment he saw you. ''So like Sir Beauchamp, with his very manner,'' he said. He had great charm, too, when he chose to use it.'

Alan was silent, thinking again of all the ruined lives if the truth were known—and the life which had been ruined because it was not. His lost grandmother walked in the shadows because of it.

Sir Hart said painfully. 'Your father—I should like to know more of him. You speak of him with such pride. *My*

son, a son *I* might have been proud of—and careless Ned
brought you here, never thinking of what he was doing.
Half in joke, I do believe…'

'My father?' asked Alan. 'Why should you wish to know
of him? You let him go lightly enough in the end.'

'You have the right to say that, sir, and I deserve to hear
it for the two great wrongs I did. One not to tell my father
what I had done straight away, and the other that I took his
word over your grandmother's death and married again
without looking for her until it was too late. Yet perhaps
before you go, you might tell me a little of him.'

'Perhaps,' said Alan, still cold, still Sir Beauchamp.
'First I must think about what you have told me—for there
are many lives whose future is at stake here.'

Sir Hart bowed his head. 'Indeed, and I must not seek
to influence you.'

'As you say. And the wrongs which you have done to
me and mine cannot be righted. You could not know, no
guess that my father would become rich and powerful, and
that he is happy with his life with my mother and his family. You say that there is no legal proof as to our rights.
The Parish Registers have gone, and the marriage licence
too, I suppose. Whether my father, or my elder brother
Thomas, would wish to make a just claim to what is rightly
theirs, I cannot say.

'Only you can testify that the claim is just, and by saying
so you would destroy many lives, including that of the
woman I love—for, Hatton or not, she is supposed to be
one. I had intended to leave for London soon, but I may
not do that now. You must give me leave and time to think
the matter over.'

Sir Hart said painfully, 'You behave as well as I might
have expected—and not like *he* would have done, I am
sure.'

By 'he', he meant Sir Beauchamp. 'Should you wish to

claim what is your father's, I could not lie again and deny
you. When I contrast you with Ned and Beverley…my pain
is worse…'

Alan said only, 'You will forgive me if I leave you, but
I need to think of all this—coldly and carefully.'

Sir Hartley Hatton lowered his head.

The hard face before him neither judged him nor, indeed,
showed any sign of what its owner thought. To be so
young, and so formidable already! Alas, he knew that Alan
would never be his willing grandson, whatever decision he
came to. He and his father and his family were lost to him
in affection. He had forfeited that right—and his pain was
the greater.

'I cannot ask you to stay or to speak further. You have
my leave to go.'

Alan left by the door to the Picture Gallery. He neither
wished to see nor to speak to others, not even Eleanor. On
the way through it he stopped to look at Sir Beauchamp.
His great-grandfather, so hard, so severe, so clever, so
cruel—and he so like him in looks and manner.

He shivered. For the wrong was Sir Beauchamp's in his
treatment of his son. The thought of being like him was
abhorrent—and all who had seen him, and had known Sir
Beauchamp in life, had said he was. Knaresborough had
immediately commented on it.

Alan shivered again. Every tale he had heard of him
testified to his cold severity. He knew that, in part, this was
true of himself. Both his father and his mother had occasionally reproached him for being hard and inconsiderate—
particularly when the rage took him. The rage he had inherited from Sir Beauchamp.

He had learned to control it because the better part of
him hated and feared it. Left to itself, the rage would have
closed the mill at Bradford, but he had ignored it. On the
other hand, he also knew that, properly controlled, it could

make him transcend himself, as it had done on the moor outside Bradford, when it had enabled him to hold Jem off for so long, despite all.

He must use it, not let it use him, lest, like Sir Beauchamp, he allowed it to destroy him, and those around him.

The old man he had left behind him gazed unseeingly at the water-drenched landscape. He was on the moors again, in the brilliant sun of a long-gone summer's day, with a pretty girl in his arms. She was saying, 'It is right, now, Hart, for we are married, and God has said that we can love one another.'

But both the boy and the girl had been lost in the mists of time, and although the past had returned it had brought him pain, not redemption.

Alan met Stacy on the stairs, and in his concentration which was almost distress, would have passed him blindly except that Stacy put out his hand to touch him on the arm and ask anxiously, 'Alan, is anything wrong?'

Alan shook his head, as much to clear it as to answer Stacy's question. 'Forgive me, my mail today was troublesome: I was thinking of Bradford, and then of London.'

This was not a lie, but it was not the truth either. He thought again of how often he did that, and wondered whether it came from Sir Beauchamp. It certainly came from his father, and Thomas possessed the same habit.

Stacy shrugged his shoulders and walked on: that something was wrong was plain, but it was not his business, and in his way Alan had told him so.

Eleanor was alone in the drawing room when Alan walked in. Her face lit up at the sight of him, but, sensitive to him now, she saw that he was troubled. She was still in the dark dress that she wore to work with Mr Rivers, and its severity enhanced rather than diminished her beauty which lay in force of character, not only in pretty colouring and youthful vivacity. Almeria had made her laugh once by telling her that one day she would be a beautiful old woman because of this.

Alan, admiring her beauty while she talked of the book she had been examining—Captain Cook's *Voyages*—unknowingly made the same judgement. The promise under her youthful high spirits, which Sir Hart had always seen, was coming to maturity. Alan suddenly wanted her most desperately for his wife and companion, his better half, who would help him to tame the rage and keep down Sir Beauchamp. To know that he also loved her equally desperately for herself and nothing else, simply because she was Eleanor, was a bonus.

While no one was looking, she patted him on the hand. The look of gratitude which he gave her was more exciting than a kiss would have been. What troubled him troubled her, and if she could not by convention tell him so, then she could give him silent support.

Ned was there, too, dressed for riding. He was due to meet Robert for a final fling with him before going off to the wedding in York with Eleanor.

After he had left, Eleanor turned to Alan and said, 'I have been indoors all day, and I would love to have a last ride with you before I go to York. The weather has cleared and the sun is shining. Besides—' and she gave him a comic conspiratorial look '—we shall be on our own. Stacy, Jane and Mrs Chalmers are returning to Culverwell Manor in the morning, and are preparing to leave. Aunt Hetta, Beverley and my mother are visiting the Lorimers, so we shall have the moors to ourselves.'

'Minx!' said Alan, smiling fondly at her and thinking, not for the first time, that to be with her renewed him. Like her unacknowledged father, she was both straightforward and frank. 'Of course I will come with you—particularly if we are to be alone.'

'We can go to the Cradle Rocks,' she said enthusiastically. 'They're called that because of their shape. We have
never been so far before.'

They dismounted at them after a hard ride, and Alan
wondered briefly if the long-gone lovers had been here, too.
It made him gentle—and careful—with Eleanor. Eleanor
had thought, nay hoped, that he might offer for her here
surrounded by the wild beauty of the savage landscape, but
she saw that his morning visit to Sir Hart had left him
distrait.

They kissed and embraced, but the controlled passion he
had sometimes shown was missing. He was loving, indeed
he could not have been more so, but there was something
bittersweet in his manner quite unlike his usual forthright
habit, so that Eleanor could not help wondering what was
troubling him.

Alan was recalling, a little sadly, what careless love had
done to Sir Hart and his grandmother. The memory of what
he had learned that morning was strong in him, and made
him particularly considerate of his dear girl, for he had no
wish to say or do anything which might end in sorrow for
them both.

'Ned and I used to ride out here when we were children,'
she told him. 'Sometimes we would bring a picnic with us
but Sir Hart never liked to visit Cradle Rocks, which I
found strange, for it has by far the best views.'

If his guess was correct, that Sir Hart and his grandmother had met here as young lovers, his reluctance was
understandable, Alan thought.

'I love it here in Yorkshire,' she told him, 'but I would
like to see the rest of the world, too.' This was as near
encouragement as she dared offer him. 'I know that comparisons are odious, but how does this scenery strike you
after that of New South Wales?'

'It is so different that comparisons are difficult. Each has its own beauty, and people are different here as well. Our society is very limited, compared with yours, both in London and in Yorkshire. But there is a vigour with us which is lacking here.'

Looking at him, Eleanor thought that vigour was what marked him off from other men. For all his deviousness, which she had long since recognised by picking up the half-truths and indirections which he employed—unlike Ned—there was still a directness about him missing from the men she knew. If Alan did not offer for her everyone else who might seemed second-best. But something was troubling him, and had obviously been troubling him all day.

Almost as if he had read her thoughts, he turned and took her small hand in his large one. He gave her a smile and said, 'Remember, Eleanor, whatever happens in the future, I love you, and all this, too.'

He swept his hand around the horizon. 'It is almost like coming home. I thought so the first time that I saw it, and think so still. London is quite another thing. If I settle in England I shall be compelled to work in the City, but I should want a refuge outside of it. Essendene, for all its beauty, is too mild for my taste.'

It was almost the long-awaited declaration, but not quite. She must be patient.

After dinner they sat and talked together of her work with Mr Rivers, of his need to return to London soon, of her visit to York and of their mutual regret that they must part for a few days.

'I shall certainly not leave before you return,' he told her—and Eleanor's hopes rose again.

Alan was restless, and after he had seen Ned and Eleanor off the next morning he knocked on Sir Hart's study door. When the old man asked him what he wanted of him, he said simply, 'The loan of a horse and a pack. I've a mind to visit the Dales on my own. Without Gurney.'

The old man immediately understood him. In some ways it was like talking to his father.

'Is it wise? And how will you know where to go?'

Alan gave him what his sister Mary called his knowing grin. 'You will tell me where I may find the Dilhorne farmhouse, to the second question, and to the first, I don't know. I don't even know what I shall do when I get there. I take it that there are inns?'

'It will be a pleasant ride in this weather. Yes, there are inns, rough ones. I cannot see any harm coming of it. You have a cool head.'

So Alan rode into the Dales in the halcyon weather of early September and found the village near to the farmhouse with the aid of the rough map which Sir Hart had given him before he left. He never looked back when he left the House, so he did not see that the old man watched him until he was lost to sight.

The inn in the village was small, pleasant and simple. The landlord was friendly when he questioned him. 'I understand that a family called Dilhorne farms in these parts.'

'Right enough, Maister, over to Leethwaite. There's a track leaves the byway nigh two miles on from here.'

He bespoke a room and food. Like the accommodation and the ale, the food was simple, but good.

The landlord and his wife were curious as to what such a fine young gentleman should be doing in these parts looking for Dilhornes' farm. They asked him his name, and where he came from.

'London,' he answered them, with the smile which always won people over. 'And my name is Smith, Alan Smith.'

He had no wish to start hares. The resemblance to Ned which had occasioned such excitement in London society and around Temple Hatton and Brinkley fortunately meant nothing here. His clothes and his horse excited more comment than his face.

He spent the morning after his arrival walking around, admiring the scenery and drinking in the flavour of the village, so far from civilisation. There was a great grey church, and he wondered if it were like the one the boy Hart had taken his grandmother to, sixty years and more ago.

It was pleasant without Gurney nursemaiding him. Lunch was bread, cheese and ale. He ate it outdoors in his shirtsleeves, surrounded by geese, an old goat, and a number of village children to whom any stranger was a curiosity. After that he resumed his fine London coat and boots and mounted his horse, and under the curious stares of the villagers he rode off towards Leethwaite, up the rough road, and then along the even rougher track, towards the farmhouse. It was a low grey building, set on a slight rise, with a cottage garden at the front and the back.

More curious stares from a burly man with dark hair and a brown face greeted him. The farmer—for his clothes were superior to those of the labourers he had seen—was tending to a shaggy pony. There were stables at some distance from the house. An idle boy was filling a bucket from a well. A woman in a sunbonnet and a print dress was carrying dried washing in a wicker basket.

Alan tied his horse to a stump which had obviously done similar duty before and walked towards the farmer and the woman, who, despite their curiosity, greeted him with a gaze so blank that it was almost hostile.

He pulled off his tall hat, another fashionable result of his friendship with Ned, and said as pleasantly as he could, 'Am I correct in supposing this to be the farm where the Milhorne family live?'

'Aye,' said the farmer, in true Yorkshire style determined

to give nothing away. In any case gentry—and this young
sprig was such obvious gentry—were always folk to be
wary of.

Since nothing further was offered, Alan spoke again. 'I
wonder if you would be good enough to answer a few
questions for me.'

'Happen. Depends what they are.'

'I understand that a Mary Dilhorne lived here nearly
sixty years ago. I know that the chances are small, but is
there anyone alive who might remember her?'

'Mary Dilhorne? Can't say that I remember a Mary,' said
the farmer.

He looked at his wife, who said hesitantly, 'Ezra might
know. He'd be the right age.'

'Aye, Ezra's my great-uncle,' he explained. 'Take the
young gentleman round the back, Lottie.'

He turned to Alan. 'The old man likes to lie outside in
fine weather.'

Lottie Dilhorne beckoned to Alan, and he followed her
round the house to a small flower garden with a wild lawn
next to beds of vegetables and some small fruit bushes. A
wooden settle was drawn up beneath an apple tree, and an
old, white-haired man lay on it, covered with a knitted blan-
ket.

He looked up at Lottie, who screamed at him, 'Great-
Uncle, here's a young gentleman enquiring after a Mary
Dilhorne. Would be about your age. Do you remember
Mary?'

'No need to shout,' said the old man petulantly. 'Of
course I remember a Mary. She were my older sister. Long
gone, is Mary.'

'Can you tell me anything of her?' asked Alan, raising
his voice a little.

'Aye, she were a bad girl, were Mary. Went to the Big
House, Temple Hatton, over the moors, she did, and go

herself a bastard. I mind my feyther's anger. He wouldn't have her back. Disgraced us all, she had. But when my mother were took ill a few years later, she swore she'd never rest easy until she knew what had happened to Mary and the child.'

He stopped and appeared to fall asleep. 'Where were I, young sir? Aye, Mary. Feyther went to the place where she'd been sent. He missed her by a few weeks. She'd been a bad girl again, so they'd turned her out, and the little lad, too. Never did know where she'd gone. Handsome little lad, they said. I mind a gentleman came round some time later, after Mother died, asking for Mary, and that were all we could tell him.'

He was silent again: lost in a world where Alan's father had been a handsome little lad, turned out with his mother into an uncaring world.

The old man looked at Alan, standing there in the pride of his youth: at his confident bearing, big and strong, his handsome face, his beautiful clothes especially made for him by Ned's tailor and his polished boots. He stared at Sir Hart's splendid horse, tethered where he could see it.

'And you, my fine young gentleman? What can the likes of you want to know about Mary Dilhorne?'

Alan debated—and then made up his mind. He was aware of the farmer's sudden interest, but he also knew that he would never come here again. The truth could not hurt.

'She was my grandmother. My father is—was—her little lad.'

'Aye, and is she still alive, then?' asked Ezra, staring at him in wonder.

'No, she died not long after your father tried to find her,' said Alan, recalling how little he knew of his grandmother, beyond her name.

'How come you're gentry?' said the farmer. 'Seeing that your father was...' He stopped, embarrassed.

'A bastard,' said Alan gently. 'My father is a clever man who made a great fortune. I'm not really a gentleman. I only look like one.' His tone was quite unoffended.

His last remark was greeted with complete disbelief, except that Lottie said, 'Ezra is your great-uncle, too, so we must be cousins.'

'Yes,' said Alan.

'A cup of tea, then,' said Lottie. 'Come into the house.'

The house had been improved recently. There was new furniture and a small piano. He was persuaded to sit down, and Lottie brought him tea in a bright china cup and saucer. They had no idea what to make of him. He was so alien to everything they knew.

It seemed preposterous that he was Mary's grandson, and the unlikelihood grew when Alan confessed that he was from New South Wales, on the other side of the world. They were almost afraid of him. Such a great gentleman to be sitting with them and claiming to be thier cousin.

The strange afternoon wore on. They asked him to wait to see their two sons, who were out working, but he refused. He had to go back, he said. It was obvious that they had nothing in common. He said goodbye to Ezra, who was drinking his tea in the open, and then he rode away.

Sixty years had gone by and Mary Dilhorne was a dream, a fading memory in the mind of a moribund old man, and her son and grandson had no place here. His presence distressed them—he was an outsider very different from those who had turned Mary away—without mourning either her—or her little lad.

Alan left for Temple Hatton at dawn the next morning. The landlord packed him half a loaf, a piece of hard cheese, some apples, and filled a bottle with water for him. He rode slowly home to Temple Hatton, noting wryly that he thought of it as home, and that, in reality, it was more his home than anyone's who lived in it—apart from Sir Hart himself.

Seated on a slope by a waterfall he ate his snap, as the locals called a light meal, and considered the world and his place in it. He would tell his father of the farm, its decency, the good, sound stock who lived there, and the fading old man who, beside his father and Sir Hart, was the last to remember Mary Dilhorne.

More than that, he had come to understand himself, and the farm had helped him there. He was Alan Dilhorne, a gentleman, whether he liked it or not. Everyone told him so, and the Dilhornes had stared at him: he was not one of them.

His rightful name was Hatton—and what a sad joke that was. He was Sir Beauchamp's great-grandson, something of which he preferred not to think but would have to, for he must be sure never to go down the dreadful road which his forebear had taken. He must—he would—control himself, so that he would never be tempted to inflict suffering for its own pleasure—or for his own ends. He was unaware that his father had faced this dragon and had conquered it.

It gave him pleasure to remember that he had not ruined his cousin Victor, that he had stayed his hand when he had fought with Ralf and had offered himself up for punishment rather than destroy Ralf for his own and Knaresborough's pleasure. He had also saved the mill at Bradford when he was sure that in his place Sir Beauchamp would have closed it. To remember him would remind him always never to treat people as things, for if the habit should grow it would destroy him as well as them.

Now he was faced with choices—as he had faced others. But choice was life and life was choice, whichever way you looked at it. He thought that he knew how his father would choose when he told him Sir Hart's story, but he could not pre-empt that choice. He was sure that the Patriarch would not choose Temple Hatton and England rather than Sydney and the Antipodes—he had renounced England long ago.

But how should he, Alan, choose between England and Australia? The pull of both were strong. Eleanor drew him to England, he had fallen in love with Yorkshire, and, if the truth were told, life in London excited him, too. To stay, though, would mean that he would lose his parents and his family.

He had no notion of what Sir Hart might do, now that the truth was out at last. Could he make a decision before he knew what Sir Hart would decide? Or was to wait a sign of weakness: that he would let someone else make up his mind for him? Alan sat so long that noon was well past before he remounted his horse and rode on, his choice still to make.

He needed a sign, he thought. His father had once said that he believed in signs and omens, and he had laughed a little at that hard, downright man for saying such a thing—but now he knew what he had meant. He rode into the deserted stableyard and Ralf came to meet him, to hold his horse as he dismounted.

'I'm right glad to see you, Mr Alan, sir.'

'Not sir, Ralf.' He felt like his father suddenly. 'Never sir. Maister Alan will do.'

'Maister Alan, then. I talked to Jem Briggs today, and of how he fought you. He said that he had his work cut out to beat you, and that there was no way I could hold you in fair fight. I knew that, and I hated you for giving me the victory. But when he told me what a brave fist you had made of it, though hungry and tired, I thought on. For all I have left in the world now is my skill, and that I am unbeaten, and you left me that rather than make a joke of me before that lord and the others. I honour you for that and for what you did for poor Nat. I should not be saying this, I know, but the talk is that you will be marrying Miss Eleanor, and we all hope that this may be so, because this place needs a man, and there will be none left when Sir Hart dies if you go.' He put his hand out when he had finished speaking and Alan took it.

'I could not have beaten you when you were champion,' said Alan.

'That's as may be. You did not fight me when I was champion. You don't mind me saying what I did about Miss Eleanor? I thought that it would be a pity to let that man spoil it for us.'

No,' said Alan slowly, 'for what you have said has decided something for me. I needed a sign, and you have given me one.'

He shook Ralf's hand and went into the House. He would offer for Eleanor and stay in England, and in some measure try to right the wrong which Sir Beauchamp and Sir Hart had done between them. He would claim his love and guard the House, which needed guarding.

Chapter Fourteen

The first thing Alan wanted to do when he entered the House was to find Eleanor who, he hoped, would have returned by now, but his duty demanded that he see Sir Hart first.

He was in his study. His desk had been cleared of everything but some letters and documents, many with large red seals attached to them. He was seated in a great chair, almost like a throne, which had belonged to the founder of the family. He no longer looked ill: rather there was a feeling about him of decisions made and conclusions reached. Sir Hart was in sight of harbour and was making the ship secure.

He motioned to Alan to sit down.

'You have decided?'

'Yes. Visiting Leethwaite helped.'

'I thought that it might. Well, sir?'

'I have decided to marry Eleanor, if she will have me. I shall return with her to Australia, to tell my father and brother of what I have learned from you. They must decide what action—if any—to take, although I think I know what their decision will be. Then I shall return to England, to settle here. That decision is a hard one, but I have made it.'

'You would never avoid a decision because it was hard, I think,' said Sir Hart. 'I have spent the time since you left me with the lawyers, and I am ready for death.'

He paused. 'All my life I have avoided making decisions because they were hard. I see now that by doing so I have always succeeded in making bad worse.'

He picked up a letter. 'This is for your father. To do with as he pleases. It tells him his story. There is a sealed copy at the lawyers'. They do not know of its contents: I have informed them that it is to be handed to you after my death—to do with as you please. These dispositions would have been different, I may add, if you had chosen not to marry Eleanor.

'This is my will, and this is a signed disposition of matters to be done—again, only if you marry Eleanor. As to the will, I had Shotton in the other day, worried that Ned refuses to learn the business of the estate and that the staff are in distress at the prospect of his inheriting. They fear for its future.

'Unfortunately, they are right. Yesterday I received letters from London. Like your cousin Loring, Ned has borrowed great sums against his inheritance. Something has troubled the sharks from whom he got the money, and they want it now, from me. I have long thought how to secure the estate from him, without completely disinheriting him, and it was bound up with my hopes that Eleanor would marry Stacy Trent. Now the burden will fall on you.

'I have set up an arrangement for the estate to be held in Trust, with you in charge of it. Ned, Beverley and Eleanor will be left incomes, commensurate with their standing, to be paid annually. Others such as Hetta and Eleanor's mother will receive legacies, but you will be responsible for the administration of the Trust. I am hoping

that Ned's resentment at not inheriting outright will be less-
ened by his loss of a responsibility which he plainly does
not want. You are strong enough to face his resentment—
should he feel any.

'I have arranged matters to provide for Eleanor and
Ned's children, but the estate will no longer be tied to the
title. I have no wish to see Beverley Hatton despoil it
should Ned have no heirs. If both Ned and Beverley die
without heirs, then everything but the title will go to
Eleanor. Of course, should your father make a successful
claim, then all this fails, too. I have tried to provide for
every eventuality. Needless to say, the lawyers know nothing of your father.'

He fell silent. Alan looked hard at him. 'You are sure
that this is what you wish?'

'Quite sure. My responsibilities are towards those who
have served me on all my lands, not to worthless grandsons
who would see them ruined in order to gain money for high
living.' His voice was bitterness itself. 'You see, I trust you
and I do not think that I am wrong to do so.'

Sir Hart handed Alan another signed paper. 'I am trans-
ferring all my guardianships to you, and this paper gives
you those rights immediately Eleanor accepts you. I am no
longer strong enough to do what should be done. I have no
wish to compound the sins of my youth.'

Alan read the paper and said, 'You are sure that you wish
this, too?'

'Most sure.' Sir Hart leaned back in his chair, relieved.
'And now I suppose that you will speak to Eleanor—the
sooner the better.'

'Yes.' Alan rose, holding the paper. 'Mary Dilhorne was
not forgotten,' he said quietly. 'There was an old man there,
her brother. He was the only member of the family who
remembered her. He said that she was pretty and that my
father was a handsome little lad.'

He moved to the door, and as he placed his hand on the knob, the old man said, 'I know that you will do your duty, Grandson. If I may so call you for the first—and last— time.'

Alan found Eleanor in the herb garden where they had sat on the morning that Nat had tormented her, and he had rescued and reassured her.

'Oh, you are back earlier than I had expected—or hoped. Grandfather said that you had gone to explore the Dales. They are beautiful, are they not? Not so beautiful as the moors, of course.'

He put out a hand to assist her from her seat. 'Walk with me a little, Eleanor. I have something to say to you.'

Eleanor knew at once what that something was going to be. She had spent the time since she had last seen him in a fever of doubt, fear and expectation. She knew that he was due to leave for London soon. We have so little time left, she had thought, and now, to her great relief, the expression on his face told her what he was going to say before he spoke.

They walked to the end of an alley giving on to a view of the House, dark ochre in the growing night. He turned to her, took her hand, and kissed it.

'Eleanor, I think that you know what I am going to say. You may even have wondered why I took so long to say it. But I had decisions to make, grave ones, before I dare ask you—but now I am free. Eleanor, my dearest heart, will you marry me?'

His face was so grave and so loving that Eleanor wished to kiss him, to lighten the gravity but keep the loving. For the first time she initiated action. She stood on tiptoe and kissed him on his brown cheek.

'Can you doubt my answer, Alan? I have been a complete spectacle in the weeks since you came here. I wonder that no one has complained of my dreadful boldness. I thought that I was going to have to be like the Maenads with Orpheus and drag you off—without tearing you to pieces, of course! Even Ned and Mother, who never notice anything, have wondered what was the matter with me.

'If you do not kiss me immediately I shall expire of frustrated love on the spot. There, I can say all that now that you have asked me. I have always been told what a bold, forward creature I am, so I feel that I really must do something to earn that description.'

He laughed at her eager, glowing face. The load he had been carrying since Sir Hart first told him the truth about his father fell from his shoulders. The day was suddenly bright again, his fears and worries banished.

'Right, my girl,' he told her. 'For that you shall get the full treatment. Your first lesson in love begins now.'

He took her in his arms and gave her her first real kiss, to set her alight and take her on the first step into her future.

Seated at dinner, Eleanor was surprised that what had happened was not plain to everyone. The thought of what had passed between them in the garden set her blushing. Afterwards she and Alan had been to Sir Hart to tell him that they had agreed to marry. He had kissed her, wished her happy, and given her his blessing. They were to inform her mother and Ned of their decision after dinner. But plans, however well made, do not always come to pass exactly as intended.

There had already been uproar earlier that day because Beverley had managed to damage and dirty with ink and crayon many of Charles's possessions. He had claimed that it was an accident and his mother had supported him. Sir Hart had been appealed to and Beverley had been threatened with exile to his room again. He had been forbidden dinner with the family, but Eleanor's mother, and his, had agreed that this punishment was too severe. A place had been laid for him and he was in it by the time Sir Hart appeared.

Sir Hart had looked his displeasure, but said wearily that, since he was there, Beverley might stay. Beverley took this victory as an excuse for being more obnoxious than ever. He kicked poor Charles, already smarting over his vandalised property, under the table. He snarled at his mother, and greeted Alan most charmingly with, 'What? Are you back again? Why could you not stay away?'

Alan fingered the paper in his pocket and looked meaningfully at Sir Hart. Sir Hart nodded. Eleanor smiled at Alan across the table. Even Beverley was not to be allowed to ruin her happiness.

He did his best to try, though. Ned was asking Alan about his journey to the Dales when Beverley cut rudely across their conversation, exclaiming, 'I wonder at you, cousin Ned, that you trouble yourself with *him*.' And he pointed at Alan. 'My uncle Harry says that he wonders at you all for allowing a Hatton bastard with your face to sit at table with you.'

There was an appalled silence at this. Both Ned and Eleanor turned white. Sir Hart sank back in his chair, grey and half- collapsed. Beverley's mother and Eleanor's exclaimed together. Only Alan kept cool in face of the gross insult offered him.

He rose to his feet, his wine glass in his hand. 'Why, Master Hatton,' he said, and his voice would have shattered glass, so cold and hard it was, 'Your speech is timely. It is not how I would have chosen to announce this, but so be it. This afternoon your cousin Eleanor has done me the honour of consenting to be my wife, and Sir Hartley, as her guardian, has agreed to it. He has also made over all his guardianships to me, from the moment of her consent— and that includes you, Master Hatton.

'What is more important is that both myself and Sir Hart are willing to swear, on oath, that neither I nor my father are bastards, Hatton or otherwise. So you may save your insults, for those who deserve them. I drink,' he said, 'to Sir Hartley and to my future wife, and ask you all to do the same.'

The company did as he bade them in the deadly silence which followed this announcement.

He put his glass down. 'And now, Master Hatton, for my first exercise in the duties of a guardian.' So saying, he strolled slowly around the table to where Beverley sat, mesmerised, spun his chair around, plucked him out of it in one rapid movement and swung him over his shoulder. Beverley began to kick and scream until Alan's large hand covering his mouth silenced him.

Alan strode to the door, where he stopped and said to Sir Hart, 'When he is fit for normal company again he will apologise to you, sir. Before that I shall wash his mouth out with soap, administer a suitable drubbing and see him fed on bread and water in order to teach him to leave Charles alone.'

Beverley's mother began to protest at this cavalier treatment, particularly since after kicking Alan hard on the shins he had received the first blow of his promised drubbing. When she had finished Alan offered her his most charming smile.

'I assure you,' he said, 'that you will not need to intercede for him so much in future. I promise you that by the week's end you will be the first person to whom he will apologise, for shaming you so often.'

With that, Alan was gone.

Ned began to laugh, and Charles gave a relieved smile on hearing his tormentor's roars fade into the distance.

'Oh, famous,' Ned cried. 'How often have I longed to do that. I congratulate you, Eleanor. I said that you would be a busy wife if you married Alan. And the likeness! Fudge to the likeness. There is nothing in it, as I always thought.'

He addressed his dinner with an appetite which told of his relief.

The colour slowly returned to Sir Hart's cheeks. He sat up again. Oh, the devil, he thought. The devious, clever devil. To turn disaster into such a triumph, to use my dreadful grandson to neutralise all scandal, and while not telling the whole truth, not lying while he did so!

He looked down the table, and for the first time since Alan's arrival he smiled at them all. At Ned, deprived of his worries, at Eleanor in her new-found happiness, at Charles, freed at last from torment, and at his two daughters-in-law, angry but resigned.

Eleanor's mother was pleased that her daughter was at last fixed, and although she was annoyed at the man she was fixed with she did not dare to say anything in the face of the united front of her daughter, Sir Hart and the formidable giant whom Eleanor was marrying. Instead of railing uselessly against fate she turned her mind to thoughts of the wedding and what she would wear at it—and what Eleanor's father, Knaresborough, would think of it.

He would approve, of course. He had made that plain to her in his direct way before he had left for London, so that when Alan returned, Beverley disposed of, she offered him her congratulations in a voice which rang true.

Sir Hart, as well as the lovers, had insisted that the wedding should not be long delayed.

'I wish to be present,' he had said, 'and it must be a grand one. In London. Never mind that the season is over.'

Privately he told Alan that it must not be a hole-and-corner affair. The likeness must be flaunted, not shuffled off, and the half-truth that Alan had uttered after Beverley's provocation would satisfy more than Ned when Ned repeated it. After all, the unlikely idea that marriage, not a seduction, had taken place, making all Sir Hart's English descendants illegitimate, would never enter anyone's head—as it had not entered Alan's before Sir Hart had confessed to it.

The wedding was thus suitably grand.

Knaresborough insisted that they should be married at his great palace off the Strand—for Hatton House, he said, was not sufficiently large to accommodate all who would wish to attend. He also brooked no refusal to his other proposition to Alan.

'I shall stand with you at the ceremony, for you need a stout fellow in your corner, your father and family being absent.'

So on his wedding day the poor felon's son was attended to the altar in a style neither he nor his family could have expected. Although there were some who commented on the likeness, there were others who said that it was not so strong after all—a trick of size and colour which later diminished when the differing lives of the two men took its inevitable effects.

Sir Hart had told Ned of the disposition of the estate, and, as is common, Ned, who had always claimed that he never wanted the responsibility or the care of Temple Hatton, suddenly found, when granted his wish, that the reality was a different thing from his imaginings.

He was rapidly reconciled, however, by the thought that he would receive his income without needing to do anything to earn it!

'That troubles me, too,' Sir Hart had said ruefully to Alan. 'It's one more opportunity for him to be careless—but were everything to have been left to him then everything would have been lost, I fear.'

The days would not pass quickly enough for Eleanor

First the wedding, and then the long journey to the ends of the earth beckoned her: something which in her wildest dreams she could never have imagined. The only worry was whether Sir Hart would live to see them return, but he had told them that he possessed more determination to cling to life than he had known for many long years.

'Do you mind all this pomp?' Eleanor whispered to Alan when they sat together at the wedding breakfast after the ceremony, surrounded by 'the beautiful ones', as Alan called them. Frank Gresham, smiling his pleasure, was seated near them.

'No.' He smiled. 'I don't usually like circumstance, but I am prepared to pay the price for it today.'

'Sir Hart said that had we been married in Sir Beauchamp's time they would have escorted us to bed, too,' said Eleanor, mischief written on her face. She was not quite sure how she would feel when bed became a reality, but she was confident that Alan would be kind to her.

'I am a married woman, now,' she told him, laughing a little. 'I can say things like that to you now and in future, should I so wish.'

Alan looked across the room to where Gurney, still the Golden Boy's watch dog, but dressed in a footman's livery today, glowered at the party.

'What worries me,' Alan whispered confidentially in Eleanor's ear, 'is that when we finally do get to bed, if Gurney thinks that you are going to do me a mischief, we shall find him waiting there for us, pistols at the ready in order to protect me. What will you do then? Think on!'

Eleanor collapsed into happy laughter at the picture this presented.

Alan took her hand and pressed it, looking into her beautiful eyes. 'I am willing to endure all this, Eleanor, because we shall be together for the rest of our lives. But I warn you, ceremony will not be a major part of them. I am a

working man and always will be, even if the Queen's
cousin stood by me at the altar.'

'Your world will always be mine,' she promised him.

Later, in the joyful transports of the night, when love and
passion became a reality, she silently vowed again that
whatever happened in the future they would, for good or
ill, always be friends as well as lovers, facing life together
whatever it might bring them.

Epilogue

Villa Dilhorne, Sydney, Australia, 1842

It was obvious, from the moment that she met him, that Eleanor was fascinated by Alan's father. Good manners precluded her from saying anything straight away, but in the evening, at dinner, he told them an amusing story of one of his business deals and Eleanor, laughing, put down her knife and fork, saying, 'You were right, Alan. It's quite extraordinary. Your father is the exact double of my grandfather, Sir Hart, as he was before he became ill.

'It's not only that you look like him, sir,' she went on, 'but you have the same droll way of telling a story as he does. I mean this as a compliment,' she added in her direct fashion, which always amused Alan because it was a feminine version of her unacknowledged father's manner.

'Ned, my brother,' she explained further, 'says that I fell in love with Alan because he is so like what Sir Hart must have been in youth. The three of you could all charm birds off trees just by looking at them. Ned's very like Alan, too, but not so serious.'

It *was* a compliment, but the effect of what she had just said was profound, if unspoken. Tom offered the company an enigmatic smile, but said nothing until he pulled Alan on one side before they retired to the drawing room after dinner.

'I think that some explanation is in order, don't you?' His expression was what his wife thought of as typical Tom, quizzical and demanding.

'Indeed, Father. In fact, Eleanor has saved me from raising the matter with you myself. She wishes to retire early tonight, being weary from the long journey here, so I propose that you, and the rest of the grown-up family, meet me later, when I will tell you the strange tale of my English adventures.'

Old Tom nodded. 'Tonight, then.' He was always short when serious.

Later, they all sat round the big table in Villa Dilhorne's great barbaric hall, as beautiful as but quite unlike that at Temple Hatton. Old Tom, Hester, his wife, and the twins, Tom and Alan, were present.

'Now,' said Tom, still short. 'An explanation. Why this strange set of resemblances? Unless, of course, your wife was exaggerating.'

'No exaggeration,' Alan told them. 'And once you have heard me out you will understand that what I have to say to you could not have been put in writing. The tale is a long one, so you must be patient.'

He began with his chance meeting with Ned Hatton and took them, in detail, through his stay in England, his arrival at Temple Hatton and his meeting with Sir Hartley.

'He was you, Father, exactly as Eleanor said. You grown very old. I was a shock to him as well, and to many others, being so like Sir Hart's father, Sir Beauchamp. Sir Hart was particularly stricken when he heard that you came from Yorkshire and that your mother's name was Dilhorne. Later he told me why.'

He led them through Sir Hart's explanation of his long-gone love affair and secret marriage, its tragic end and his own adventures in England, and finally his marriage to Eleanor.

'And she knows nothing?' asked Tom.

'Nothing. None of them know. The matter remains a secret between Sir Hart and myself. He has given me a letter for you, setting this all out. It is for you to do with it as you please.'

'This beggars belief,' said Thomas. 'That you married your long-lost illegitimate cousin without her knowing the truth.'

'You might say so,' said Alan, who had not told them that Eleanor was Knaresborough's daughter and not a Hatton at all—he saw no useful purpose in so doing, and did not wish Eleanor to be hurt. Sir Hart had accepted her, and that was that.

'She knows nothing of this. That was my agreement with her grandfather. I had told her that my father was very like Sir Hart, but, as you all saw, it was still quite a shock for her to meet him. Now, Father. Sir Hartley said that once you had read his letter the choice was for you to make, and he would abide by it even if you wished to claim what, after all, is rightfully yours.'

He handed his father the letter Sir Hart had given him on the day he had proposed to Eleanor.

They were all agreed that Tom was the one to decide. It was he who had been the most wronged. Hester put out a hand to take his.

'Do?' he said, without opening the letter. 'Why, nothing! Put it this way. Leaving it as it is there is only one bastard, myself, and I've lived with that all my life. But if I make my claim there's two generations of a whole family ruined and nameless—and for what? I ceased to care long ago.'

He looked at Thomas. 'Do you wish to be Sir Thomas

badly enough to ruin the lives of all the Hattons in England?'

Thomas shook his head. 'No,' he said decisively. 'I don't want to be Sir Thomas at all. I don't care about England, either. My life is here. Leave them in peace.'

'And you?' said his father, turning to Alan. 'Do you want to destroy your wife's family? You wouldn't have married her if you did.'

He surveyed his two sons with pride. 'Besides, even if I were mad enough to try to claim my due, I know them. They'd fight like the devil. Win or not, we should be the losers. No, let it go. I've made a better life here. I might have turned into an idle wastrel if things had gone differently and I'd been Tom Hatton. Let it go.'

He picked up the letter, weighed it in his hands a moment, said, in his most dismissive manner, 'Baggage I do not want,' and tossed it, unopened, into the fire.

Alan stood up. 'I knew you'd say that, Father. There is one thing more, though. Thomas wants to stay here, and that's fine by me. But I like England. If you are all agreed, I intend to go back, take over the business there, and my mother's interests, too. Thomas can have what is here. Agreed?'

They all nodded. The possibility of future friction between them both about their share of the business had always worried the twins. This seemed a good, if sad solution. Alan would be lost to them, but there would be gains.

After the twins had retired to bed—Thomas and his wife, Bethia, were staying overnight—Hester took her candle upstairs to wait for Tom, as she had done for nearly thirty years. This night he was long in coming, and after a time she went down to find him staring at nothing, looking older than his usual self.

'Well, Sir Thomas?' she said simply.

He smiled at her. The smile which could still wrench her heart with love for him.

'Very well,' he said. 'The best part of the tale was that my mother told me the truth. She *was* married, and the boy whom she married did not willingly desert her. The rest is nothing.'

'So Alan did the right thing?'

'To say nothing until he saw me? Yes. His judgement is as sound as ever.'

He put his arms around her and pulled her to him. They sat there like that for some time.

'No regrets, Hester?'

'None. I only hope that Alan and his wife will be as happy as we are.'

He laughed. 'She's a lively piece. But he'll keep her in order.' He laughed again. 'As I did you—which means not at all! Let's go to bed, my dear. Tomorrow is another day.'

Alan slipped gently into bed so as not to disturb Eleanor, tired as she was from her long journey. She was not asleep, however.

'Alan?' Her voice was urgent.

'My dear? I hoped that you were asleep.'

'I was, but I awoke a little while ago. I am stupid. We were all stupid back home. You are beginning to teach me to think, and I have thought. The likeness: it is not an accident, is it? It cannot be. It is not possible that your father should be so like Sir Hart as I remember him before he grew so very old. Nor that you should be so like Ned and Sir Beauchamp, so that even Knaresborough could see it. I am not wrong, am I?'

Indirection would not do here, nor could he lie to her. Neither could he tell her the absolute truth.

'No, Eleanor, you are not wrong. There is, was, a connection between us all. A distant one. But it is over. It cannot affect our lives. It belongs to the past, and a dead past at that. I cannot tell you the whole truth, for it is not mine to tell, and because you are my wife, the past does not matter.'

She sat up suddenly. 'You know that I shall always trust you, so you need tell me no more. I have to confess that I like your family enormously, Alan. And I can see why you are as you are. Thomas's wife and your mother were so kind to me that I shall be sorry to go back to England— but it is our duty, is it not? We promised Sir Hart.'

'Bethia is always kind. She is very like my mother,' said Alan, taking her into his arms and laying her head on his chest. 'Do I take it, then, that you are pleased with your Australian family?'

'Yes,' she said, turning in his arms to kiss him. 'Most particularly with the one I married.'

* * * * *

Watch out in November for
AN INNOCENT MASQUERADE
the next exciting installment of the Dilhorne family

MILLS & BOON®

Makes any time special™

Mills & Boon publish 29 new titles every month. Select from...

Modern Romance™   Tender Romance™

Sensual Romance™

Medical Romance™   Historical Romance™

MAT2

FREE

2 BOOKS
AND A SURPRISE GIFT!

We would like to take this opportunity to thank you for reading this Mills & Boon® book by offering you the chance to take TWO more specially selected titles from the Historical Romance™ series absolutely FREE! We're also making this offer to introduce you to the benefits of the Reader Service™—

★ FREE home delivery
★ FREE gifts and competitions
★ FREE monthly Newsletter
★ Exclusive Reader Service discounts
★ Books available before they're in the shops

Accepting these FREE books and gift places you under no obligation to buy; you may cancel at any time, even after receiving your free shipment. Simply complete your details below and return the entire page to the address below. *You don't even need a stamp!*

YES! Please send me 2 free Historical Romance books and a surprise gift. I understand that unless you hear from me, I will receive 4 superb new titles every month for just £2.99 each, postage and packing free. I am under no obligation to purchase any books and may cancel my subscription at any time. The free books and gift will be mine to keep in any case.

HO3EC

Ms/Mrs/Miss/Mr ....Initials ....

BLOCK CAPITALS PLEASE

Surname ....

Address ....

....

....Postcode ....

Send this whole page to:
UK: FREEPOST CN81, Croydon, CR9 3WZ
EIRE: PO Box 4546, Kilcock, County Kildare (stamp required)